DEFECTOR

Also by Susanne Winnacker

IMPOSTOR

DEFECTOR

SUSANNE WINNACKER

Hodder
Children's
Books

A division of Hachette Children's Books

To my mother; for always defending me
against the doubters.

Für meine Mutter. Dafür, duss du mich immer
gegen die Zweifler verteidigt hast.

PROLOGUE

The floor of the helicopter vibrated against my ballerina flats. I could feel the constant buzz humming through my body, and my heartbeat seemed determined to keep up with it.

In the distance, the mountains of Glacier National Park rose against the darkening sky. Their peaks were framed by crimson as the day bled away. Was Major already waiting for us? We'd be in for an ass-kicking after what we'd done. Maybe the sky wouldn't be the only thing bleeding tonight.

Alec squeezed my hand, and his grey eyes briefly darted towards me, as if he could feel the worry rolling off me. This had been a difficult day for both of us. Nobody understood me like he did. I looked over to him. His dark brows were drawn together on his tanned face. My eyes glided lower to where the snarling head of a dragon peeked out of his black shirt. He'd loosened the top buttons and it had slipped, revealing his right collarbone and strong shoulder with the top of his tattoo. He was focused on the controls of the helicopter, but he was smiling encouragingly. I wanted to lean against him and breathe in his scent – cinnamon and something spicier – to convince myself that this moment was real.

Only two hours ago, Alec had admitted that he wanted to be with me, that he'd finally ended his relationship with Kate. But now that the news had time to sink in, I couldn't help but wonder: how would she react when we got back to headquarters? Alec had emphasized that their relationship hadn't been about love, but I was sure she wouldn't give him up without a fight.

His black hair was all over the place from running his hands through it earlier. I loved that it was a little longer than how he usually wore it – or rather how Kate had wanted him to wear it. It made him look more rugged.

'You're so quiet,' Alec broke the silence. 'What are you thinking?'

Heat slithered up my neck. It was almost like he'd read my mind. 'Just about the mission.'

'Do you want to talk about it?'

The events of the last few weeks still weighed heavy on me. I'd completed my first mission as an FEA agent, and it hadn't been easy. Ultimately, I'd performed successfully, but I could just as well have died.

My palm rested over my rib cage, where a serial killer had cut an A into my skin – the mark he left on all of his victims. It was a wound I'd sustained while pretending to be someone else, but it didn't disappear once I changed back to my own body. I'd keep the A forever: a constant reminder of a mission that had come dangerously close to breaking me. Despite my layers of clothes, I imagined I could feel the rough edges of the scar. My chest vibrated against my palm; I wasn't sure if it was from the helicopter movements or because I'd started trembling. I dropped my hand before Alec could notice it.

I had no doubt that upon our return, Major would be furious with Alec and me. As the head of the FEA – Forces with Extraordinary Abilities – he was our boss and the person responsible for overseeing all of our actions. We'd gone against his orders by returning to the place of my mission. But it was something I had to do for closure. I was grateful that at least Alec understood that.

He dipped the controls forward, and we began to decline, the skids of the helicopter almost brushing the treetops. The huge grey FEA building came into view, surrounded by small cottages, forest, the glass dome of the swimming pool and our training grounds.

This, I reminded myself, was my home.

Alec steered the helicopter towards the landing strip at the back of the property, which was illuminated by red fog lights. And as I let my gaze stray further north, I could see a wall of white mist creeping toward us. I shivered violently. Alec's eyes swivelled to me, away from the landing strip.

I forced my body to relax, remembering that returning to head-quarters meant good things too, like getting to see my best friend, Holly, again. Whenever we were separated, it felt like a small part of me was missing.

After a moment, Alec turned his attention back to our landing. There was no hiding now: the hissing of the propeller blades would alert Major and everyone else to our arrival. This was the moment of truth.

The skids touched the ground, and with a jerk, we halted. I could still feel the vibration in my body. In combination with my trembling, it created a strange rippling, not unlike the feeling I got during a shape-shifting transformation.

The blades slowed, their hissing dying down.

A heavy weight settled in my stomach.

Alec brushed a strand of hair from my forehead. The auburn lock had stuck to my sweaty skin. 'It'll be OK. I'll be at your side,' he said softly.

At Alec's touch, my trembling halted. I undid the buckle, slid open the door, and jumped outside. My breath left my mouth in small clouds, and iciness slithered through the thin soles of my shoes and into every inch of my body. It was April, but this year the winter was particularly hard in Montana. Alec rounded the helicopter and took my hand. For two years, I'd been longing for this moment, for his touch, and now I had what I'd always wanted. I tried to savour it despite the circumstances.

I tugged at Alec's arm. 'Come on. Let's go,' I said. 'I want to get this over with as soon as possible.' *And as long as my new bravery lasts*, I thought.

We hurried across the slick pavement – it must have

rained recently, and the water had frozen in a thin layer. My eyes darted towards the building looming threateningly in front of us.

Whoever had built FEA headquarters must have been a fan of Bauhaus architecture, with its square forms, clear and simple without any flourishes. If I didn't know better, I'd have sworn Major had commissioned it. But headquarters had been built in 1948, well before Major was born.

When I'd first glimpsed the headquarters after Major and Alec had picked me up more than two years ago, I'd been disappointed. I'd expected an old manor with brick chimneys, ivy-covered walls and stone gargoyles on the ledges of the roof. Instead I'd gotten a run-of-the-mill office building. But once I'd seen the wide corridors that prevented me from losing my way and the picture windows in the rooms, I changed my mind. And it was better than anything I'd experienced before. This time, though, the inside of the building wouldn't bring me comfort.

I could already see Major standing behind the floor-to-ceiling window of his office, arms crossed, waiting for us.

CHAPTER 1

Date night. My favourite night of the week – along with my evenings spent doing 'girly stuff' with Holly (her words). Sometimes it was still hard for me to grasp that Alec and I had been dating for a couple of weeks, that it had been that long since I'd returned from my first mission. The time felt like a blur.

Though Alec and I didn't go to the movies or out to a fancy restaurant (or even leave headquarters) for our dates, they were a big part of the reason why everything between us started to feel real. Holly had tried to talk me into dressing up. She'd even laid out an array of four outfits for me to choose from. Maybe she took this a bit too seriously. I'd explained to her in carefully chosen words that it would have felt wrong to get dolled up. Alec had seen me at my worst: crying and sobbing over my mother, beaten up and covered in blood. It would have felt as if I was putting on a mask if I'd dressed up for movie night. It was bad enough that I had to be someone else for my job; I didn't want that in front of Alec. This evening was about Alec and me as we really were.

Despite Holly's disapproving frown, I wore my favourite shorts and my Ten Rules to Survive a Zombie Apocalypse T-shirt. Alec greeted me with a peck on the lips as I slipped into his room. A small smile of endorsement spread on his face when he noticed my shirt. Happy that my instinct had been right, I stepped out of my shoes and lay back on his bed while he pushed the DVD into the player. With a buzzing, it snapped shut. A swarm of butterflies fluttered in my belly as I watched the muscles in Alec's lower back and shoulders flex beneath his white T-shirt when he straightened. Alec kicked off his sneakers and locked the door. Date night number three, and it was the first time he'd done *that*. My imagination went into overdrive, and the fluttering in my stomach turned into a riot.

Alec turned slowly, as if he'd only just realized how his actions might look. His eyes were cautious as he glanced at me. Did I look nervous? 'Because of Tanner. I don't want him to barge in.' Then he added with a hint of annoyance, 'Again.'

Good thinking. Tanner had already walked in on us kissing on the bed *twice*. If I had to bear his teasing and kissy noises one more time, I'd shave his beloved mohawk off while he was sleeping.

I gave Alec a smile, though the mix of nerves, embarrassment and excitement had me feeling like I was going to combust. Nobody would interrupt us tonight;

anything could happen. Alec was experienced – after all, he was older than me, and he'd dated Kate for months. How far did he want to go? How far did I want him to go? This felt momentous somehow.

'I can unlock it, though, if that's what you prefer,' he said softly. It was pretty obvious from his expression that it wasn't what he wanted, but it made me happy that he was trying to make me feel comfortable.

'Don't be stupid. Come here.' I patted the bed and made more room for him. His expression lit up, but I could still detect a hint of uncertainty in the way he moved. He was always worried about me and constantly protective of me. That would probably never change. I had to show him that I wasn't some breakable porcelain doll. I had extraordinary abilities; I'd recently survived a serial killer, for goodness' sake.

He sank down beside me and stretched out his long legs. Then he paused and pointed at a big, round red candle on his nightstand. 'Do you want me to light it?'

That was too much. I couldn't help it. I burst into laughter. 'Did Holly put you up to this?' I could imagine only too well how she'd followed him around, trying to teach him what constituted a romantic date. Alec smiled sheepishly. 'Maybe.'

'OK, well, I'm not the candlelight type. The glow of a light-saber is more my thing.'

'Thank god. This thing smells like apples and cinnamon, and I hate the stench.' The last bit of tension leaked from

Alec's body, and he sank into the crisp (the laundry staff loved starch) black cushions with Chucky's face on the front propped up against the dark wood headboard. I pressed myself against his chest, breathing in his woodsy smell as he wrapped his arm around me. I couldn't stop myself from wondering what his date nights had been like with Kate. Had she liked candlelight? He pressed a kiss against my temple, and I looked up, bringing our faces closer together. Our breath mingled. I leaned forward, trying my best to bury my worries. He was mine now.

'You can trust me,' he said quietly, grey eyes earnest and open. Once again, it was almost like he'd read my thoughts.

I inched towards him until I could almost feel the heat of his mouth. I kissed him and smiled against his lips. Besides Holly, Alec was the only person I'd ever allowed myself to trust completely. The feeling was comforting and thrilling at the same time. 'I know.' My skin tingled from the friction as I spoke.

His lips moved against mine, softly sliding over them, tasting, claiming. The prickle of his stubble sent a sliver of desire into my belly. My eyes fell shut, and I relaxed against the mattress. Alec's hard body pressed against me, hipbone to hipbone. His hands travelled up my throat into my hair, fingertips feather-soft. My palms marked his back as mine, pressing him tighter against me. His muscles flexed beneath my hands. His kiss was slow, unhurried and spread fire in my body before it pooled in my belly. His lips brushed the corner of my mouth, then moved to my chin and throat. A sound tumbled out of my mouth – a sound I hadn't known I was capable of. When I opened my eyes, Alec was watching me. A small smile played around his lips. I pushed my fingers into his black hair, relishing in the silkiness. With a groan, he climbed on top of me, careful not to crush me with his weight, and pressed his lips against me again. Feeling his body on me, his warmth seeping into me, his smell surrounding me, I felt safer than I'd ever felt before. I felt at home. He kissed the hollow of my throat, and I tilted my head back to give him better access. His tongue darted out and flicked across my collarbone. I gasped and dug my hands into his arms. His muscles twitched under my grasp. Something was unravelling inside me – a feeling unlike anything I'd ever felt before. There was no use holding it together – I felt no need to. His hand, warm and strong, crept under my shirt. His palm rested on my stomach, friction of skin on skin raising goose bumps all over my body. But then his fingers travelled up to my rib cage, and I froze.

His fingertips rested on the mark. The glaring red of the A had faded, but the scar hadn't. It had entirely lost feeling, but it was there and always would be. Alec stopped kissing me, closed his eyes and rested his forehead against mine, releasing a harsh breath.

'Sorry,' I whispered, feeling inexplicably sad – and just as guilty for ruining the moment.

'No,' Alec said fiercely. He pulled back to look at me, and his grey eyes held mine with a startling intensity. 'Don't you dare start feeling guilty for this.' He brushed his fingertips across the scar. I shivered.

I stared at the candle, the way its wick was bent. 'I know it bothers you. I mean . . . it's ugly . . .' I trailed off, unsure what else to say.

'It doesn't bother me because of how it looks. It bothers me because it reminds me of the danger you faced and how I failed you, how you could have died. How I couldn't protect you from that monster,' Alec said.

'Alec, you won't always be able to protect me from everything. I'm capable of protecting myself. There'll be missions in our future that we'll have to do alone. It was my first time out in the field. I let my guard down when I shouldn't have, and this scar is a reminder of that.' I touched his arm and kissed his cheek. 'It's in the past.'

I could tell that Alec didn't want to drop the topic, but he pulled me against him and settled us against the pillows. His lips hovered against my temple, tension coiling in his body. He released a harsh breath and started the movie. The screen turned black before the quote 'Revenge is a dish best served cold' appeared.

'*Kill Bill*,' I said, laughing with approval. 'That's my kind of movie for a romantic evening.' I grinned, and I could feel the gloom of our conversation fall away from me.

The tightness around Alec's lips vanished. 'I know. That's what makes you so perfect.' A blush crept up my neck, and I hastily put my head down and rested it against Alec's shoulder so he wouldn't see it. The opening song, 'Bang Bang (My Baby Shot Me Down)', started playing, and I hummed along with it. The *Kill Bill* soundtrack was one of my all-time favourites. And when Alec whistled 'Twisted Nerve' along with Black Mamba in her nurse costume, the moment was perfect. But no matter how much I tried to allow myself to relax, a thought haunted me. 'Does she still try to talk to you?' I asked, my voice strangely hoarse.

'Hmm?' Alec's fingers stopped tracing the skin on my arm. 'What did you say?'

'Kate,' I clarified. I could see his body tense, feel it in the shift of his muscles, and I regretted bringing it up. 'Does she still try to talk to you?'

'Tessa, do you really think this is a good time to talk about Kate?'

Of course it wasn't. But would there ever be a time when talking about his ex-girlfriend wouldn't be hurtful and awkward? 'I need to know. Kate's been between us for such a long time, and somehow in some way it feels like she still is.'

Alec stopped the movie. 'All right,' he said slowly. 'But you know that there was never anything *real* between Kate and me. We were friends, but the spark was never there. We were clinging to the relationship out of habit and because it seemed like the right thing to do.' *That was a strange thing to say*, I thought. Why was keeping up a relationship the right thing to do?

He continued, 'She's still pissed, and she never misses a

chance to make that clear to me. She even tried to blackmail me, but—'

'Blackmail?' My neck bristled. What could Kate possibly use against Alec?

He was silent for a moment. 'Yeah,' he said reluctantly. 'We spent so much time together on our joint mission that we were bound to share a few secrets.'

'The mission where you and Kate first became a couple?' I still remembered the utter shock and heartbreak I'd felt when Kate and Alec had entered headquarters as a couple for the very first time. And just as vividly I remembered the twisted smile on Kate's face and the triumph in her eyes when our gazes had crossed. I'd thought I would never hate someone more than I hated her in that moment.

Alec nodded, but I could tell from the set of his jaw and the tightness in his shoulders that that mission – or the secrets that went along with it – wasn't something he wanted to talk about.

'There must have been something between you two to make you get together in the first place?' The words escaped me, even though I knew I should stop before I got a reply I didn't want to hear.

'The mission formed some kind of bond between us. I guess that happens if you aren't allowed to talk to anyone else about it. We only had each other, and we couldn't help but grow closer. Our relationship was born out of practicality.' I could sense he was keeping something from

14

me, but it was obvious that he had absolutely no intention of telling me more.

I opened my mouth, but Alec silenced me with a kiss. 'Don't let Kate ruin this evening. The relationship was a mistake. All that matters now is what's between us.'

I nodded reluctantly and relaxed against him, though part of me didn't want to let the topic go. Alec turned the TV back on. But suddenly seeing Kiddo's pursuit of revenge wasn't so funny anymore, because I was pretty sure Kate would be on a similar quest soon – not to kill me, but she would certainly make my life hell.

I woke with a start. Someone was trying to beat the door down. I sat up, brushing back a few unruly locks of hair that had fallen into my face. Straining, I blinked against the light. It was then that I realized I wasn't in my room. I didn't own bed linen with Chucky on them, or a Freddy Kruger figurine. My eyes found Alec, already on his feet, sliding his jeans over black briefs. My skin flushed with heat, and I hastily stared down at myself. I was still dressed in my T-shirt and the shorts I'd been wearing last night. I must have fallen asleep before Alec had taken his jeans off.

He gave me a quick smile. 'You look adorable with your hair all over the place.'

I groaned. I knew exactly how I looked after waking up, and it definitely wasn't adorable. My hair was naturally curly, but in the early morning light it tended to look like someone had given me electroshock therapy. Alec frowned,

15

as though he could read my thoughts. I tried to smile, but when that failed, I trained my gaze on the *Alien* poster on the wall.

The knocking at the door grew even more insistent and made the door shake on its hinges. A tiny ball of unease gathered in my stomach. What could be so urgent this early in the morning? Had something happened?

Alec unlocked the door and pulled it open. Tanner stood in the doorway, and before I could hide under the blanket, his eyes settled on me. His eyebrows shot up – they were the same neon green as his mohawk. Somehow he pulled it off, and it looked impossibly cool with his dark skin. I waited for his teasing remark, but it didn't come. That's when I knew something really was wrong. I untangled myself from the blanket and staggered to my feet.

'What's the matter? It's not even eight on a Sunday,' Alec said, but the anxiety in his voice ruined the flippancy of the words.

'You can get your beauty sleep on another day. Major wants to see you,' Tanner said. 'Another agent has disappeared.'

CHAPTER 2

Tanner left without further explanation to fetch Kate. Our only directions were to head to Major's office ASAP. In the hallway we almost bumped into a group of older agents deep in conversation, voices panicked and expressions strained. Word about another abduction must have already got around.

My stomach tightened. What had happened? Who was the newest victim?

When Alec and I stepped into Major's office, I was surprised to find that Devon and Phil were already there. There was a moment of hesitation in their expressions. Even after living at headquarters for almost a week and seeing me pretty much every day, they still seemed to struggle with seeing me in my 'real' body, and not as the person I'd pretended to be back during the Livingston mission. Devon's blue eyes held mine briefly before his gaze quickly anchored somewhere else. It had been like this ever since he arrived at FEA headquarters, and I couldn't really blame him. I couldn't have forgiven him either if I'd been in his position. I just wished he'd give me a chance to talk to him, but so far his evasive tactics had worked.

Phil occupied the second chair across from Major's desk, and unlike Devon, he definitely wasn't trying to avoid me. Quite the contrary, he stared at me with unmasked curiosity like I was a puzzle he needed to figure out. His eyes were a pale, watery blue, like the colour had been washed away, and his hair was so light that it was almost white. Like the very first time I'd seen him, the sight of him gave me the creeps.

Someone cleared his throat, and I jumped. Major stood behind me, holding a tray with tea, the steam curling up from the cups in smoky spirals. The china had a blue, flowery pattern, which seemed at war with Major's personality. The scent of bergamot flooded my nose. Earl Grey – Major's favourite. I wondered why he didn't let his secretary, Mrs Finnigan, handle the tray, but realized she was probably still asleep. After all, Sunday was the only day everyone at headquarters didn't have to work – at least on a usual Sunday.

Major's dark eyes took in my crumpled clothes and unkempt hair, but he didn't comment. He didn't need to, his disapproval clear on his tanned face. 'I'm glad you finally decided to join us,' he said neutrally as he strode past Alec and me and into his office, setting the tray down on his desk before handing a cup to each of us. 'Sit,' he ordered in a clipped tone. Alec and I sank down on the glossy, black hardwood chairs across from Major's desk, which was spotless, as usual. Despite the dark wooden surface, not a finger-print or a trace of dust could be seen.

'Major, what happened? Who is missing?' Alec asked, voice businesslike. This Alec – public Alec – was light years away from the person I knew when we were alone.

Phil began sipping his tea casually, his eyes watching me from the side as if I was the morning entertainment. Why was he so fixated on me when there were much bigger things at hand?

Major sank heavily into his desk chair. 'Agent Stevens.'

I let out a small sigh. I was glad it wasn't someone I was close to, but I immediately felt bad for thinking like that. Stevens was a fellow agent. I'd met him a couple of times during my first mission, but I barely knew anything about him. I became acutely aware of the freezing temperature in the office as the cold from the linoleum floor seeped into my bare feet and spread through my body. Or maybe it was my anxiety that turned my blood into ice.

Who knew what his captors were putting him through? Or whom they were going to target next? Four agents had already been abducted, and the FEA had been incapable of stopping it. I shivered and began rubbing my arms for warmth.

Alec reached for my hand, and a wave of calm overcame me. I smiled gratefully. As long as Alec was at my side, everything would be fine. I don't know how he did it, but his presence alone always managed to soothe my worries.

'Sir, what exactly happened in Livingston?' I asked, but Major raised his palm. 'In a second, once everyone is here. I don't want to tell the same story twice.' He drummed his fingers against his desk, then stopped abruptly when he felt my eyes on him. Major never showed nerves. Ever.

A knock sounded at the door, and a moment later Kate stepped in, freshly showered, blonde hair still wet, and neatly dressed in clean clothes.

'Tanner briefed me on the situation,' she said in the same businesslike voice that Alec had used earlier. She settled herself into the only vacant chair – beside Alec. Her strange coppery eyes met mine for a second before I dropped my gaze. I didn't want to make eye contact and allow her to read my mind. But she must have gotten a glimpse of last night, because her eyes narrowed slightly at me before she gave Alec a curt nod and smile and turned to Major.

'Now,' Major began, 'as I said before, Agent Stevens has disappeared. All we know is that he didn't give his usual status update and we couldn't reach him by phone or email. Given our experiences with previous disappearances of FEA agents, and the similar patterns of all recent events, I think it's safe to say that Abel's Army is involved.'

'But, sir, what makes you so sure? Do we know why Abel's Army chose Agent Stevens? What is the deciding factor? What are the perceived reasons for the abductions?' Phil sounded like an analyst.

20

Kate's eyes cut to me. I tensed. Why was she staring at me like that?

'Their main aim is to weaken us. The FEA is, and always has been, their enemy. So far they've abducted agents who weren't living in headquarters and thus were an easy target. I believe, however, that their tactics might have changed. If they want to grow stronger as an organization, they'll need reinforcement – Variants with useful talents. The mission in Livingston might have revealed five very interesting new Variations to them.' His gaze glided over us, and I sank deeper into my chair. If Abel's Army really knew all about our talents, and I was almost certain they knew about mine, then we were all in danger. Alec squeezed my hand, and some of the tension left my chest.

Phil nodded, wide-eyed. His entire body was tense, the cup in his hand tipping precariously to the side. It was only a matter of time before he'd spill the hot liquid all over himself.

Devon's fingers were turning white from their grip on the arm-rest. He hadn't touched his tea yet. If his stomach felt anything like mine, he was probably afraid of regurgitating whatever he'd eaten for breakfast.

'I've been expecting their focus to shift, to target you. That's why I made you join the FEA a couple of weeks before the agreed date,' Major said with a nod towards Devon and Phil. They tilted their heads in understanding, as if they, or I, knew what the hell that meant, as if we had the slightest clue what Abel's Army was capable of.

'But still, if they were after us, then why take Agent Stevens?' Devon asked.

'He'd been tasked with guarding you while you were still in Livingston. He knew details about your Variations and your personal lives. He can give away important information about all five of you. He's the first abducted agent who has a certain degree of insider knowledge that could potentially hurt us.' Major pressed his lips together in disapproval, as if he couldn't believe Agent Stevens had dared to get caught.

'If he told them about your healing power' – he nodded towards Devon – 'and about your capability to produce toxin' – he looked at Phil – 'I'm sure Abel's interest will be peaked. Your Variations are quite useful, after all,' Major said with an appreciative look. I wondered if they'd noticed Major's choice of words. *Useful*. It was a term he loved to use.

Phil looked miserable. 'But I can't control my glands.' He stretched out his arms, gloved palms upwards. 'It's not like I'm a biological weapon or anything.'

Major emptied his cup with a grimace. 'The dose usually isn't enough to kill a human, you're right. At least, not a grown up. But with training and the right incentive, I'm quite sure that Abel's Army could turn your Variation into something that's worth being afraid of,' he said. My face must have shown my shock. Major gave me a pointed look. 'That's the problem with Abel's Army. They wouldn't hesitate to use your talents to kill and maim, while the

FEA wants to teach you to control your Variations.'

'So you believe that we could be next,' Kate said, a hint of impatience in her voice.

'Given your involvement in the last mission and Abel's interest in that case, I've come to that conclusion, yes. The Variations gathered in this room are too valuable for them to ignore. Appropriate security measures must be taken.'

'Alec should be safe, though, don't you think?' Kate gave a delicate shrug. 'After all, there's nothing he can do that a machine can't do. Strength isn't *that* valuable.'

I couldn't believe her audacity. Even in a situation like this, when agents were going missing and all of us were potential targets, she didn't have anything better to do than continue to attack Alec. His fingers tensed in mine, but his face remained a stony mask.

'Alec is a very important asset,' Major said sharply. *Discussion over.* I smirked at Kate, but the expression on her face wasn't the one I'd expected – not rebuffed, rather challenging. Kate had never defied Major openly. What the hell was going on?

'Until further notice, FEA headquarters will be on high alert. *You* will be on high alert. We have to take all necessary precautions to prevent another abduction from happening. Any kind of suspicious behaviour must be reported immediately. Are we clear?'

'Clear,' we echoed as one. I wondered if the others were as confused about the meaning of suspicious behaviour as I was. Everyone began rising from their chairs. Alec didn't look half as freaked out as I felt. He even managed a smile for me, even though he usually kept our romantic interaction to a bare minimum.

'Alec, Kate,' Major's voice lashed through the room like a whip. 'A word with you.' I hesitated and glanced at Alec, Kate and Major. None of them gave anything away. Alec released my hand with an apologetic smile. 'See you later?'

I nodded and, with a last glance at him, left the room and closed the door behind me.

When I arrived back at my room, Holly was awake and reading an email on our shared computer. But as soon as she heard me, she quickly clicked the browser window shut before I'd even closed the door – before I could catch a glimpse at what she'd been reading. Holly and I didn't keep secrets from each other. 'Hey,' she said without turning around. Her voice was too high. *Strange.*

I walked up to her slowly, hoping to catch a glimpse of something on her screen that would give me a clue. But her desktop background – a photo of us in front of the Christmas tree in the common room, wearing red Santa hats and huge grins – was the only thing greeting me. 'Everything OK?' I asked, touching her shoulder. She tensed, then put her hand over mine and turned around in her chair, giving me a smile. 'Sure.'

I searched her face for any kind of a sign, but it didn't give anything away. It was Holly's cheery face, the same face that had brought me through many dark moments.

Maybe all this high-alert talk from Major had turned my brain cells to mush. Holly was the one person besides Alec I could trust completely. End of story.

I sank down on the bed, and a moment later Holly joined me. 'Hey, you, why the gloom face?'

I put my head down on her shoulder and told her what I'd heard about Stevens and about Major's suspicions. 'Oh, wow, I suppose it's a good thing that I keep messing up with my Variation. At least that means I'm not valuable enough to be a target,' she said with a laugh. But even that sounded off. I raised my head. 'Holly, I don't know what I'd do if . . .' I swallowed. Even thinking about it made me all choked up. 'If something happened to you.'

She blinked quickly, then hugged me. 'Oh, please. I'm safe. You heard what Major said. Only useful Variants should be worried. I still can't get my invisibility under control.' She pulled back and changed the topic. 'So! You spent the night with Alec?'

'Just sleeping. Nothing happened,' I snapped back, feeling a blush creep up my neck.

She grinned, then her eyes darted back to her laptop. A small envelope had appeared and then faded. A new email.

'Who are you emailing?' I asked casually, but a feeling of concern wormed its way into my brain. I couldn't stand the thought of Holly doing something without telling me.

She kept staring at her laptop before finally turning to me. Tears sprang into her eyes.

'Holly, what's wrong?'

Her gaze dropped to her lap, where she was wringing her hands. 'It's . . .' she began, then sighed deeply. 'It's just my parents. My mom emailed me to say that Dad lost his job. She's taken on a part-time job, but she can't really do more. Someone has to take care of my brothers and sister. Noah has been sick a lot. His medicine is expensive.' Holly had two younger brothers and a younger sister, and her parents had always struggled to make ends meet.

'I'm sure he'll find a new job soon,' I assured her.

'I should be there to help them. It'll still be a couple of years before I'll really earn money as an agent.'

That gave me pause. Somehow, being with the FEA had felt more like a way of living than a job, but Holly was right: as full-fledged agents, we'd get paid for our work.

'Maybe you can ask Major if he can help out. I mean, we're practically doing this agent-trainee thing full-time, so we might as well get paid for it.'

'I don't think Major would agree. I mentioned it once, but I got the feeling that he'd prefer that I break ties with them.'

'Are you sure? That sounds so callous.'

'You know he doesn't care all that much about normal people. And look around: most FEA agents are either orphans or were abandoned by their parents. I'm pretty much the only one who stays in contact with their family, except for Kate and the few others with Variant parents.' She had a point.

'Maybe you could ask Major again? Or I could ask Alec to talk to him. Major listens to Alec.'

Holly shook her head hastily. 'No, no. I'll have to figure out another way. I wish I could live with them for a while to help take care of my siblings, so my Mom can work full-time. But Major would never agree.'

The FEA took us away from our families. Major seemed to think it was the duty of every parent to hand their child over with pride. But if he expected us to serve the FEA, he should at least make sure our families were doing OK. I wondered if parents had ever refused to send their child to the FEA, but somehow I already knew the answer. I didn't think Major knew the meaning of no.

CHAPTER 3

That night Holly, Alec, Tanner and I sat around a table in the common room, playing poker. Holly already looked much more cheerful, thanks to Tanner's jokes. Sitting beside each other – Tanner with his green mohawk and septum piercing, Holly with her fury-red pixie hair – they looked so cute together. I knew their admiration was mutual, but apart from an awkward kiss months ago, they'd yet to make a move.

Meanwhile, Alec kept touching my hand, my knee, my thigh beneath the table whenever he didn't need to put down a card. It seemed like he couldn't stop touching me, and it made me ridiculously happy.

'So what's really the deal with Abel's Army?' Holly asked as she dealt out cards.

'What do you mean?' Tanner asked distractedly as he sorted his hand. 'I thought you knew the gist already. They broke off with the FEA decades ago and are doing their own thing. Mainly illegal stuff.'

'Yeah, but what exactly are they doing?'

'They're working for the highest bidder. The Russian, Italian, or Chinese mafia, international terrorists – whoever pays the most,' Alec replied with an intense look at his cards. But something told me the cards weren't why he'd tensed.

'But if they work for all kinds of gangsters, how can they keep Variants a secret? If they care about money so much, wouldn't someone have bribed or blackmailed them and sold the knowledge to a newspaper or TV station?' I said.

Alec popped a few chips into his mouth, considering how much he should tell us. 'You should know that what I'm telling you now are only rumours. I don't know for sure, but I heard that Abel's Army has a Variant in their ranks who can alter or even remove memories. The ability to instantaneously brainwash someone.'

'Holy shit,' Holly said.

Tanner nodded in agreement, but it didn't look like Alec's words had been news to him. I was too stunned to say anything. I'd always joked with Holly that I'd love to know someone who could wipe out a few of my less pleasant memories, like when my mother told me I shouldn't call her ever again or that I was a freak and had ruined her life, or all the drunk, messed-up guys she'd dated back when I was a child. But it was scary to consider that someone could do that – change my memories, steal entire parts of my life so it was like they'd never happened. Alec was watching me as though he knew exactly what was going through my mind. His childhood had been filled with heartbreak just like mine.

The door to the common room swung open, and Phil and Devon entered. They glanced tentatively at our table, apparently unsure if they could join us.

'We still have room for more players,' Tanner said. He pointed at the vending machine in the back of the room, behind the sofas and the flat-screen TV. 'Get yourselves some provisions!'

'We don't have any money on us,' Devon said as he walked towards the vending machine.

'You don't need money for drinks,' Holly said. 'They're free! The vending machine is just for show.'

Phil and Devon got their drinks, while Tanner took care of the chairs. He raised his hand, and immediately the black folding chairs leaning against the wall beside the vending machine began floating towards us. Phil and Devon watched Tanner's show with obvious admiration. I rolled my eyes at Tanner, but he just winked and carefully lowered the chairs to the ground beside our table. Devon sat down across from me, and Alec's eyes darted between Devon and me with inquiring intensity. Alec didn't like Devon very much. They had barely spoken two sentences since Devon had joined the FEA. As implausible as it was, I suspected that Alec might be jealous of him.

I took Alec's hand beneath the table and squeezed. A shadow of stubble showed on his jaw. I wanted to press my cheek against it. I loved the prickly feeling. His smile widened as if he knew exactly what I was thinking.

'So you're the toxic guy, right?' Tanner asked as he handed cards to Phil. Only Tanner could say something like that without sounding rude. A deep flush spread across Phil's pale face. It was obvious that he wasn't used to attention, or to hanging out with friends.

He slid off the fingerless black gloves he wore most of the time. There were tiny glands embedded in the spot where his palm met his wrist. They looked like the lachrymal glands we have for tears, only slightly bigger. Maybe it was from nervousness, but they were already coated with poison.

'So if I touch it, I'll fall asleep?' Holly asked, her fingertip a centimetre from the gland.

Tanner tensed at her side. 'Holly,' I said in warning.

'You'd likely pass out,' Phil said quickly. For his next words, he lowered his eyes. 'Or fall into a coma.' He put the gloves back on, his fingers shaking.

'Well, I'm sure Devon could save the day,' Alec said with a forced smile.

Devon shrugged. 'I probably could.' Our eyes met, and memories crashed over me. Was he thinking of the time he'd saved my life back in Livingston?

'Let's get this game going,' I said with forced cheerfulness.

It was way past midnight when we stopped playing and finally returned to our rooms. More accurately, I went to my room only to change into pyjama shorts and a top before I hurried back to Alec's room. My cheeks were still

31

glowing from the way Holly wiggled her eyebrows at me as I retreated.

I found Alec already sitting on top of the covers on his bed, pulling a shirt over his head. I touched the long scar hidden beneath the dragon tattoo on his right shoulder, halting his movement.

'When you mentioned that Variant who could alter and remove memories, I thought of all the things in my life I've wanted to forget. And I wondered if I would ask them to, you know, erase some parts of my life.' I traced the scar as I locked eyes with Alec. 'Would you?'

Alec took my hand and kissed my palm, his lips warm against my skin. His grey eyes were serious. With him sitting on the bed and me standing in front of it, we were almost the same height. 'No,' he said quietly. 'I wouldn't. The past made me who I am.' That was such an Alec thing to say.

'But it hurts, remembering. Knowing that our parents didn't want us because of what we are. That they didn't care what would happen to us as long as it meant they could get rid of us.'

Alec pulled me down on to his lap. I straddled him, my hands resting on his shoulders. 'It does hurt, and that won't ever change. But remembering is what stops me from becoming like them. Their actions make me want to be better.'

I pressed my forehead against his and closed my eyes. 'Maybe. But sometimes I feel like a dog chasing its tail. Like

I'm looking for something I can't ever have, only I haven't realized it yet,' I murmured.

Alec shook his head in disagreement.

'You'll have your own family someday.'

'Yeah,' I agreed, but I knew it wasn't the same as having loving parents and siblings. 'Do you sometimes wonder what they're doing now?'

'No, because I know they aren't thinking about me either.'

'So you never think about contacting them again? Maybe they miss you.'

He didn't reply right away, and for a moment I wondered if I shouldn't have brought up this topic at all. 'No. I can't forgive them for what they did, and I don't want to. I don't need them. I have the FEΛ, and I have you.'

That was what I always tried to tell myself, too, but sometimes I wondered if I was only lying to myself.

A yawn slipped out of my mouth. 'Time to sleep,' Alec said. He let himself fall back on to the bed and took me with him. I lay sprawled on top of him and let sleep wash over me, banishing my dark thoughts.

CHAPTER 4

I knew it was only a matter of time until I had to face Kate. But when she knocked at my door the next day, I couldn't do anything but stare at her, my fingers gripping the edge of the doorframe. She was only a few centimetres taller than me but always managed to make me feel small in more than one way. As usual, she was styled to perfection: blonde hair in a neat ponytail, dressed in black pants and a crisp white blouse. I was wearing grey sweatpants and a rumpled T-shirt.

'Oh, hi,' I said stupidly. Holly was doing laps in the swimming pool, and I suddenly wished I'd gone with her to avoid this confrontation.

Kate's face was carefully controlled, her coppery amber eyes unreadable. If she wanted to strangle me, she did a damn good job of hiding it. 'We need to talk.' She glanced over my shoulder into the empty room. 'Are you going to invite me in or not?'

I strongly leaned towards 'or not', but it would have

been childish, and I wanted to get the conversation over with. I stepped back and opened the door wide enough for her to enter.

Without another word, Kate strode inside and hovered in the middle of the room. Her eyes took in the *Alien* and Freddy Krueger posters hanging over my bed. She nodded smugly. 'So that's where Alec got his bad taste from.'

I bit back a snappy comment. She just wanted to get a rise out of me, and I wouldn't give her the satisfaction. I stayed close to the door in case I had to make a quick escape. 'Kate, I'm sorry for how things went down. I—'

'No you're not,' Kate interrupted me. 'And don't pretend otherwise. You've been pining for Alec for years, and now you've finally got what you wanted.'

'It's true. But that doesn't mean I'm not sorry for what you lost.'

'No.' She shook her head forcefully, but not a single strand escaped her ponytail. My curls would have been all over the place. 'Don't you dare feel pity for me. I'm a big girl. I'm not crying myself to sleep because Alec left me. There are other fish in the sea. Bigger fish.'

I was still holding the door handle. It wasn't too late to throw Kate out. 'Then why are you here?' I asked.

'Look, Tessa, I came here to warn you.'

I dropped my hand from its perch on the handle. 'Warn me?'

A resentful smile flickered across her face. 'I don't think

you should go into this . . . relationship with Alec blindly. You deserve to know the entire truth.'

'What truth?' I didn't buy that Kate had come here to help me. She was here to drive a wedge between Alec and me. But she was wasting her time: nothing could shake my trust in Alec.

'Alec's been lying to you from day one. He's been manipulating you—'

I shook my head. 'You're just jealous that he left you for me. I don't have to listen to your lies. I should have known that you'd been planning this.'

'If you think I'm here because I'm jealous, you're even more delusional than I thought,' Kate said with a sneer. 'Tell me: in all the years you've known Alec, you've never felt that something was off, never had a twinge of suspicion?' She scanned my face, and one corner of her mouth quirked up.

Anger slithered through my belly at her tone and words. What reason did I have to be suspicious of Alec? My fingers clutched the hem of my shirt. I wanted to claw at her. 'I know Alec better than you, better than anyone.'

'Oh, please!' Kate snorted, her eyes cruel and merciless. 'I knew he had you wrapped around his little finger. But this? It's ridiculous.'

'Kate, talk to someone who cares about your bullshit.' I opened the door, determined to leave, but Kate grabbed my upper arm, her nails digging into my skin. The scent of her flowery perfume flooded my nose.

36

A dozen self-defence images fluttered through my head, but I pushed them back. A fight with Kate would lead to nothing. I was above her games. 'Let me go.'

'You'll listen to what I have to say, and you'll listen well,' she hissed, having completely disposed of her pleasant mask, her face an angry grimace. 'Whatever's going on between Alec and you, it's doomed. Because no matter what you think, you don't know the first thing about him.'

I tried to shake her off, but her fingers tightened on my arm. She slammed the door shut, and my hair whipped into my face from the force of it. I blinked at the smooth white surface of the door, forcing myself to breathe calmly. We were alone in the room once again. A quiver went through my body. Nothing she was going to say would break my trust in Alec. Nothing, I swore to myself.

But her softly spoken words wormed their way into my head. 'He's been lying to you all these years. Alec's a Dual Variant, and he never told you, and he never will.'

My legs felt weak. If Alec was a Dual Variant, that would mean he had a second Variation – one he'd hidden from me all along. I stepped away from her, my back bumping against the hard wood of the door, and she let go. 'He's not. You don't know what you're talking about,' I protested. Alec wouldn't have kept a Variation from me . . . would he?

Kate shook her head with a sneer. 'Still eager to defend him. But let me tell you something. Alec isn't only strong; he's an Empath. He can control emotions. Think about it.

When you're with him, are you sure you've felt what you felt?'

'You're lying,' I whispered, but it felt like something was stuck in my throat.

'Whenever you feel something around Alec, he knows. And if he doesn't like your emotions, he has the ability to change them. He can make you feel exactly what he wants you to feel. He can manipulate you, and believe me, Tessa, he has done so in the past. Are you sure your emotions are your own?'

I felt like I'd been ambushed. I couldn't believe what I was hearing.

'Go,' I croaked.

'Wake up, Tessa. It was time that someone told you the truth. Believe me, Alec and Major would have kept you in the dark forever.' Something flickered on her face, maybe worry or regret, like she realized that she shouldn't have told me as much as she did. Beyond whatever Alec wanted, Major would probably throw a fit if he found out. Without another word, Kate walked out of the room. I pressed my face against the cool wood and sank to my knees as the door slid shut.

I tried to convince myself that she'd lied, that her words had been the result of jealousy, her way of revenge, but the seed of doubt had been sown, and now it was taking root. A couple of months ago, when Alec and Major first accompanied me on the Livingston mission, I'd felt like someone was trying to manipulate my emotions. But I'd put it off as nerves. What if Alec had used his Variation to calm me back then? And that wasn't the only time I'd felt magically calmed in Alec's presence. Was it nothing more than a trick? Had he been using his Variation on me? And what else had he done without me noticing? How could I be sure if anything I felt around Alec was the truth? Every memory, every kiss, every smile . . . everything felt tainted now.

I closed my eyes, trying to get the whirlwind of emotions and thoughts in my body in order. I clenched my fists and staggered to my feet. I didn't want to believe it. But deep down I knew that something had always been off about my feelings when I was around Alec. I started trembling, and sickness washed over me. If I couldn't trust the one person I thought I could love completely, what was left? Holly. I had to talk to Holly.

I opened the door and peeked into the hallway to make sure Kate was gone. I didn't want her to see how much her words had rattled me. The corridor was empty. I slipped out and hurried down the stairs toward the swimming pool. Kate's perfume still clung to my clothes – just like her words clung to my mind. A woman from the cleaning staff disappeared into the laundry room, and I waited until she'd closed the door before I slipped past and entered the swimming hall.

Holly was doing dolphin butterfly strokes. Her red hair popped in and out of the water, her moves fluid and fast. She didn't see me as I crouched at the edge of the pool. My hands and legs were still shaking, but I felt somewhat calmer. Ten minutes passed before Holly eventually stopped at one end of the pool. She pulled her neon yellow goggles off and immediately spotted me. Her face broke into a smile, but just as soon it disappeared. Her narrow brown brows pulled together as she swam towards the ladder and got out. My legs ached when I straightened from my crouch to hand her a towel. Her eyes never left my face as she dried her hair. 'Did something happen between you and Alec?'

'Sort of. Kate and I had a talk,' I said slowly, trying to keep the worry from colouring my voice. But my emotions were right beneath the surface; Holly could probably see them shining through my skin like neon signs.

'Oh no. What did she do?' As she threw the towel into the hamper, I couldn't help but stare just beyond it, at that spot on the ground. That was where Alec had found me a few weeks after I'd joined the FEA, crying hysterically because my mom had said that I should never call her again. Alec had consoled me that day and countless times since then. What had stopped my tears each time, his words or his Variation?

'Tessa?' Holly touched my arm, leaving fingerprints of water on my shirtsleeve. I snapped out of my thoughts and turned away from the hamper. Water lapped over the edge of the pool only to be sucked back into the filter system. I slumped down on to a bench against the wall, and Holly sank down beside me, shivering in her yellow bikini.

'Spill,' she demanded, and I told her everything Kate had said. With every word, my voice got higher, and it felt like a bubble was building inside my body and ready to burst. When I was done, I gulped down a deep breath. I expected, *I hoped*, Holly would laugh and tell me how ridiculous I was, but she didn't. Her eyes became distant, a frown creasing her brows. 'Kate might be jealous, and she's certainly out to hurt Alec, but why would she make up something like that?' she said softly.

I nodded. 'It's not just that. Sometimes when I'm around Alec, my feelings take a quick turn for the better, you know? I always thought it was because of him, because of my feelings for him, but . . .'

'But now you aren't sure any more,' she finished the sentence for me.

Holly gnawed on her lower lip. Water ran down in narrow rivulets over her face and arms. She'd probably get a cold if I kept her from changing into proper clothes for much longer. 'You know how my Variation is always messing up?'

I gave a nod; of course I knew. 'Major made me take all these additional classes with Summers, but they didn't really help. With every class, I felt more like a total failure and kept messing up even worse. But then one day Major sent Alec instead of Summers, and magically my mood and my Variation improved. Remember when I told you afterwards how amazing classes had been that day?'

I didn't move. I remembered. Holly hadn't lost control

41

of her Variation once that day. She was as happy as I'd ever seen her.

'I'd felt calm and sure of myself, and suddenly my invisibility worked without fault. I'd thought it was because Alec wasn't making me as nervous as a real teacher, but now that I think about it, I'm not really sure if my emotions that day were entirely my own.'

I stared down at my palms, which were red from clenching my hands. 'It sounds exactly like what I've been experiencing.'

'I . . . hmm . . . maybe,' Holly was fishing for explanations, for excuses, but there were none. 'Do you think Major knows?'

I smiled mirthlessly. 'Major knows everything.'

Holly nodded. 'Yeah, he probably thinks we don't need to know. He always knows best.' The last part rang with bitterness. I got it. I really got it. I was so tired of being treated like a second-class agent, like I couldn't handle the same knowledge that Major or Alec or even Kate could.

'I have to talk to Alec.'

'Are you positive? If you confront Alec, he's going to give you an answer whether you like it or not.' Holly wrapped her arm around me. I shivered as my clothes got soaked through and the cold crawled into my body.

'I know. But I have to know for sure. I have to hear him say it. I can't just forget what Kate said. Who knows, maybe there's an explanation.'

'OK,' she said slowly, looking doubtful. 'Do you need backup?'

'No,' I said. I got up. Her arm slipped off my body. 'You get dressed and make sure you don't get a cold.'

Holly gave me a small, encouraging smile as I turned around and headed for Alec's room, but she didn't manage to wipe the doubt from her face.

CHAPTER 5

My fingers shook as I arrived in front of the white door to Alec's room. Alec and I had originally planned to meet in two hours to have dinner together in the cafeteria. I brought my fist up against the door, but I didn't knock, just rested my knuckles against the smooth surface. Maybe Holly was right. Maybe I shouldn't talk to Alec. But how could I pretend nothing had happened?

'Alec's in the dojo.'

I whipped my head around. Tanner stood behind me, dressed in workout clothes, covered in sweat, a towel hanging around his neck. Two guys stood a few steps behind him. One of them was Ty, Tanner's older brother. He was in his twenties and had been gone on a mission in Afghanistan or Iran or something like that until very recently. He looked remarkably like Tanner – same dark skin, long limbs, almond-shaped eyes, but he had shaved all of his hair off and his nose was slightly crooked, as if it had been broken and not treated properly. The look in his eyes was distant. I didn't recognize the stocky, muscle-covered guy beside him.

After a quick nod in their direction, I turned to Tanner. 'Huh? What did you say?'

'Alec is giving Devon and Phil kickboxing lessons in the dojo. He'll be there for at least another half hour,' he said. There was a hint of curiosity in his voice.

'Oh, thanks.' I forced my lips into a smile. Tanner stopped rubbing the towel over his mohawk. The guys must have sensed the rising awkwardness because they excused themselves and headed off to their rooms.

'Something wrong?' Tanner asked.

I shook my head. 'No. I'm fine.'

'You sure?'

'Yeah, I'm sure,' I said. 'I just need to talk to Alec. Thanks for telling me where to find him.' I hurried past him, but I could practically feel his eyes burning into my back. If I was acting that rattled around Tanner, it was unlikely that I could hide my feelings from Alec.

When I arrived on the ground floor, I could already hear panting and the sound of someone kicking and hitting the punching bag. I hesitated in the doorway to the dojo, unsure if this was a good idea. Alec had always been the one thing at the FEA that I could count on. This could be the end of my relationship with him, of the thing I'd been longing for since I joined the FEA. What would I do if that disappeared?

The familiar scent of the dojo welcomed me: rubber

from the new green workout mats mixed with the pungent odour of sweat. I'd spent so much time surrounded by the smell that it didn't even bother me any more.

Alec was pulling off his boxing gloves and began unwrapping the protective tape from his fingers when he glanced my way. He gave me a quick smile before he turned back to Devon, who was punching the bag, his face furious and determined. Phil was sitting on one of the green mats on the ground, arms wrapped around his knees. His head was tomato red, his clothes drenched in sweat. It was obvious that he wasn't as fit as Devon and Alec. The workout clothes hung loosely on his wiry frame, their fit much too big on him.

When Devon stopped pummelling the punching bag, he glanced in my direction, but as quickly as his gaze settled on me, it moved on.

The smile that had been playing on Alec's lips died. Could he feel my inner turmoil? Alec's eyes rested on mine, and our surroundings became a blur. I could hear Phil talking, could see him struggle to his feet from my peripheral vision, but nothing could penetrate the whooshing in my ears.

Alec said something to Devon and Phil, who both glanced at me briefly before they grabbed towels and water bottles and walked past me out the door. When they were gone, Alec moved towards me. His hands were still taped, but he didn't bother unwrapping them further.

'What's the matter?' he asked softly as he came to a halt

in front of me. I searched his grey eyes, looking for a hint of something, anything, to keep me from saying what I was about to say. He touched my shoulder. 'Tess?'

I took a step back so his hand slipped off me. I couldn't focus when he was touching me. I could see the confusion on his face, but there was something else mixed with it. Compassion? Understanding? Regret? Or maybe I was just looking for things that weren't there.

'Kate came to my room today. She told me everything about you,' I said. I was proud that I managed to keep my voice from cracking. I fought the urge to cross my arms in front of my chest, to create a shield between Alec and me.

He froze, his expression slipping from shock to anger and then to dread. 'What did she say?'

'She told me that you've been keeping something from me all this time – that you're a Dual Variant and that your secret Variation is reading and *manipulating* other people's emotions.'

Alec stared at me, every muscle in his body so tense it looked like he might combust. 'I—' Alec was lost for words. That was something I hadn't seen before. And that more than anything else made me realize that Kate hadn't lied.

'Tell me the truth,' I said quietly. I could see on his face that he was struggling to come up with a lie, and part of me wanted him to. Maybe I could pretend my talk with Kate never happened. Maybe I could pretend Alec hadn't kept a secret from me. But I wouldn't do that to myself. I was worth more than that. I'd put up with enough while he was torn between Kate and me.

Alec hung his head, the tension leaking from his body. 'It's true. I am a Dual Variant. Major thought it would be wise to keep my ability a secret, since it was something people often didn't take kindly to.'

No kidding. 'Everyone knows about Kate's variation. I think they could have dealt with yours as well.' It was easier to talk about it in general terms, but other questions burned in my chest. Questions I was scared to get the answers to.

Alec began picking absentmindedly at his tape. Was he buying time? Considering once again how much to tell me? 'Kate doesn't have a second Variation she could have hidden her mind reading behind. Major had no choice but to let everyone know,' he said eventually. 'And people are more concerned about hiding their emotions than their thoughts, in my experience.' He took a step closer once again but didn't try to touch me. 'I wanted to tell you.' His face looked so earnest and imploring, my heart gave a thud. But this time I wouldn't let it turn me into a fool.

'Then why didn't you?' I demanded, anger slowly but steadily taking the place of my hurt.

'Major forbade me. He thought it would endanger our community.' He hesitated, like there was more, and my anger flared again.

'You should have told me once we started dating. I had a right to know.' I clenched my fists. 'I *trusted* you, Alec. When I was broken and thought I could never trust anyone after how my mom treated me, you gave me back my ability to trust.'

His expression turned pleading. 'I know, and I'm sorry. But I wasn't allowed to, and I knew you'd hate it if you knew that I could read your emotions.'

'I bet you were glad that Major's order gave you a justification not to tell me. At least admit that.'

'No,' he said. He gripped my hands. 'I hated that I had to lie to you. Please, you have to believe me.'

I wanted to believe him. But that didn't change the fact that he'd violated my privacy without my knowledge for the past two years. 'So you always knew what I was feeling? And even now you can read my emotions, right?'

We stared at each other. He dropped his gaze and sighed. 'Yes. But it isn't something I can just switch off. Even if I don't want to, and, believe me, most of the time I'd be glad to be spared having to deal with everyone's emotions all the time. Sometimes I manage to tune it out, but it's not always easy.'

I tried to imagine how it must be, to be overwhelmed with the myriad of emotions from people around me, with their fears and worries. Sometimes I could hardly stand seeing the sadness on Holly's face. How much worse would it be if I could actually feel it like it was my own? A tiny part of me felt sorry for Alec, but the bigger part held on to my anger.

'Have you ever manipulated me?' I asked.

'I could manipulate people's emotions if I tried,' he

said slowly. 'But it would be a breach of FEA rules, you know that.'

'That doesn't mean you've never done it. Answer my question. Yes or no. Have you ever manipulated me?' *Please say no*, I thought. But I knew that he'd be lying if he did.

'Only for your own good. I wanted to help you,' he said reluctantly. 'I couldn't stand to see you scared. I shouldn't have done it.'

'They are *my* emotions. I can handle them.'

Alec shook his head in despair. 'Tess,' he whispered. 'I'm really sorry.'

Sorry that I found out? I wondered, but I didn't say it. How could I ever be sure about anything around him?

'You don't trust me,' he said.

'Did you just gather that from my feelings?' I asked.

He sagged against the wall of the dojo. His eyes looked tired. 'I know you're upset, but even if I couldn't read your emotions, I'd know it from the look on your face.'

I wrapped my arms around my chest, as if that could stop him from looking into my heart, from seeing everything I didn't want him or anyone else to know. I thought of all the times I'd lusted after him and all the nights I'd imagined kissing him. Even now, thinking about how he must have felt my desire for him every time we were close made me want to run and hide from the shame. But what if he had been responsible for my feelings? 'So you never made me feel something I didn't?' I whispered.

He frowned, then his eyes widened. 'You mean your feelings for me?'

I couldn't bear looking at him, so I stared at the floor-to-ceiling mirrors lining the other end of the dojo. One of them had a crack in it that had been there for months.

He touched my shoulders, bringing our bodies so close together that I could feel his warmth. 'I'd never have done that, Tess. What kind of person do you think I am?'

'I don't know what to think any more. I thought I knew you, and suddenly it turns out you've been keeping a huge secret from me. I have to think about it. I – I just feel so unprotected.' Even that admission made me feel even more vulnerable. But what did it matter around Alec? All of my feelings were fair game.

Alec's hands slid off my shoulders. 'I always hated that part of me. It was why my parents hated me, why they couldn't stand being in a room with me, much less looking at me. It's why they wanted me gone. I always knew that this Variation more than my strength would scare people.'

I took a deep breath. 'I think we need a few days away from each other. I still—' *Love you.* I didn't say it. I couldn't, not when a part of me hated him at the same time for what he was capable of, for knowing me better than I probably knew myself.

He touched my cheek, and for the briefest moment I leaned into the touch but then turned away. I needed to leave before he broke through my resolve. He probably didn't even need his Variation for that.

'I love you, Tess,' he said quietly when I was halfway through the door.

The words felt like someone had thrust a knife into my heart. I'd wanted to hear those words from Alec, had long imagined and dreamed of the moment when he'd finally say them, had pictured the happy glow on my face when I'd hear them and how I'd pull his face down to mine to kiss him and whisper the words back to him over and over again. Today wasn't that day. And now that day would never come. Without looking at him, I strode away from the dojo, towards the elevator. Alec didn't try to stop me.

CHAPTER 6

'This is so messed up,' Holly said.

I scratched my pencil over the paper, doodling black twirls around the list of names I'd written down with Holly's help earlier. A dull fury burned under my skin. It covered up the underlying sense of betrayal and loss. But nothing was lost yet. Alec and I hadn't broken up. He still wanted to be with me, and I wanted to be with him. And yet it felt like something had been broken in a way that couldn't be fixed.

'Do you really think Tanner could be a Dual Variant? He doesn't seem like the type to keep a secret.'

'Neither did Alec,' I said. Though that wasn't exactly true. Alec was the more secretive, brooding type. 'He's Alec's best friend. Even if he isn't a Dual Variant himself, that doesn't mean he didn't know about Alec's extra Variation.'

'I don't think Alec would have told him, if he didn't even reveal it to you,' Holly said thoughtfully.

I wanted to believe that Alec was the only one who was

hiding something, but I couldn't trust any of them. Not yet. Not after finding out that the person I'd trusted most besides Holly had lied to me from the start. 'I have to talk to Major,' I said finally. Maybe he'd tell me the entire truth, now that I knew about Alec.

Holly's eyes grew wide. 'Whoa. Have you lost your mind? Major will go ballistic if he finds out that you know about Alec. He won't tell you anything.'

A crackling sounded from the speakers in the ceiling. Holly and I raised our heads at the same time to stare at the white painted squares. My insides felt like someone was squeezing them. What were the odds that Major would message me or Holly on the day I found out about Alec's Variation?

'Holly, Tessa, in my office in ten minutes,' Major barked, and with a hiss the speakers went out again. Silence followed.

Holly glanced at me. 'Uh, why do I think this isn't good?'

'Because it isn't.' I glared at the picture of Alec and me on the digital frame on my nightstand. We'd taken it only two days ago. A red gummy bear was wedged between our lips, our eyes crinkling with laughter. A moment later, he'd swallowed it. When I'd protested, he'd silenced me with a kiss. That seemed like a lifetime ago.

'Come on. Let's go. We can't afford to be late.' Holly jumped up from her bed and dragged me to my feet. The desk chair groaned as it spun from the sudden movement. A good reflection of the way I felt.

* * *

'Sit down,' Major waved a hand at the two free chairs. The third was already occupied.

Alec. Of course he was here. His eyes followed me as I crossed the room and sat in the far left chair so that Holly ended up between him and me. It was ridiculous and childish, but if this talk was about what I thought it was – me finding out about Alec's Dual Variation – then I needed the space, or I'd end up strangling him. Kate would have been here if she were the one who'd told Major about her slip of the tongue. So that left only Alec. I could still feel his eyes on me. They seemed to burn into me, ignoring Holly and Major completely. He could probably feel my anger, and for once I almost welcomed it.

Major's gaze darted between Alec and me, and his frown threatened to swallow his eyes. 'I'm sorry, did something occur that I should be aware of?'

The question leaked some of the tension from my body. So he didn't know.

'No, sir,' Alec and I said at the same time. Major's frown and the lines around his mouth deepened as he narrowed his eyes in suspicion. I'd faced that look too often to be intimidated by it. Realizing it, he stared down at a file lying opened on his desk. Holly relaxed visibly in her chair.

'So why did you want to see us, sir?' Alec asked, his voice all business. I wished I had his talent to switch off my emotions. I bet his Variation factored into that. Outside the picture window, it had started hailing, and the icy stones lashed angrily against the glass.

'I have a new mission for the three of you,' Major said, shuffling a few pieces of paper around.

'So soon?' I blurted. It had been only a few weeks since I'd returned from my first mission in Livingston. There were classes to complete before I was sent out into the field again. And my previous mission still haunted my dreams.

'I thought we'd agreed to keep Tessa in headquarters for a while until we've determined if Abel's Army will target her,' Alec said disapprovingly.

Why did he make it sound as if I was the only target? The clunk-clunk of hail hitting the window filled the awkward silence of the room. Holly watched the scene with wide eyes. This would be her very first mission. I scratched my shoes over the grey tiled floor, unsure what to make of Alec's strange reaction.

Major's lips thinned as he folded his fingers on the desk in front of him. 'It's not my decision, sadly. A politician has been getting death threats, and one of his bodyguards was seriously injured during a recent attack. Secret Service is convinced that we're dealing with Variants. Apparently the government may have done some bargaining with shady individuals. Now this is mob business, and Abel's Army might be doing some of their dirty work for cash.'

'If Abel's Army is responsible, Tessa can't be involved in the case. It's too dangerous,' Alec said urgently.

'What would our mission entail?' I asked, tired of everyone discussing my safety as if I wasn't there.

Major's lips turned up into the semblance of a smile. 'Our main job is to catch the people responsible for the death threats and the attacks.' He turned his attention to me. 'But in order to do that and keep the politician safe, certain people think you should impersonate him.'

'Who is he?'

'Senator Jack Pollard,' Major said. I didn't know him, but a senator? 'He was with the FEA a while back, then he turned politician and started working for the State Department. He tried to establish a cooperation between our government and foreign organizations that were similar to the FEA.'

'There are Variant agencies in other countries?' I asked. Somehow it had never occurred to me that there might be Variants around the world, not connected to the FEA.

'Yes,' Major said. 'So far his cooperation efforts haven't worked out though. Not that we've been revealing anything about the FEA to other countries, so why would they?' He paused. 'Anyway, now he ensures that the FEA prison abides official regulations, though he's never actually set foot inside.' It didn't take much to hear the contempt in Major's voice. 'Mainly he's an advisor for the government on matters of organized crime.'

'So he's fully aware of the involvement of Abel's Army with the mob and other crime organizations?' Holly guessed.

'Indeed,' Major said. 'His affiliation with them is likely the reason for his becoming a target.'

'How long would I need to pretend to be him?' I couldn't imagine living someone else's life again so soon after my last mission.

'You're not going to take anyone's place,' Alec interrupted me. 'Not when Abel's Army is involved.'

I stared at him, speechless. What the hell had gotten into him? His grey eyes were boring into me as if he was trying to send me some secret message. I was so sick of him deciding what was best for me when he couldn't be honest himself.

'That's not for you to decide.'

'You don't know how serious this is, Tessa.'

'Enough,' Major said sharply. 'This is an order. I won't tolerate your insubordination. If you can't keep your emotions in check, I'll pull you from the mission and will send Tanner as protection for Tessa and Holly.'

Alec's face turned to stone. 'No. I have to be there.'

Major searched his face for a long time, then nodded and turned back to me. 'You're going to take Senator Pollard's place for one event. The senator has been invited to speak in front of a few hundred law students.'

'He'll talk about us?' Holly asked in a hushed voice.

'Of course not,' Major said curtly. 'He'll give a speech about organized crime.' He turned to me once again. 'Apparently the Secret Service believes that this'll be the perfect opportunity for Abel's Army to strike. It'll be your job, Tessa, to replace Senator Pollard. You'll be giving his speech, and you may need to talk to a few people, if

58

necessary, but we'll try to keep your contact with outsiders to a minimum.'

'So I'll have to memorize his speech and learn everything about organized crime?'

'I doubt you can learn everything in two days. But it can't hurt for your future missions to get familiar with the structure of the mob and similar organizations.'

'Sir,' Holly said meekly. 'What's my job?'

'You and Alec will accompany Tessa for her safety. While Alec will be part of the official security staff, you'll be keeping an eye on things discreetly, using your Variation. It's time that you're finally part of a mission.' Major's eyes narrowed. 'Summers and Alec assured me that you can do this. Do you agree?'

Holly nodded hastily. 'Yes, sir. My Variation has improved a lot. I can stay invisible for several hours.'

'That will do for now. You should make sure that your record is over a day by the end of the year,' Major said.

Holly shrunk on her chair and cast her eyes downwards. Why couldn't Major praise her for her improvement? Didn't he realize how difficult it had been for her?

'Do Pollard's bodyguards know of the mission?' Alec asked.

Major glanced up from his desk. 'No,' he said. 'No one else knows. The senator thought it wouldn't be wise to tell them about it.'

'But they know about the FEA and Variants?' I said.

Major's lips twisted. 'No, apparently it's hard to come

by entirely trustworthy security personnel, unless you're the president.'

Well, that made me feel safe.

'Pollard will visit headquarters tomorrow. He'd like to meet you before entrusting his reputation to you, and since you'll have to touch him to gather his DNA for the mission, I agreed.' He gave a dismissive nod. 'That's it for now. You can return to your rooms.'

Alec tried to catch my eyes as we left Major's office, but I ignored him. The moment we were outside, he grabbed my hand. 'We need to talk. Just one minute.'

Holly waited for me a few steps away. 'Should I wait?'

'No. It's OK. You go ahead.' After she disappeared into the elevator, I followed Alec to the other end of the corridor, far away from Major's office and his ears.

'You'll have to trust me for this mission, Tess,' he said. We were standing far too close. I craned my neck to look into his eyes, and the emotion there stopped me from stepping back. 'That's rule number one for bodyguards and their charge.'

'Don't worry. My feelings won't disturb the mission. I'm sure you won't let them,' I said coldly.

'Don't you get it? I don't give a damn about this mission. I'm scared for you. They're using you as bait again. Just like last time. I couldn't protect you then, and you almost died. I won't let that happen again.'

Words rose into my throat, but I couldn't bring them out. Despair and worry crowded on Alec's face. His palm felt warm against my cheek. What did it matter that he could read my emotions? It didn't change what I felt for him. Alec leaned down until our breath mingled, and I could practically feel the heat of his lips on mine. One kiss and maybe everything would be OK.

Don't, a tiny voice warned, but it couldn't compete against Alec's warmth, against the smell of him, against the look in his grey eyes. Our lips collided, and it felt like the world around me had faded to black, like nothing mattered but him and our kiss. I jerked away. How could I know he hadn't planned this, gauging my emotions until they told him what he was waiting for? How could I know that I wasn't just feeling what he wanted me to feel?

Alec slumped against the wall. For a long time, we just stared at each other, and the look in his eyes almost killed me. I whirled around, away from the pain on his face. I had bigger things to worry about: Abel's Army and the next mission. If what Alec said was true, Holly and I were in great danger.

CHAPTER 7

My hands were sweaty when I stepped into Major's office the next morning to meet Senator Pollard. It felt more like an assessment than a meeting.

I was surprised to see Summers leaning against the wall beside the glass cabinet, her sinewy arms crossed in front of her chest. As usual, she was dressed in all black: black muscle shirt, tight leather pants and combat boots with steel toe caps. She gave me a curt nod. Her ash-blonde hair was pulled back in a messy ponytail. It looked as if a brush hadn't come near her for days. Sometimes I wondered if Summers deliberately dressed like a man so that people would show her more respect. Or maybe she just hated make-up and other girly things. I supposed she was involved in the mission because of Holly. After all, it was her evaluation that had convinced Major that Holly was ready for the field.

Major stood in front of his floor-to-ceiling window, his back turned to the man in the chair across from his desk.

The door fell shut behind my back with an audible thud. I winced. Major turned, his face lined with a deep frown. The senator twisted in his chair to look at me. He was the epitome of a successful politician. Every detail of his appearance was perfect, from his black designer pinstripe suit, his light blue tie, his neatly smoothed-back grey hair and his attractive, clean-shaven face. Nothing was out of line. Even his high-wattage smile looked like it took weeks to perfect in the mirror.

'So that's her?' he asked in a voice even smoother than his outward appearance. His smile twisted and suddenly turned cruel. I was pretty sure that was his behind-closed-doors smile. 'That tiny slip of a girl? You're losing your touch, my friend.' He let out a superior laugh while watching me the way one would regard a bothersome fly. I was stunned into silence and glanced at Major. Was that man for real? It seemed his perfect appearance was trying to overcompensate for his ugly persona. What a douche.

Summers straightened, her square jaw tightening. Her leather pants squeaked as her legs moved.

Pollard looked at me, blue eyes no longer amused but calculating. 'You, come here.'

The annoyance must have shown on my face, because he let out a deep laugh. 'Oh-ho-ho, a firecracker,' he whistled. He glanced at Summers as if he thought she'd agree with him, but from the look on her face, she would have liked to crush him under her black boots.

I walked up to him without a word, rearranging my face

into a smile. Nothing I wanted to say would have improved my situation. Not that I thought I'd have gotten in trouble with Major. Whatever insult I might have chosen, I was sure he had a worse word in mind for the senator. But this was about professionalism. In future missions, I'd often work with people I didn't like or who would be rude to me. The trick was to remain above the fray.

'So you're the one they're all salivating over?' He didn't even try to hide his doubt and amusement. His hands were smooth, with the skin of someone who'd always had other people to do his work, and neat nails as if he'd had a manicure recently. When he reached out to touch my arm, it still took all my willpower not to flinch. He was rude and slimy and I didn't want him anywhere near me. The second his skin came into contact with mine, I could feel my body absorb his data, incorporate it somehow into my memory and DNA. 'This little girl is supposed to take my place, huh?' His eyes burned into mine, never wavering.

I bristled, but stopped myself from saying something. I returned his gaze. I wouldn't let that man intimidate me.

'She's more than capable,' Major said through gritted teeth. His expression made it plainly clear how little he thought of the man in front of him. But I thought that went both ways. There wasn't any love lost between them.

'Then get on with it, missy. Show me what you got,' he said in a deep southern drawl, all charm and smile. He seemed to find himself very funny.

Since he'd already touched me, I'd already collected the

DNA I needed to shift into his form. But then I hesitated. I had a better idea. I let the familiar rippling sensation wash over me, felt my bones grow and shift, saw my skin darken to caramel. The man let out a whistle. 'Holy moly. Not bad.' He glanced between Major and me. 'I can't tell who's the real one.'

A self-satisfied smile tugged at my lips, but it died when I noticed the look on Major's face. His lips were set in a hard line, eyes burning with anger. He'd never said as much, but apparently changing into him was off-limits. I glanced at Summers for help, but her face didn't give anything away.

'You know, Antonio,' Senator Pollard said snidely. Major tensed at the use of his first name. Only Martha was allowed to call him that. 'She actually manages to make you look better. I guess that's because she isn't so tense and stuck up.'

With a violent shudder, I hastily changed back to myself. I didn't want to give Senator Pollard any more reason to provoke Major, who already looked close to exploding.

'As you can see, Tessa is the perfect agent for the job,' Major said curtly. 'She'll make sure this mission is a success.'

'She'd better. Some people would love to see her fail and have your trust in her be thrown in your face.' His cold eyes settled on me. 'You're being watched.'

I didn't dare ask what that meant, and Major's scowl made it clear he wouldn't tell me. And maybe it was for the best. It would only distract me from the mission. Major dismissed me with a nod, but as I stepped out of the office, Senator Pollard's words made me pause. I slowly closed the door behind me, stopping to listen to as much of their conversation as I could. 'Someone has stolen the files about the FEA prison.' I was glad that the senator saw no reason to keep his voice down. I held my breath and pressed my ear against the door.

'Why has no one informed me of this before?' Major demanded.

'I suppose they think it's my concern.'

'Your concern? You haven't been there once in all these years. If you had any sense at all, you wouldn't have kept sensitive information in a building full of non-Variants. This is FEA business.'

'That's where you're wrong, my friend. You can't just build a prison and think the FBI and federal government won't keep an eye on it. You're given a lot of leeway with your decisions, but we have to at least pretend to work under federal laws.'

'You don't realize the consequences of your incompetence.'

'And you are a drama queen.' I had to stifle a gasp. But Senator Pollard continued as if he hadn't just insulted Major. 'What can they do with a file? So what if they know who's been locked up in our prison?'

I heard some rustling, and the door opened. I stumbled back, but it was too late. Summers had seen me. She slipped the door shut behind her and cocked a blonde eyebrow. 'Poking your nose into things that aren't your business?'

I was about to reply, but she didn't give me the chance. 'Curiosity killed the cat. Some things better stay a secret, *believe me*,' she added, then she strode down the corridor.

Was she talking about Alec's secret Variation? Or were there more secrets – even darker secrets – I didn't know?

CHAPTER 8

Tanner was the one who brought me the clothes I was to wear as Senator Pollard: a dark grey suit, a white shirt and a red tie, as well as white cotton briefs and an undershirt. I hadn't considered that I'd have to wear his underwear too.

Tanner leaned against the doorframe, twisting his septum piercing. His expression was too serious.

'What's up?' I asked.

'I need to talk to you,' he said. 'About Alec.'

Dread settled in the pit of my stomach. That was the last thing I wanted to talk about.

'Can it wait until later? I need to change.' I couldn't even look him in the eyes. He was Alec's best friend. He'd probably been in on his secret from the start. I knew which side he was on.

'I won't take long.' He moved closer, but then he thought better of it and stopped in the middle of the room. He looked uneasy, as if what he was going to say next was way out of his comfort zone. 'Alec loves you. You know that, right?'

Of course I knew. Alec had said the words to me, but hearing Tanner say them made them seem more real. 'Love isn't the problem,' I said quietly. I glanced at the photo of Alec and me on my nightstand. Why did things have to go wrong so fast? There had been a time in my life when I'd thought Alec admitting his love for me would make me the happiest person alive.

'All you need is love. Want me to sing the song?' he joked. But the grin died on his lips when he saw my expression. 'Not a good day to make jokes, eh?'

I shook my head. I stared down at the clothes clutched in my hands.

'Alec's beating himself up because of the whole thing,' Tanner said. He was rubbing his checkered sneakers over the floor, back and forth, back and forth. I focused on them instead of his face. 'He wanted to tell you. But things aren't that easy when Major is involved.'

I raised my head. 'So you know about his Dual Variation?'

Tanner hesitated, his dark eyes cornered. 'Yeah, but—'

'Did he tell you?'

Tanner gripped his mohawk. 'Jeez, Tessa, I'm making a mess of things.'

'So he told you but not me?'

'It's complicated.'

I pointed a finger at him. 'Oh no, not you too. I've heard those words so often, and I'm sick of it.'

'Alec was worried about how you'd react if you found out. But believe me, he wanted to tell you.'

'Did he send you to talk to me?' I demanded.

Tanner snorted. 'Alec? Please. You know him. He tries to deal with stuff on his own. He'd probably kick my ass if he found out I was here.'

'I really need to change into Pollard now,' I said.

Tanner nodded and moved towards the door. His hand on the handle, he turned to me once more. 'You two need each other. You should give him another chance. Everyone makes mistakes.'

'Believe me, I know. And I never said I wouldn't give him another chance. But I'm upset, and I really need to focus.'

Tanner hesitated as if there was more to say, but then he slipped out and closed the door without a sound. I stared at the white surface for a moment, trying to calm my raging emotions before I started undressing. How was I supposed to focus now?

I didn't bother to put Senator Pollard's clothes on since they would have been too big for my current body.

My transformation started off slow because I was distracted, the rippling decreasing to a gentle tremble. But I returned my focus, and within seconds I had changed into Senator Pollard.

Holly came out of our bathroom, and her eyes widened as her gaze travelled over the foreign body. 'Oh my God,' she breathed, flushing pink.

It took me a moment to realize why she was reacting like that. I stood naked before her – in Senator Pollard's body. There wasn't any part of it that was covered. Laughing, I staggered towards the pile of clothes and thrust my legs into his underpants.

Holly helped me get dressed. I jammed the hem of the shirt in my zipper three times before she stuffed the fabric back into the trousers and zipped me up. She didn't stop giggling.

'I hope you don't have a laughing fit during the mission. I think people might get suspicious if the empty air starts to make a sound,' I said. It was meant as a joke, but I regretted the words when I saw the anxiety on Holly's face. This was her first mission, and her Variation hadn't exactly been reliable in the past. I put a heavy, long-fingered hand on Holly's shoulder. 'Everything will be fine,' I told her in Senator Pollard's deep voice. 'Alec is there. He won't let you fail. If things get tough, he'll just use his freaky Variation to manipulate your emotions.' I could almost taste the bitterness on my tongue.

Holly peered at the hand on her shoulder with a little frown before she burst into laughter once again. 'I'm sorry. This is just too absurd.'

'I know,' I said with a smile, glad that her dark mood had disappeared. When the suit was in place, Holly and I headed for the heliport.

Major and Alec were already waiting for us. 'I'd like a word with you, Tessa,' Major said, walking away from

Holly and Alec, and leaving me no other choice but to hurry after him. He stopped abruptly, and I almost ran into his back. It was the first time that I had to look down on him; Pollard was quite a bit taller than Major. 'Listen, if it was up to me, you wouldn't be part of this,' he said. 'We still don't know enough about the threat, much less if the attackers will strike today. I don't like the thought of being in the dark like this. And I don't think this is a good time for you to leave headquarters.'

I nodded, though I didn't understand his reasoning. Why was he telling me this if I still needed to go?

'But you think Abel's Army has something to do with the death threats?' I asked.

Major frowned. 'I don't see why they'd bother with Senator Pollard, unless they misjudge his importance. It's not like his advisory role in matters of organized crime is stopping anyone, and even his involvement with us isn't worth mentioning. I think there's more at play here. And frankly, I don't trust Senator Pollard.'

That surprised me.

Major glanced at his watch. 'It's time to set out. We don't want you to be late,' he said. 'Alec will make sure that nobody's up to something, especially the security staff.'

'You mean by reading and manipulating their emotions?' I wasn't sure why I'd said it.

Major's eyes snapped to Alec, as if he thought he might have revealed his secret to me. 'He didn't tell me,' I murmured. 'I figured it out by myself.' This would have been my chance to get Kate in serious trouble, but for once she wasn't the one I was angry with. Without her, I'd still be in the dark. I supposed I should be grateful to her, even if her reasons for telling me weren't innocent.

'Why didn't you tell me?' I asked.

Major raised his eyebrows. 'There was no reason to. But we'll discuss this further once you're back from the mission.'

'It's time!' Alec shouted, pointing at his watch, before he boarded the helicopter. The blades began rotating. I hurried towards Holly, and together we climbed inside. Major gave a nod before he closed the door and backed away. Then we lifted off – towards my second mission.

CHAPTER 9

It was sweltering. Without a word, Connors and Orlov, Senator Pollard's usual bodyguards, positioned themselves next to the windows. They were solid, pretty much walking wardrobes. I could see the muscles bulging under their suits. If I'd met them in a dark alley, I'd have run as fast as my legs would have taken me. Orlov especially: with his square jaw, hard features and cold steel-grey eyes, he could have played the hit man in every Hollywood production. Neither of them even glanced Alec's way. He was new and, it was pretty obvious, unwanted. Of course they judged him on his appearance. They didn't know about the power hidden beneath his lean muscles.

Sweat gathered at the nape of my neck. I twisted my head back and forth in an effort to widen the collar. But it was useless. The suit and the button-down shirt felt confining. I didn't think I could fight in them – even if I didn't have Pollard's unfamiliar body to consider.

I inched a finger into the gap between my neck and the

clammy collar to try to loosen its hold once again. Nothing. The fabric was stiff with starch and resisted my tugging. I sagged against the brown leather couch. The dark green carpet smelled flowery in an artificial way, as if someone had used a carpet cleaner shortly before we'd arrived. The smell tickled the inside of my nose.

'You all right, sir?' Orlov asked in his thick Russian accent, taking a step closer to me. I waved my hand dismissively. 'I'm fine. Do your job and watch the windows.' I hated how rude I had to act towards them, but I couldn't step out of character.

Alec came up to me – without asking for permission and thus breaking protocol. His expression reflected the worry that he couldn't voice in front of the others. 'What are you doing? Go back to the door,' I snapped, Senator Pollard's voice emerging rough and clipped from my throat. Alec's lips tightened, but he strode back to his designated spot. Elation flared up in me at my position of power over him.

I was glad to have some distance between us. Something brushed my arm, the touch warm and comforting. Holly. Her form hadn't once flickered during the thirty minutes we'd been waiting in this room. Her invisibility seemed to work just fine. I hoped it was her own doing and not Alec's manipulation.

I wanted to smile at Holly to show her that I'd felt her comforting touch, but I didn't move a muscle. Senator Pollard's bodyguards and Alec were all watching me.

Though Alec seemed busy guarding the door, I knew he would never take his eyes off me.

Outside the door, I could hear the current speaker wrap up his speech. I was next.

I dug Senator Pollard's fingers into my legs and tried to feel nothing. I focused on my breathing, on the way the trousers clung to the back of my thighs, on the way the strange hair growing in my ears tickled. Slowly a wall of calm came up around me. But my reprieve was short-lived. Applause rose outside, and someone knocked at the door. Alec stepped back, a hand over the gun at his waist, as he opened the door a gap. The same middle-aged woman with a tight ponytail who'd first taken us to the green room appeared in the corridor. 'It's Senator Pollard's turn,' she said politely.

I hoisted myself to my feet and followed the woman to the back of the stage, Alec taking up my front and Orlov and Connors my rear. I could feel Holly moving at my side, and it was her presence more than theirs that eased my nerves. Five hundred people made up the audience – law students and journalists and possibly someone intent on Senator Pollard's death.

'You're safe,' Alec said under his breath. 'Don't worry. Security measures were tripled.'

'If it's so safe, why am I here and not Pollard?' I whispered, glaring at his back, as I lumbered up the stairs on to the stage. A wave of applause welcomed me, and I raised my arm in Senator Pollard's trademark greeting.

Every gesture, every move was perfect. Nobody would realize I wasn't him – not even his enemies. I walked up to the speaker's podium in the centre of the stage as the clapping ebbed away. I let my gaze swivel over the audience, looking for anything out of the ordinary. But there was nothing. Most of the blue chairs were occupied by men and women in their twenties. They'd probably fall right off their seats if they found out a sixteen-year-old girl was actually the speaker.

I cleared my throat and opened my lips to recite the speech, but the words faltered in my mouth. Something was off. The hairs at the base of my neck rose. I wasn't exactly sure what caused my discomfort. A wall of silence lay before me as people stopped talking to stare at my mute form. I coughed and glanced at the notes on the speaker's desk in front of me.

My voice was calm and businesslike as I started the speech. I'd seen videos of Senator Pollard giving speeches and knew that he was a good orator. He possessed the natural charisma and verbal skills to grab an audience – which made what I was about to do that much harder. I forced myself to look up every now and then to smile at my audience and search the auditorium for anything suspicious. A few minutes into my speech, I raised my head again, my mouth already dry from reading, and the words died in my throat. Every muscle in my body bristled with anxiety.

My eyes landed on a familiar face in the audience. It was the man who'd been watching me a few weeks ago back in

Livingston, the man who was most likely a member of Abel's Army. He was leaning at the back of the auditorium, returning my gaze with unsettling calm. Brown hair, pale skin, dark sunglasses, unidentifiable age. He wore a long beige coat. What was he hiding beneath it?

Alec stared at me, then followed my eyes across the room. Of course he hadn't seen the man before, but he could feel how nervous I was. The man was wearing exactly the same sunglasses and coat he had worn last time. Was he the only Variant in the room? Was he here to enact some sinister plan?

I took a deep breath and continued my speech. The audience was starting to whisper about my strange behaviour, and I couldn't risk losing their attention. Alec gave me a tiny nod and moved off to the side of the auditorium as he tried to make his way towards the back. The man's eyes flitted briefly to Alec but then returned to me, as if Alec wasn't even worth his attention. I couldn't sense Holly anywhere near me. Where was she? Maybe she was also heading for the strange guy.

Connors and Orlov had picked up on the tense atmosphere, of course (they weren't that bad, no matter what Major might think), and were watching Alec's progress across the room with barely hidden contempt.

Maybe I should give them a sign to follow Alec. I didn't like the thought of Holly getting involved in a possible fight.

A loud boom sounded in the auditorium, and with a

rumble, a shockwave thrust me backwards. A second later, everything was pitched into darkness. I tumbled down the stairs of the podium, unable to stop Senator Pollard's tall body from hurtling forward. My face smashed against the ground, and I tasted blood in my mouth, coppery and warm. My nose was clogged with liquid, and when I touched it, pain shot through my face. Probably broken. I gagged. My ears rang, but slowly my hearing returned. Screams and shouts surrounded me on all sides. The auditorium was filled with bitter greyish mist that stung in my eyes and nose.

I tried to jump to my feet, but the ground had started shaking. I knelt, trying to find my balance. Pollard's body was more difficult to manoeuvre than my own, and the trembling ground wasn't helping one bit. Panic flashed through me. I had to do something. Could I risk changing back to my own body? I still heard shots and shouting. How could anyone fire when they couldn't possibly see their targets in the darkness?

Where were the others?

'Tess!' Holly's scream echoed in my skull. I stumbled to my feet and changed back to my own body. The ground vibrated under my feet, and a sudden burst of motion sickness hit me. I forced myself to remain calm. My clothes began to slip off, much too big for me now that I was no longer Senator Pollard. I hastily changed into Alec's body, which was better for fighting. Tightening the belt a notch, I looked around. 'Holly?' I called in Alec's deep voice.

'Holly, where are you?' She'd sounded so scared.

Orlov lay sprawled on the floor beside the speaker's podium. I couldn't tell if he was alive. The shaking ground made it look as if he was having spasms. Keeping my eyes on my dark, misty surroundings, I bent over him and pressed my fingers against his throat. The moment his pulse thrummed against my fingertips, I straightened and hurried past him, ignoring the tightness in my chest and the way my eyes watered from the gas.

'Tess!' Holly screamed.

I whirled around towards the sound. It was coming from somewhere to my right, from the seating area. A few people were still running around in panic, and half a dozen were lying on the ground, unmoving. I could only hope they'd lost their balance, hit their heads, and lost consciousness when the shockwave collided with them. Thankfully, most of the audience seemed to have fled the auditorium. But I still couldn't see Holly.

My eyes swivelled around the room. In the back I could make out a struggle between several forms. I headed that way and was halfway there when suddenly Holly appeared in front of me, her body slowly flickering into view. Her blue eyes were wide when they found me. 'Holly!' I'd never heard Alec's voice sound that scared. Realization flashed across her face. 'Tess,' she said quickly, fearfully. 'We have to leave.'

Her legs were materializing inch by inch when a man popped into view behind her. 'Grab the girl! It's her,' another man screamed. Did he mean Holly or me? But then I realized I was in Alec's body right now. They didn't even know I was a girl.

'No!' I screamed, but he didn't even look at me as he wrapped his arms around Holly's waist. Her eyes grew wide with fear and she clamped up. She had to fight! But she seemed paralyzed with terror. I stormed towards them, staggering from left to right as the ground's vibrations picked up once more. I had almost reached them when they disappeared into thin air. My fingers closed around nothing. Holly was gone. One moment they had been there, and then they'd vanished. I stared at the spot, trying to make sense of what had just happened. I turned around myself. 'Holly?' There was no answer.

Tears sprang into my eyes. Where had she gone? Alec ran in my direction then jerked to a halt when he saw that I looked like him. I shuddered and returned to my own body, not caring if anyone saw it. But there was no one around who was able to pay attention. The trousers fell off my body, but I couldn't even bring myself to care that I was only wearing a dress shirt and a tie. Blood was streaming out of my nose, over my lips, and down my chin. 'Holly,' I groaned.

Alec bridged the last few steps between us. His clothes were torn, and his grey eyes were wild. He touched my shoulder. 'Are you OK?'

I blinked up at him, and somehow it seemed to happen in slow motion. 'Holly,' I said voicelessly.

'What? What's the matter, Tess?' His grip on my arms was the only thing keeping me upright. 'Holly,' I croaked. 'She's gone.'

'Where to?' Alec looked around like she might be springing up from the ground any second.

'She vanished. She was right there.' I pointed towards the spot behind Alec. 'And then a man grabbed her, and they vanished into thin air.' A hysterical laugh burst out of me.

'Hey,' Alec said softly as my legs buckled and he picked me up. I wasn't sure if it was the gas or Holly's disappearance, but I was cracking up completely. 'I caught one of them. He's over there.'

Alec carried me to the back of the building, where I'd seen the man with the sunglasses. He stepped over unmoving bodies without stopping to check if they were alive. 'Are they dead?' I whispered. The taste of blood was overwhelming.

Alec's grip on my legs tightened. His fingers felt hot against my naked legs, and I shivered in only the thin dress shirt. How could I have thought it was sweltering just minutes ago? 'I didn't have the time to check them all. But the ones I did were alive, just unconscious. We have to hurry. I already called Major to tell him about this. He has to make sure that law enforcement doesn't get wind of it. We can't risk them finding out about us. We should be gone by the time they arrive.' I could already hear sirens in the distance. Alec stopped beside a body on the ground.

'Can you walk?' he asked quietly. I nodded, though I wasn't sure. My legs shook when he set me down. He didn't let go of my arm.

'I'm OK,' I said firmly.

'I need to carry that guy towards the helicopter so we can get away,' Alec said with a nod toward the unmoving form.

'Is he Abel's Army?'

'It seems that way. What else would he be doing here? And he tried to kick my ass with two other guys.'

He was right, then – we'd need to bring him back to headquarters for questioning. Maybe the guy knew where Holly was. Alec wrapped his arm around the man's back and hoisted him to his feet. I gasped. I knew him. It was the last agent who had been kidnapped, formerly one of our own. Agent Stevens.

CHAPTER 10

I'd never seen Major this furious. His entire face was twisted. The blades slowed down, and Major ripped open the door of the helicopter before it even stopped moving. Two older agents were at his side in a blink, and they helped him heave Stevens outside.

'They took Holly,' I said again, my voice muffled by the blood in my nose. I'd said it out loud at least a dozen times, but it still didn't seem real.

'Alec already informed me,' Major said distractedly. 'This isn't the end of it. I'll demand an explanation from Senator Pollard.' His scowl was fixed on Stevens, but the agent wasn't intimidated. Something was different about him. When I'd last seen Major and Stevens in a room together, Stevens had cowered under Major's stare and tried to make himself as small as possible, but not today. He held his head high and returned Major's gaze without hesitation. He looked confident, defiant, completely at ease with himself.

'Why did you take Holly?' I shouted at him, taking a step in his direction. He opened his mouth, but before he could reply, Major raised a Taser and stunned him. He sacked to the ground, face slack. I was frozen. Why had he done it? Stevens wasn't being aggressive or struggling against his restraints. There was no reason for the violence.

Major's face was a mask of stone as he bagged the Taser again and straightened his collar.

'Sir, what about Holly?' I asked as I watched two agents pick Stevens up from the ground. He hung limply in their grasp. I could feel Alec's hand on my shoulder, steering me away from the helicopter. It had started raining again. I couldn't stop shivering.

'We'll talk later, Tessa. I don't have time for this now. Return to your room and try to get some rest,' Major said sharply.

'But I want to be there when you interrogate Agent Stevens,' I insisted.

Major shot me a quick look, his eyes lingering on the blood on my face and shirt. 'That isn't your place, I don't think that would be wise. You heard what I said. Get some rest.'

I stared at his back as he followed Stevens and the two agents who were carrying him into the building. 'Alec, I need to have a word with you,' he called without turning around.

Alec was still touching my shoulder. 'I'll bring you to your room.'

'No, it's OK,' I said mechanically. 'You shouldn't let Major wait. Maybe you can find out more about Holly. Will you?' I looked at him pleadingly.

He gave me a sad smile. 'Of course.' He leaned down and brushed his lips across my forehead. But I barely felt it. My body had gone numb. I watched as he hurried after Major before I dragged myself towards my room.

Devon was waiting in front of my door when I arrived. Major must have warned him about my injuries. His eyes moved over my naked legs and the bloody shirt until they came to rest on my nose. I hadn't seen myself yet, but from Devon's expression of horror, I was a mess. He wrapped an arm around me, and I gladly accepted his support. He only let go of me when I'd sunk down on the bed. 'It's just my nose,' I said quietly.

'What happened?' He touched his fingers to my cheeks.

'I – I don't think I'm allowed to talk about it.'

'Aren't we on the same side now? FEA, fighting for the right thing?' he asked, but there was a trace of sarcasm in his voice.

He rested his palms on my face, and after a few seconds the dull throbbing in my nose ceased. Slowly, he removed his hands. 'Do you need anything else?' he asked in a careful voice.

I began to shake my head, but my body began trembling uncontrollably. I gasped. 'Holly was taken.'

Devon reached for my hand. 'Shit,' he murmured. 'I'm so sorry, Tessa. I haven't been in headquarters for long, but I can tell how close you two are. I'm sure the FEA will find her.'

His blue eyes bored into me, and suddenly I couldn't take it anymore. 'Devon, I'm sorry, but I need to be alone.'

The understanding on his face nearly undid me. When he closed the door after him, I dropped to my knees in the doorway to the bathroom. It took a while before I found the strength to stand.

I couldn't stop staring at Holly's empty bed. Her sheets with the huge sunflowers (she couldn't stand the stark-white FEA-issued sheets) were crumpled, and the pink teddy bear that her younger siblings had given her last Christmas was perched on the pillow. I'd caught Holly pressing it against her chest more than once in the middle of the night. She'd always denied it with a happy little smile. My stomach clenched painfully at the memory.

Now she was gone.

Gone.

What would they tell her family if she never returned? Would anyone tell them? Or would Major just make up a story?

I'd fought the tears back for hours, but now I couldn't stop them. The floodgates opened, and they poured down my face. I still wasn't sure what had happened. But somehow I knew they hadn't intended to take Holly. It was why everyone had been so afraid to let me go. They'd been given orders to take the auburn-haired girl from the

Livingston mission. Me. And because I had looked like Alec, the guy had thought Holly was his target.

The door to my room opened, and Alec stepped in. Deep shadows spread under his eyes, and he was still wearing the suit he'd worn for the mission, but he'd loosened the tie and unbuttoned the top two buttons of the white shirt. Red dots sprinkled the collar and parts of the front. Alec followed my eyes. 'It's your blood,' he explained, like I could have forgotten that my nose had been broken earlier that day. He scanned my face. 'Devon was here?' he asked neutrally.

I nodded. Slowly, I tried to stand, my legs wobbly. 'What did Stevens say? Did he tell you where they took Holly?' I wished I could have been present during the interrogation.

Alec looked exhausted. 'He didn't tell us anything.'

'But he must have said something! He knows where Abel's Army is.' Despair rang out in my voice. It seemed to fill every fibre of my body.

'Maybe he doesn't,' Alec said softly. 'If it's true that they have a Variant who can alter memories, they might have done that to him, because he was new and they weren't sure about his loyalty.'

'Why?' I whispered. 'Why would he work for them?'

'I'm sure they promised him money or power.'

My legs gave way, and I sank down on to the bed. Money and power? That seemed too easy. I covered my face with my hands, unable to stop the sobs. The mattress dipped as Alec sat down and pulled me against him. I buried my face in the crook of his neck. He felt so solid and strong. My fingers clutched at his arms, and my tears soaked his shirt. I couldn't stop them. 'I'm so scared. What if they hurt her?' I gasped. My throat felt swollen and raw. 'God, Alec, I love her. If something happens to her, I . . . I . . .' I didn't even know what I'd do. If anything horrible happened to Holly because they'd mistaken her for me, I wouldn't be able to live with myself.

'I know,' he whispered against my hair, kissing the top of my head over and over again.

And I knew he did. For once it was a relief to know he could feel what I felt, that no words were necessary. He tightened his hold on me.

'This is all my fault. They wanted me. I know it,' I said miserably.

'Don't say that. It wasn't your fault, and you don't know that they wanted you. Abel's Army wants to hurt the FEA, and they don't care who gets in their way.'

'Alec, they said, "Get the girl". Why would they have orders to catch Holly? I was the one they saw in Livingston,' I said. 'They wanted me.'

Alec didn't argue again. He just held me and let me cry until I had no tears left. I hung limply in his grasp, forcing myself to breathe in and out. His familiar scent surrounded me, brought me back to better memories, and slowed my pulse.

'Everything will be all right,' Alec said eventually. 'We'll find Holly. I'm sure Major will find a way.'

But was Holly really Major's top priority? The FEA came first, and Abel's Army was the enemy. He wouldn't negotiate with them even if it meant saving Holly.

'Maybe I could talk to Stevens?' I said quietly. 'Maybe if he sees what he's done and how much I miss Holly, he'll feel pity.' But could someone who'd betrayed the FEA, who'd worked for a known murderer like Abel, even feel pity? He would probably laugh right in my face. But I had to try.

Alec shook his head. 'Stevens is scared of Major. If that didn't loosen his tongue, nothing will.' But he hadn't looked scared when I'd last seen him. 'And Stevens will be transported to the FEA prison today. He'll be placed in a high-security holding cell, and neither you nor I will be allowed to visit him there.'

I stiffened in Alec's embrace. 'When?' I asked. I pulled back and stared at him. 'When will he leave?'

Alec glanced at the clock. 'Any minute now.'

I freed myself from his hold and stumbled to my feet, determination coursing through me.

'What are you doing, Tess?' Alec looked alarmed.

'It's worth a try. I need to see him.' I staggered towards the door, Alec only a few steps behind me. 'Don't,' he protested. 'You'll only get hurt.'

I walked faster and faster until I was sprinting through the corridors. 'I have to.'

A wall of cold hit me when I stormed out of the front

door and hurried towards the heliport. I could hear the sound of rotating blades roaring over the wind. My lungs constricted as I sped up even more and rounded the building until I had a free view of the helipad.

A man I didn't recognize sat in the pilot seat, and Major sat beside him in the front, with Stevens riding in the back. The moment I reached the helicopter, I pulled open the back door. My hair lashed against my face and my eyes watered from the blasting blades. Stevens's eyes widened when he spotted me. Blood crusted his lips and chin, and his nose was askew. I couldn't remember if Stevens had had the injuries before the interrogation.

'They won't give up. Not until they have the one they really want,' he said. He let out a scratchy laugh. From the corner of my eye, I could see Major opening his door to get out and remove me from the helicopter. I didn't have much time.

I gripped Stevens by the collar, and he winced, eyes growing wide. He couldn't defend himself since his hands were cuffed behind his back. 'Where is Holly? What will they do to her?'

He smirked. It made him look even more like a hawk. 'Who knows? Abel wants you, not her.'

I *knew* it. 'Where is she?'

His eyes stared at something behind me. I shook him and didn't even stop when someone gripped my shoulder. 'Tell me,' I hissed.

The grip on my shoulder turned painful.

Stevens looked into my eyes, and suddenly he leaned very close, his breath wet against my ear. I had to stop myself from shuddering. 'You have his eyes, you know? It's so obvious. Too bad you're blinded by their lies.'

Major pulled me away forcefully, and I stumbled backwards and would have fallen, if Alec hadn't grabbed my arm. 'Whose eyes?' I shouted.

Major closed the door, but I couldn't stop staring at Stevens through the window.

His lips twisted in triumph before he mouthed something. I wasn't the best lip-reader, but I didn't need to be to know what he'd said.

Abel's eyes.

CHAPTER 11

Major glared at me from the passenger seat as the helicopter lifted off the ground. I knew my actions would have consequences, but I couldn't bring myself to care. The stench of aviation fuel streamed into my nose.

You have his eyes. Abel's eyes. That's what Stevens had said. Why had he said *that*? An awful inkling blossomed in my mind.

Alec touched my shoulder. My clothes were soaked from the mist, which I hadn't even noticed before. 'I told you it was useless,' he said, his eyes still following the black dot in the distance. His hand was scorching my skin. In the last few hours, I'd felt so cold; when would that stop? 'Stevens doesn't know anything.'

'He said I have Abel's eyes,' I whispered.

'What?' Alec exclaimed, his widened grey eyes flashing down to mine. There wasn't surprise in his voice. Instead, he sounded angry.

I tried to force my body to stop trembling and to

really focus on Alec's expression. 'Stevens said I have Abel's eyes.'

For a moment, the howling of the wind was the only sound between us. It filled my head. Then Alec let out a laugh. 'That's ridiculous. Don't let the traitor mess with your mind.'

But something about the way he said it was off. I gripped his arm. 'Why did he say that?'

'Who knows why? You shouldn't believe—'

I tightened my hold on him. 'Don't you dare lie to me again, Alec.' My voice shook, and a new crop of tears spilled out of my eyes. 'Tell me the truth.'

Alec's eyes reflected his conflict, but there was also pity and sadness in them. 'Tess,' he said softly. He released a long breath. 'Maybe you should talk to Major.'

I dropped his arm. The horrible suspicion I'd had was festering in me. 'Abel. He's my father, isn't he?'

Alec didn't say anything. I took a step back and clapped a hand over my mouth. I felt sick. 'It's true. He's my father.' I couldn't breathe. 'Oh my god.'

Alec pulled me into an embrace. 'Tess, we're not responsible for the actions of our parents,' he said, but I was only half-listening.

I was the daughter of a man who was responsible for the deaths of several people. A criminal, a murderer and Holly's abductor. Major knew. So did Alec. And Alec hadn't told me. That was another secret he'd kept from me, but it wasn't his secret to keep.

* * *

A few hours later, after I'd thrown up my stomach's contents and finally escaped Alec's care, I scraped myself together and knocked on Major's door. I'd seen him return with the helicopter thirty minutes earlier. He didn't seem surprised to see me.

'Good that you're here. I wanted to have a word with you anyway,' he said as he stepped back and let me enter the office. Anger simmered under my skin. I had to resist the urge to smash his stupid glass cabinet and trample on his tin soldiers. There was never a speck of dirt on them. That's probably how Major spent his nights, polishing his stupid toys until they sparkled. Sometimes I was sure he cared more about them than about his agents.

'Tessa, your recent behaviour has been erratic, to say the least. We have rules, and they apply to everyone.' He spoke with obvious disapproval. He rounded his desk in measured strides and pulled back his chair.

After everything that had happened, he wanted to give me a lecture? 'I know about Abel,' I blurted. 'Why didn't you tell me that he's my father? Were you just going to keep that a secret forever?'

Major froze as if I'd touched a stun gun to his skin. 'What did you just say?'

'I know that Abel is my father. Agent Stevens told me.'

Major turned his back to me for a moment, as if he was scared his face would give away more of his secrets. Why couldn't he be honest with me for once? Didn't I deserve the truth? Slowly he turned, his expression perfectly controlled, and sank down into his chair. In that moment he looked older than he ever had before. 'I didn't want you to find out like this.'

'Then why didn't you tell me? Why, in all the talks we've had about Abel's Army or my missing father, did you not mention that they're the same person?' I was shouting, and I didn't care that Major hated it when we raised our voices against him. I was so far beyond the point of caring, it wasn't even funny anymore.

'I wanted to protect you,' Major said.

I snapped my mouth shut, too stunned to speak. Protect me? I swallowed my surprise. 'I don't understand.'

'I knew you were special from the day I met you. And I knew Abel would stop at nothing to recruit you and use your power for his own goals, if he ever found out about your Variation. That's why I've been trying to keep you hidden from him.'

'But he found out about me when I was on my mission in Livingston?'

Major nodded. 'That's my take on things, at least. If a member of his army saw your eyes, they would have known you were Abel's daughter.' He looked up. 'There's no mistaking those eyes,' he said, something dark crossing his face. He'd known Abel for a long time, and somehow I knew that their hatred for each other had started before Abel's Army even existed.

Turquoise eyes like mine. It was the first concrete

image of my father that I had gotten. I couldn't remember anything about him. I'd been too little when he'd left. I tried to imagine how the face around those eyes might look, but I came up blank. 'Why did he leave my mother and me?' An ache spread in my chest at the other unanswered question that I didn't ask and never would. *Why didn't he care about me?*

Major considered his answer for a moment. Was he planning to add another lie to the two I'd already discovered? 'I assume that he left you because you hadn't shown any sign of a Variation at that point and therefore weren't of use to him. He isn't someone who keeps people around for their emotional value.' Then Major and Abel should have gotten along perfectly. I didn't think Major knew how to love anyone. If I lost my Variation today, he'd let go of me and never think about me again.

'What about my brother? That must mean he's a Variant?' I knew I had a brother, but he was a black void in my memory, a void full of what-ifs and childish hopes. My mother had never talked about him, and I couldn't remember anything. The only thing I knew was that he was two years older than me.

Major leaned back in the chair. 'I can't tell you. But I hope for his sake that he has a useful Variation, or Abel would have gotten rid of him by now.' He said it like a mechanic might talk about a defective car.

I held on to the backrest of the chair in front of me. I wasn't sure if my legs were going to hold me for much longer. This was all too much to take in. 'You really think he'd kill his own son?'

'Oh yes. If you knew Abel as well as I do, you'd believe it too.'

How well did Major know Abel? How much wasn't he telling me?

'What about my mother? Did she know about Abel?'

'Your mother has always been weak. Exactly the kind of woman people like Abel prey on. She was under his spell. He knew what he was doing. And then he knew when she was no longer of any use to him.' There was a hint of emotion in his voice that I couldn't place.

'But I still don't get why you kept it a secret? I deserve to know about my family,' I said.

'I knew it would only bring you grief if you found out.' Since when did Major care so much about the emotional welfare of others? He was a highly rational man who didn't let emotions get in the way of what he thought was necessary.

'Sir, I know the man who kidnapped Holly mistook her for me. But if they know who I am – if they know about my eyes – why would they take her?'

'In the confusion of the attack, mistakes can happen. And since they know about your Variation, eye colour isn't really something they could trust. Plus the chaos would have made it hard to look very closely. You could have been anyone in the auditorium. If they saw Holly's appearance flicker, they could have easily mistaken her for you.'

Major folded his hands. 'We should also consider the possibility that they took Holly as bait. They know they can't ever be sure you are who you are, but Holly is your best friend, and they might hope that you're going to be part of the mission to rescue her. That would lead you straight into their arms. But this is just speculation.'

'But if Abel realizes I'm not going to look for her, and if we aren't able to find her right away, what will they do to her?'

'I have agents who are working incessantly on finding Holly and the other missing agents, Tessa. We are doing the absolute best we can.'

That didn't answer my question. 'Will they hurt her?' The mere thought made my hands shake.

'Her invisibility is a useful talent; she's worth keeping around. I don't think Abel will harm her. If Holly is smart, she'll pretend to go along with whatever he asks of her.' Major's tone was indifferent. It was clear that this topic wasn't his main concern.

'I want to help. Let me search for her,' I pleaded.

Major rose. 'No, Tessa. I can't allow that. Didn't you hear what I just told you? That's exactly what they want.' I had to bite my lip to stop myself from saying I didn't care if this was a trick to lure me into their trap. I needed to save Holly; that was all that mattered.

'Abel will stop at nothing to get his hands on you, and if he does, you're lost. There are people in his army who would twist your mind. And if they couldn't get you to work for them, they'd kill you. You can't help Holly if you're dead. If you get yourself captured, you'd only make things worse for all of us. You can't leave headquarters until things have calmed down.' The phone rang, but Major kept his gaze trained on me. 'You understand that, don't you?'

I swallowed before I nodded. 'Yes.' But I wasn't sure I did. Right now, it felt like I didn't understand anything. Major picked up the phone. I knew this was my cue to leave and that our conversation was over.

Slowly I walked out of his office and closed the door. Alec was already waiting in the corridor. Had he followed me?

Alec pushed himself away from the wall he'd been leaning against. 'What did he say?'

'He confirmed that Abel is my father and demanded I stay in headquarters. He doesn't want me to help rescue Holly.'

Alec wrapped an arm around my shoulders. 'Maybe you should listen. Major has fought against Abel's Army for many years. He knows what he's doing. You can't help Holly by putting yourself in danger.' It was almost exactly what Major had said.

He and Major, they always acted like they had my best interests at heart, but I couldn't ignore the fact that they had lied to me twice. And they weren't just small fibs. They were huge, earthshattering lies. How could I be sure that they'd told me everything? How could I trust them to tell the truth this time?

'I'm tired,' I said. It wasn't true. I was physically exhausted, but my mind was wide awake. I wanted to get away from Alec's piercing eyes. From the way my body yearned to be close to him, despite my mind's warnings.

Alec's brows dipped. 'Are you sure you don't want some company? Maybe you shouldn't be alone right now.' His face was so full of concern, I almost changed my mind. I shook my head and slipped out of his embrace. 'No, really, I need some time to myself.' The weak part of me wanted to snuggle against his chest and let him whisper soothing lies into my ears, but I was tired of being lied to – even if it was to protect me. I needed to know the truth about Abel's Army and, more importantly, about me. And from the look in Alec's eyes, I was pretty sure he knew. If I asked him to go against Major's order to help me save Holly, maybe he'd do it. But first I needed to find out what was really going on. Alec took a hesitant step towards me until our chests were almost touching. I gave him a small smile, and he took it as permission to plant a soft kiss on my lips. I relaxed into his embrace and allowed myself to forget everything for just a moment – the lies, the hurt, Holly. Alec was there for me – he had always been and would always be.

'I meant what I said yesterday, you know? I love you.'

I touched his cheek briefly. 'I know.' Disappointment flickered across his face. Before the conversation could go any further, I turned around and walked away. Maybe he'd expected me to say it back. But I couldn't do it. I did love him, there was no doubt about it. I'd loved him for a long time, but in the last few days, in the last few hours even, so much had happened that had shaken me and made me doubt the world I thought I knew. I needed time. And I needed to reveal the real dimension of secrets, because I had an inkling that Major hadn't told me the truth, not even half of it. He was probably the only one who knew the full extent of things. And there was only one way to find it out. I would become him.

CHAPTER 12

I waited for nightfall before I headed down to the laundry. I took the stairs down to the ground floor and then walked all the way to the back of the complex, to the swimming hall. The laundry room was right next to it, so the wet towels didn't have to travel a long way.

The black letters on the white door were chipped and faded. I looked around before I pressed down the handle and slipped inside. I stared into the darkness and carefully slid the door shut before I felt the wall for a switch. The stench of bleach, detergent, and starch crept into my nose. After a few seconds, the room was bathed in bright light from the halogen lamp on the ceiling. My eyes stung. After the time in the dark on my way here, they had to get used to the sudden intrusion of light.

It was only my second time in the laundry. The last time had been almost two years ago, a few months after my arrival. I'd forgotten a photo in the pocket of my jeans – the only remaining photo I'd had left of my mother and me from my childhood. The woman who worked in the laundry had watched me with wide eyes while I'd searched everywhere for the photo, but I hadn't found it. Of course, the woman wasn't there now. Heaps of dirty clothes stood piled in front of the five huge washing machines on the naked concrete floor. In the corner with the ironing boards – Major thought a mechanical press didn't do a good job – I spotted a batch of freshly pressed white shirts, and beside those was a row of suits and uniforms on hangers. I grabbed one that I recognized as Major's, along with a white shirt. Then I spotted Holly's pink shirt with Ernie and Bert as a gay couple emblazoned on the front on top of a pile of clothes. I picked it up and pressed it to my nose, as if it would smell of her perfume. But all I could smell was the freshness of detergent. I considered putting it back down, but then added it to the stash of Major's clothes over my arm and headed for the door. I turned the light off before I peeked out into the corridor. Everything was dark and silent. I crept out and gently clicked the door shut behind me.

My bare feet were noiseless as I tiptoed past the entrance to the swimming hall. A wave of chlorine smell entered my nose, and I froze. Why hadn't I noticed it on my way to the laundry? Holding my breath, I inched towards the glass door. It was ajar. Someone must have left it open. A dark shape appeared behind the door. I stumbled back, swallowing the scream that rose into my throat.

The door glided open, and the shape moved away.

It was too dark to make out much, but when he came closer, I recognized Devon's blond hair. 'Tessa?' he whispered. I was glad that he had the sense to keep his voice down.

'Yes,' I answered. I moved very close to get a better sense of his reactions, but it was too dark to make out more than the white of his eyes. 'What are you doing here?'

'I don't sleep very well, since . . .' He trailed off. He didn't need to say it. I knew his sister's death kept him awake at night. 'I was taking a swim.'

'In the dark?' I asked.

'I didn't want anyone to see me and ask questions.'

I reached out to check whether his hair was wet, but I misjudged how close we were, and my fingers brushed his naked chest. He sucked in a breath while mine caught in my throat. I snatched my hand back, feeling my cheeks heat, glad that he couldn't see it. 'I'm sorry,' I mumbled.

'You thought I was lying,' he said. There was a hint of amusement in his voice.

'Sorry,' I repeated. My fingertips still tingled from the touch. 'I should probably head back to my room.'

'Hey,' Devon said quietly. His warm hand touched my shoulder, and I was acutely aware that I didn't know what exactly he was wearing. I glanced down, but I couldn't make out much. 'You haven't told me why you're sneaking around in the dark yet.'

I hesitated. 'There's something I need to find out, and I have to do it in private.'

'I won't tell anyone,' he said. 'Will you tell me what you're looking for?'

'I can't right now. But maybe later.'

'OK,' he whispered and released my arm. 'Good luck then. Sleep tight.'

'Thanks. Maybe later,' I repeated with a smile before I hurried away. I wondered if his dimples had appeared during our conversation. And as soon as I did, I wanted to kick myself for that thought. I should have been worried that Devon had caught me sneaking around. But he hadn't seen Major's clothes, and somehow I knew that even if he had, Devon wouldn't run to Major and tell him about it.

Back in my room, I hastily put on the stiff white shirt and the rest of the uniform before I let the rippling wash over me and changed into Major's appearance. For a moment I stared at my reflection. Physically, I was identical, but something about the way I held my mouth wasn't quite right. Maybe I wasn't bitter enough to carry off Major's expression. Not yet, at least. The next part of my mission was tricky. I wasn't sure about the security measures Major had put in place and what I'd have to do to overcome them. I decided against taking the elevator down beyond the basement. It was off-limits at certain times of day, and it was quite possible that an alarm would inform Major if someone pressed a button that led there after-hours.

My breathing was slow and even as I descended to the floors that lay below ground. I became calmer the closer I got to the restricted parts. Maybe because no matter what lay before me, I was finally getting closer to the truth.

When I arrived on the floor marked –2, I hesitated before the huge metal door. This was it. The ultimate breach of rules. If I got caught, I'd be in serious trouble. Surprisingly, the door wasn't locked when I turned the handle. I strode through the hall. The floor was bare, uncoated concrete. The white of the walls had greyed over the years, and cobwebs crowded the ceiling and corners. Even the cleaning personnel didn't have access to this part of the building.

At least a dozen metal doors led to catacomb rooms I'd never set foot in. Which was the right one? It would take me weeks to search them all. But then I spotted the door at the end of the hall. A red light was blinking beside it – the only door with that level of security. I hurried towards it. The red light was coming from a small square box equipped with a fingerprint reader and an eye scanner. As Major, that would be a piece of cake for me. But the accompanying keypad could turn out to be a problem. I pressed my fingers – Major's fingers – against the touch pad, and a moment later the outline of my hand glowed green. 'Accepted' flashed across the screen above my hand. My fingertips tingled when I removed them from the touchpad. A mechanic female voice instructed me to use the eye scanner next. I froze and looked around, as if someone could have heard it, though everyone was sleeping several floors above me.

I brought my eyes in line with the two red lasers so they could read them. I had to force myself not to blink as the red flashed across my pupils. My eyes started to water from keeping them wide open. After a moment it flashed green, and the voice rang out again, asking for the four-digit password.

My fingers hovered over the keypad. I had no clue what the password might be. Major wasn't the type to use his birthday. Maybe some random numbers? But that would probably go against Major's sense of order. And would he really be that careful? Would Major expect anyone in headquarters to have the audacity to walk down here and try to break in? Without access to his fingerprints and eye shape, there weren't many people who could have done it. Actually, there was only me. I rested my fingers on the keys and then entered 1948, the year when the FEA was officially founded. I held my breath while 'Processing' flashed on the screen, and released a sigh of relief when the green light flashed and I could hear the lock open.

I walked into the storage room and closed the door behind me before I turned on the light. Dust tingled in my nose, and the smell of old paper and musty staleness filled the air. There were rows upon rows of grey metal filing cabinets in the room. A fine coat of dust covered everything. An aisle of maybe three feet was left in the middle for walking. I ran my eyes over the tags on each drawer, lingering on one named 'Mallard'. That was Tanner's last name. I didn't recognize the others, but it seemed the drawers weren't sorted by alphabet. Almost at the end of the aisle was one with 'Abel Crane' written on a tag, and the one immediately next to it was labelled 'Heather Crane'. I did a double take. Heather was my mother's name. I stared at the tag for a moment. Crane. Was that my real last name? My mother and I had changed our names so often, I didn't even know what my real one was. She'd always refused to reveal it to me. Tags with different last names followed after those two drawers – various names my mother and I had used over the years – with the estimated period of time when we had used them. So the FEA had kept tabs on us – on me. Sure enough, the last drawer in the line was labelled 'Tessa Crane'.

I was about to go straight to that one when I noticed the fine print under the names. Below my mother's name was a tag that said 'Volatile'. I couldn't move. Volatile? That was a term used to describe Variants who were labelled a risk because they were either prone to mental illness or because they'd lost control of their Variation. I'd never seen my mother display any kind of extraordinary talent, and she had never mentioned anything to me – nor had Major, even after I'd directly asked him about my father. Another lie – or, as Major would probably call it, an omission.

I opened the drawer and pulled the first file out. The cardboard was soft and creased from use, as if someone had held it and opened it many times. I cracked it open and peered down at the yellowed pages. My eyes flew over the letters, drinking it all in. It said that my mother's

109

Variation was regeneration. I had to pause for a second to let that sink in. My mother was a Variant, just like me. And yet she'd hated me for what I was.

Regeneration. Her cells could repair themselves, she didn't ever have to grow old. It had been more than two years since I'd seen her, but I knew that she'd had wrinkles and crow's-feet. My eyes scanned the page. It said she'd joined the FEA when she was fifteen and had lived in headquarters for twenty years following that. That didn't make sense. She'd been in her mid-twenties when she had me, and I definitely hadn't been born at headquarters. That could only mean she'd used her Variation to make herself appear younger.

What had happened then? Had she joined Abel's Army? Did Abel's Army even exist then? Or had she and my father lived together as a family? I was about to pull out the next page when a distant noise made me pause. A soft whirring, like the sound of the elevator. It was moving up. Someone had called it. If someone was looking for me, that didn't give me much time, and I still hadn't looked into my father's and my files. I slid the file back into its slot and closed the drawer before I moved on to the one with Abel's name on the front. My hands shook as I pulled it open, and for a moment I was scared to take a look. But the thought of helping Holly gave me strength. I needed to find out as much about Abel's Army as possible. I grabbed the first folder. Taking a deep breath, I swung it open and stared at a photo of my mother and me – the same photo that I

110

thought I'd lost more than two years ago. How had it gotten into the file? Anger bubbled up inside me. The laundry lady must have found it and taken it to Major, who had decided to keep it. Or maybe he'd stolen it from my room in the first place. But why?

I was standing in a room containing every single reason behind his actions. He wanted to make me forget about my parents, about where I came from, so I never figured out the truth. I traced a finger over my mother's face in the photo. Her contours were softer than I remembered them, and she gazed at me with a kind smile. In the picture, I was a toddler, maybe a year old, grinning widely with chocolate all over my face. My mother held a spoon in her hand. I didn't remember that particular moment or any other moment when my mother had taken care of me. But I wished I could. Who had taken the photo? My father? At that time they could still have been together. I lifted the photo and saw what was beneath it, and time seemed to grind to a halt. There were more photos. In the first was a family: a woman glancing down at a small baby in her arms, a man with his arm around her, and a tiny boy with brown hair and turquoise eyes sitting on the man's shoulders, grinning a toothy smile. My family. My mother. My father. My brother.

For a moment I couldn't breathe. We looked happy. We looked like a normal family. We looked like everything I'd always longed for. I gingerly pushed the photo aside to look at the third photo. It was a close-up of a young Abel,

111

turquoise eyes – my eyes – sparkling in the photo as he cradled a tiny baby against his chest. With trembling fingers I turned the photo around. 'My little princess' was written on the back in unfamiliar handwriting. Had my father – had Abel – written those words? Had he called me his little princess?

I closed my eyes. This was too much. How could a man who called me his little princess have done all the horrible things Major had told me about? How could he have left me?

I bent the three photos carefully and slid them into the pocket of Major's trousers. I'd have to remember to take them out before I returned his clothes to the laundry. I didn't care if Major found out I'd taken them. He'd had no right to keep this part of my life from me, to make me believe I'd never been loved.

I browsed the file for any snippet of information that might tell me where I could find him. Apparently, Abel's Army was headquartered in Alaska for a while before they moved south. Their whereabouts weren't known, but the file said hints pointed at a headquarters somewhere in the American Southwest. Abel had been seen near Las Vegas a few times, but there was nothing conclusive known about the current headquarters. Eventually I came across a handwritten note at the top of one page saying it was rumoured that Heather Crane had established contact with Abel Crane multiple times over the course of the last year. My mother was in contact with Abel? How was that possible? Maybe she knew something that could lead us to Holly. The sound of the elevator came again, and I hastily put Abel's file back in the drawer where it belonged. Before time ran out, I did what I wasn't sure I was strong enough to do: I picked up my own file.

My eyes landed on a red stamp at the top of the first page – just like the one from my mother's file. It said 'Volatile'. I glanced again at the cover of the file to make sure that it was really my own. Why did it say 'Volatile'? I wasn't unstable. I'd always thought I was the trophy Variant, the ultimate weapon. My eyes flew down the page and stopped at the section I was looking for. My fingers shook so much that the words kept blurring before my eyes.

Status: Volatile (not confirmed)
Risk factor: Parents – Abel Crane (Volatile), Heather Crane (Volatile).
Brother – Zachary Crane (suspected Volatile – not confirmed).
Comments: No signs of insubordination. In control of Variation.
No contact with risk factors.
Course of action: Surveillance of emotional and mental stability
(Internal mission 010)
Prognosis: Positive
Promotion to agent status: Possible (awaiting final results – I.M. 010)

A dizzy sickness overcame me, and I held on to the filing cabinet for support. They were monitoring me. Someone had kept watch over my emotional stability. Dread settled in the pit of my stomach. I could hear the whir of the returning elevator getting louder. But I couldn't move. I didn't care if I got caught. I needed confirmation. I needed to see the file about mission 010.

I pulled file after file from my drawer until I got to the one with the tag I'd been looking for. For a few seconds I stared at the ceiling, my heart pounding, scared of what I knew I'd find. It would change everything. Slowly I lowered my gaze to the file.

Two names were written right below the description of the mission. The two agents who'd been responsible for the surveillance – my surveillance.

Kate and Alec.

CHAPTER 13

I'm not sure how long I stood there staring at the page in disbelief. It was probably seconds, but it felt like hours. I hadn't yet moved when Major walked in. I wasn't sure how long we stood like that – me still posing as him – staring at each other. The file was still in my hand. My palm was sweaty. He wasn't wearing pyjamas, and he didn't seem the least bit tired. Maybe he slept in his uniform, or maybe he didn't need to sleep at all.

There was a stillness to his face that should have scared me, warned me of the fury that was simmering beneath his controlled mask. But I felt hollow. Deep down I could feel a fire burning, an anger more intense than anything I'd ever felt before, and I wanted to grasp it and harness it and unleash it on the man in front of me, to show him what this betrayal had done to me. The FEA had been my family, a home after all the years of despair and negligence, and now that was gone. Ripped from my hands by what I'd just read. The FEA had taken me in because of my worth to them, but they'd never trusted me or fully treated me like I was worthy. My life here had been a lie.

And Alec. My heart, my entire body ached so much when I thought about him and the time we'd shared. Tears stung my eyes, but I didn't let them fall. Had Major told him to start a relationship with me to guarantee the success of their spying? Had Kate only told me Alec's secret to test me? How could I know if he'd meant a single word he'd said? Had everything been lies? The touches, the kisses, the tender looks? I had been so stupid to think he loved me, to think he was on my side, that he'd help me. He was Major's soldier through and through – had always been.

The knife of his betrayal was wedged deep in my soul. He and Kate must have had a wonderful time spying on me. That's why he'd never talked about the mission they'd shared. Because the mission was me and my presumed instability. The ticking time bomb known as Tessa. Kate's triumphant looks made even more sense now. Shame washed over me, determined to banish my other emotions, but I clung to my anger. Anger was all that would get me through this. It was all I had left.

'Come with me,' Major said tersely. I put the file down slowly and followed him to the elevator. I wasn't sure how my body managed to go through the motions when I was pretty sure I was falling apart inside. With every step, another part of my carefully constructed happiness crumbled away and was crushed under Major's perfectly polished boots.

I couldn't help but wonder how often Alec and Kate had discussed my feelings behind my back. They must have had many good laughs about my stupid infatuation. Neither of us spoke in the elevator and on our way to Major's office. Arriving there, I sank down on the edge of the hard chair. My fingers curled around my knees, nails digging into the skin. I let the familiar rippling wash over me until I was back to myself again. The uniform hung loosely on my body.

Major positioned himself in front of his desk. I had to crane my neck to get a good look at his face. I could see that he was fighting for self-control. His jaw twitched, and a vein in his throat throbbed furiously. 'You had no right to be in there. This is a serious breach of the rules. I hope you are aware of that.'

If he said something about trust and gave me some line about how the FEA was built on it, I'd go off on him like the time bomb that he thought I was. Only a few days ago he'd said he'd never violate my privacy by using Kate. But what was this? He knew how much I cared about Alec, how much I trusted him, and yet he'd used him against me. Or maybe that had been his plan from the very start. Maybe when Alec had consoled me more than two years ago after the devastating call with my mother, he'd been acting on Major's orders. I realized Major was still watching me and probably expecting a reply. I reached for the fury deep within, used it to make my words come out hard and accusing.

'And you had no right to monitor me like a criminal and keep the truth about my family from me,' I said. 'You lied to me, and you betrayed me. What am I to you? Some kind of marionette you can use as you please? And what's Alec, your puppeteer?' I wanted to smash his office, destroy his too-clean desk and his stupid model soldiers. I wanted to tear him and Alec to shreds like they had done with my heart and my trust.

Major's lips thinned to a white line on his tanned face. 'I won't tolerate that tone from you, Tessa. The FEA and I have been very good to you. We gave you a home, a purpose and a chance at a normal life.' I didn't think Major had ever sounded so cold when he'd spoken with me. A few times, especially at the beginning of my life at headquarters, I'd even wished he were my dad.

'Normal?' I repeated in a whisper. There was nothing normal about me or my life, and certainly not about Major and his surveillance.

'As normal as someone like you could ever hope for. Where do you think you'd be now if the FEA hadn't taken you in and taught you about your Variation?'

I'd asked myself that question so often and always come to the conclusion that I'd have been lost without them, but now after seeing the photos of my father and brother, I felt like there might have been more out there for me.

Major continued, 'I don't think you're aware of the dangers your previous way of life entailed. You were without protection, and if Abel had found you, that would have been it. Because no matter how much you despise me and my methods in this moment, they are nothing in comparison to what Abel's capable of, if he suspected that one of his soldiers was setting a toe out of line.'

Maybe he was right. Maybe getting in the hands of Abel would have been ten times worse, but that didn't mean I had to like how Major and the FEA had treated me, how he'd used Alec against me. That didn't make their actions right. Major shook his head. 'You leave me no choice,' he said sadly. My stomach tightened. 'You've been acting erratic and irresponsible over the last few days. I think your emotions are spiralling out of control. I realize that you've gone through a lot and that I've asked a lot from you, but that doesn't excuse what you did today.'

'What do you mean?' I whispered.

'I think you need a few weeks to consider your actions and to recover from the trauma you sustained during your first mission and again when you lost Holly. We have a state-of-the-art facility that treats our agents when they suffer from PTSD, depression or other emotional deficiencies. I'll call them this morning and ask them to take care of you for a few weeks.'

'You're going to lock me in a psych ward?'

Major sighed. 'This facility isn't a prison. It's not a punishment. I just want to be sure your emotional instability is treated before it spins out of control. You're a capable agent, Tessa, and I'd hate to lose you. In a few weeks, when you come out on the other side of this, you'll see that it was for the best.'

I was unable to speak. Major was going to lock me away and let the FEA's psychiatrists mess with my mind. I didn't trust them and Major to stick to the usual therapy methods of regular shrinks. They'd do something to my brain until I was an obedient little agent.

I knew I had to tread carefully now. There was no way in hell that I'd let anyone take me to the FEA's loony bin. I hung my head with a sigh, so Major couldn't see my face, and tried to suppress my tremor of panic. 'You really think they can help me? I don't want to turn into my mother, or become a murderer like my dad.' I shuddered for effect.

Major touched my shoulder, and I fought the urge to push him away. If I'd had a knife, I wasn't sure what I would have done. Maybe thrust it into his heart and asked, 'How does it feel?'

'Your mother could have been a great agent too, but she didn't want to accept my help. She thought she wasn't at risk. I won't make the same mistake with you.'

I nodded, my mind racing to find a way out of this. 'I wish it could have been different. Why do my parents have to be so messed up?'

Major squeezed my shoulder reassuringly, as if I would ever let him *console me* again after what I'd found out today. 'We can't help who our parents are. We can only aspire to be better.'

Had Alec heard that gem from Major before he'd

repeated it to me a few days ago? Anger seemed to eat a hole into my stomach, but I forced it down. I couldn't risk Major suspecting that I was going to run away. And just as quickly, I realized that that was my only option. I had to find my mother so she could tell me where Abel was – if she really was in contact with him – and then I would do everything in my power to find and free Holly.

I covered my face with my hands and let out a sob, hoping this would really drive it home. Major had to believe I was a stupid, lost, desperate girl. 'I'm worried Alec will leave me after all this. Do you think he'll wait for me while I'm away getting healthy?'

'Alec knows about the emotional baggage you're carrying.' I bet he did, I thought bitterly. *Traitor*. 'He'll be glad that you're seeking help. Alec and I want you to be well.'

I looked up, regret and embarrassment undoubtedly playing across my face. 'I'm sorry for today. I just lost it. I'm so worried about Holly. I feel like I'm falling and there's nothing to catch me.' I hated how close to the truth the last part was, hated how everything I'd cared about and loved seemed to be ripped from my life.

Major gave me an understanding look, and it was all I could do not to punch him. Maybe that evaluation in my file wasn't that far off. Maybe I had the potential for becoming a Volatile, but if I really went off the deep end, I knew who was to blame. Major and his lies.

'I'm tired,' I said quietly. 'I think I need to get some sleep.'

'I'll take you to your room,' Major said as he straightened before slipping something from his desk drawer into his trouser pocket. I couldn't see what it was. He walked around the desk, and we headed out of his office. My expression fell, but I hastily rearranged my face into a serene smile.

So Major wasn't that easily placated. He didn't even trust me to head back to my room alone. Did he think I was going to run? Or was he just worried I'd return to the basement to snoop around some more?

Major followed close behind as I walked to my room. I could feel his eyes bore into my skull and back. I stepped into my room, and without a word he entered after me. What was he going to do? Watch me while I slept to make sure I didn't do something stupid?

'I have these for you,' he said as he took a small plastic bottle with pills out of his trousers.

I frowned at him. 'What are they for?'

'They'll help you sleep,' he explained as he placed two pills on to my palm. I stared at the small white squares.

So he was going to drug me to sleep. That way I wouldn't run anywhere. Panic wanted to make an ugly appearance, but I pushed it down. There would be time for it later. 'Here.' Major took the water bottle from my nightstand and handed it to me. 'You have a few minutes before they take effect. That should give you enough time to change into your sleeping clothes.'

Only a few minutes. How was I supposed to escape if I

was under the influence? I was sure Major would knock at my door first thing in the morning to keep an eye on me until the shrinks came to take me with them.

I accepted the bottle and thrust the pills into my mouth before taking a huge gulp of water. For a brief moment I considered hiding the pills under my tongue or in the back of my mouth, but I had a feeling Major would notice and then he'd probably tie me to the bed and ruin any chance I had at escape. I swallowed the pills and grimaced at the bitter taste they left on my tongue; they tasted like hopelessness and defeat.

Major scanned my face, and I expected him to ask me to open my mouth, but he seemed satisfied with what he saw. 'Get some rest.' He walked out and closed the door behind him, but I didn't hear his steps move away. I rummaged in my nightstand and shut it with a bang so he would hear it. Then I hastily slipped out of Major's clothes and into my pyjamas, in case he decided to check on me. Street clothes would have looked suspicious. I slipped the photos of me with my mother, Abel and the one of my whole family into my pyjama pockets. My movements became slower, my limbs felt heavier, my mind was starting to turn fuzzy. The pills were taking effect faster than I'd thought. Panic corded up my throat. I was never going to make it. Resignation washed over me. Maybe it wouldn't be so bad if the FEA's shrinks took a look at me, maybe they could turn a switch in my head that would make me happy.

No.

I staggered towards the bathroom and turned the tap on. Major would expect me to brush my teeth, though how he expected me to do it when my brain was shutting off so fast, I didn't know. I dragged myself towards the door and pressed my ear against the cold wood, glad for the feel of it against my body. My legs buckled under me, and I sank down on my knees. Black dots flitted in and out of my vision. I felt heavy and weightless at the same time.

Those hadn't been normal sleeping pills. They were supposed to knock me out. Major still hadn't moved away. What if he was going to check on me in a few minutes? I crawled towards the bed, extinguished the lights, covered my body with the blanket, and pretended to be asleep. I was scared of closing my eyes, scared that I wouldn't be able to open them again, that I'd drift off to sleep immediately. After a few seconds I wasn't even sure where the mattress ended and my body started. My legs felt numb. And my mind wanted to shut off.

I dug my nails into the soft skin of my inner thigh, and the pain banished some of the mist from my head. I heard the door open and lay very still as steps came up to the bed. Suddenly Major gripped my wrist. Without the pills already turning my body into mush, I would have flinched. What was he doing? He turned my arm so my palm was facing upwards and then he pressed something hard and cold against the skin below the crook of my elbow. There was a click, and something sharp pierced my skin, sending a stabbing pain through my arm. What had he done?

He released my arm, and after a moment his steps retreated and I was alone again. This time Major didn't wait in front of my room. He left.

Relief surged through me, but then came the realization that my body was too heavy to move and I still didn't know what he'd done to my arm. I rolled over, closer to the edge of the bed. With my arms – which were getting heavier by the second – I heaved myself out of bed. My face pressed against the floor. I was so tired. My eyes were just slits. The world was nothing but cotton and mist. Cotton and mist.

With my elbows, I slithered towards the door. I glanced up at the door handle. It was so high up. With a groan, I raised myself up on my arms and gripped the handle. My fingers slipped off, and I smashed back to the ground. But the door was ajar. I pried it open and peered into the corridor. It was dark and abandoned. Major must have gone to his room on the floor below.

There was only one person who could tell me everything and help me find Abel's Army and Holly. My mother. And there was only one person who could help me find her. I crawled across the hall, raised my fist a few centimetres above the ground, and hammered against the door. What if he didn't hear?

I felt myself drifting away when the door opened. I peeked up at Devon's surprised face, surrounded by a halo of murkiness, then my head dropped and my world turned black.

CHAPTER 14

Slowly, I came to my senses and my vision returned. A soothing voice trickled through the darkness. I tried to cling to it, to let it pull me out of unconsciousness.

'Tessa?'

I blinked against the blurriness. The shape of a face hovered in front of me. After a few seconds, it became clear. Devon looked down at me with a deep frown. My head rested on his lap, and he was stroking my hair.

Where were we? I tried to sit up, but stars erupted in my vision. Devon touched my temples, and suddenly the heaviness was gone from my limbs and the dizziness disappeared from my head. But I didn't try to sit up again. I quickly took inventory of the situation; I was in Devon's room, sprawled out on the floor, and his door was closed.

'Did anyone see us? You didn't call Major, did you?' I croaked.

'No,' Devon said gently. 'I didn't know what was wrong with you. And to be honest, I'm not sure if I trust him.'

That made me smile. At least I wasn't the only one. With Alec it had always been obvious that he was on Major's side, that the FEA was the thing that mattered most to him. 'You shouldn't.'

Devon's blond brows drew together. 'I shouldn't what?'

The smile crumbled. 'Trust him.' I wished I had come to that realization months ago. It would have spared me a lot of heartache.

'Why did you take sleeping pills and then crawl across the hall?' Devon asked softly.

'I didn't take them,' I explained, and a new wave of anger washed over me. 'Major made me.'

Devon's eyes narrowed. 'Why did he do that?'

'Because he wants to stop me from running away.' I was shocked to hear the words out loud. I never thought I'd even consider leaving. What was left in my life without the FEA? *Holly*, I reminded myself. She needed my help. I couldn't rely on Major to save her. She wasn't important enough to him. Holly would understand if I told her my reasons for leaving headquarters. Maybe we could build a new life somewhere. 'You want to run? I thought you liked being with the FEA?' Devon's words brought me back to the present.

I closed my eyes when I reminded myself of the full extent of the FEA's and Alec's betrayal. Slowly I sat up, fighting a sickness that had nothing to do with the sleeping pills. 'Thanks for waking me,' I said. I realized we'd talked more in the last few minutes than we had in the weeks he'd been living at headquarters. He was still watching me intently, waiting for a reply. I'd once loved living with the FEA, but that didn't matter any more. My eyes darted to the nightstand with Devon's family photo. I realized I couldn't have chosen a better person to confide in. 'No,' I said slowly. 'I have to run away. Tonight. And I was wondering if you wanted to come with me.' He had no reason to help me. Not after the way I'd deceived him during my last mission, but he was my only hope. There was no one else I could ask. I tried to convince myself that I was doing this for him, that I wanted to protect him from Major's game, but that was only part of it. Deep down I knew my selfish motives were stronger. I wasn't sure if I was strong enough to go through this alone.

'What happened?'

I didn't want to tell him, but then the words started tumbling out and I told him everything I'd found out today. I ached when I was done. I crossed my arms over my chest, shivering. Devon wrapped his arm around my shoulder. I couldn't believe that we'd finally managed to leave the awkwardness behind. 'I thought the FEA were the good guys,' Devon said distractedly. I could see that he was mulling over something.

'Sometimes even the good guys cross a line,' I said eventually. But I wasn't even sure if the FEA were the good guys. Did good guys actually exist? Maybe the FEA and Abel's Army were just two sides of the same coin. Different shades of bad.

'So,' Devon began, his voice tight. 'Wasn't Abel's Army responsible for the killing in Livingston and for Holly's abduction?' He grimaced when the name of his hometown crossed his lips. It probably brought too many bad memories back.

'That's what Major said,' I clarified. I realized I sounded defensive. I was trying to defend Abel – my father. Where had that notion come from?

'You're right. We don't know if Major told the truth,' Devon said. He started to rub my arm absentmindedly, and somehow it managed to relax me. He seemed so calm. 'And after what you just told me, we should definitely leave immediately. I don't need anyone messing with me. I'm messed up enough.'

I let out a laugh. 'Me too.' The way he looked at me stirred something. In a strange, twisted way, it reminded me of Alec.

Sadness wound its way through my body. I looked away and played with the hem of my pyjama shirt. Devon's hand on my arm stilled, and he stared at it, as if he had only just realized what he was doing. I wasn't sure if I wanted him to stop.

'So,' Devon said, casually dropping his arm. 'What's the plan? How do we get away?'

'Are you really sure you want to come with me? If Major catches us, we'll both be spending the next few weeks in the FEA's loony bin.'

'I'm sure.' He touched my hand. 'You uncovered my

sister's murderer. I owe it to you.'

I looked down at Devon's hand on mine. It was good that there was someone who hadn't betrayed me. *Yet*, a cautious voice reminded me. Somehow I was sure that Devon had his own reasons to join me on my quest to find out the truth about Abel's Army.

'Headquarters is pretty much in the middle of nowhere. The next farm is about five miles south,' I said. 'It would take hours to get there by foot.'

'So that's out,' Devon said thoughtfully. 'What about a helicopter? Can you fly one?'

I shook my head. 'No, I mean, I don't think I can. I've only had a few hours in the simulator, never in a real helicopter. And the sound of the blades would wake everyone. Major would just send another helicopter after us.' He'd hunt us down. If I left tonight, he wouldn't stop chasing me until I was back in his hands.

'So let's take a car. I can drive.'

I nodded, thinking it through. 'As soon as someone notices that we're gone or if anyone hears us leave, they'll send a car or a helicopter after us.'

Devon pulled a chocolate bar from a backpack and started munching on it. 'It helps me think,' he said apologetically. He held another one out for me, but I shook my head. 'Where does that leave us?'

Yes, where? An idea crossed my mind. But Major would be ready to kill me if we went through with it. 'We take a car,' I said calmly. 'But before we leave, we cut the fuel pipes of the cars and the helicopters. It'll take a few hours to fix that.'

'Won't Major just call for help?'

'Major would never involve outsiders or the police, even if he needed backup. He'll want to strangle us himself,' I said. I felt better already. Just talking with Devon and knowing he was on my side gave me hope for the first time since I'd made my discovery. I glanced at the clock on Devon's nightstand. It said 2:37. 'Major always gets up at five to run a few laps on the track. We should hurry. I want to be far away when he realizes that we're gone.' I stood. My legs were steady, and no hint of dizziness remained. 'What about Phil?' Devon asked as he rose to his feet. He wasn't quite as tall as Alec but still almost a head taller than me. 'Shouldn't we take him with us? Or at least warn him?'

I paced the room. He was right. Poor Phil was new to the FEA. He didn't know what to expect, and he was far too gullible and excited to see the truth. After all, it had taken me two years to realize what was going on, and I was pretty sure I still didn't know half of it. I glanced at Devon, at his square jaw and the way his eyebrows were drawn together in concentration. What if I was leading him straight to his death?

'I'm not sure if Phil is cut out for this, but we'll ask him. Let him make up his own mind.' I paused. 'Are you sure he's not going to run off to Major and tell him about our plan?'

Devon ran a hand through his hair as he stared intently

131

at the wall that separated his room from Phil's. 'I don't think he would.'

My eyes found the clock once again: 2:45.

'Maybe we could send him a message once we're already gone. That way he'll know to be careful and not to believe everything Major tells him,' I said.

'I know he kept his mobile phone. We could send him a text or an email.'

'Good.' I nodded. All the planning distracted me from the emptiness deep inside me. The place that had been filled with my loyalty for the FEA and my love for Alec.

Devon nodded and began stuffing clothes and a few other things into a bag. He removed the photo of his family at Disney World from its frame and put it on top. Checking the hall, I tiptoed to my room and packed my backpack with essentials, including the three photos of my real family. My eyes found the photo of Alec and me. We looked so happy. The look in Alec's eyes made me almost believe that his feelings were real, that he hadn't messed with me for a mission. I put the frame back, facedown. I couldn't even bear looking at it. This part of my life was over, and taking this photo with me wouldn't change that. I hastily grabbed a pen and a piece of paper. My fingers shook when I began my letter to Alec.

Alec—

When I came to the FEA, I didn't trust

anyone. I didn't know what it meant to have people care for you, what it meant to have a home. But then when you told me about your family and held me in your arms, I started to trust you. I knew I wasn't alone with my feelings. And during all the nights we spent watching movies because I was too scared of nightmares, I started to love you. And suddenly I knew what happiness meant. I had a home, a family and I'd learned what trust and love meant.

I trusted you and the FEA. I loved you. I thought the FEA was my home.

And today I found out it was all a lie. I finally realized how stupid I've been. I gave you my trust and love, and you threw it back in my face.

I know about mission 010.

I hope it was worth it.

Whatever there was – or wasn't – between us, it's over.

Tessa

Devon appeared in the doorway. He looked at the letter in my hand.

'It's for Alec,' I said. I folded the letter with steady hands. Now that I knew what I had to do, I felt better. I knew that would pass too, but for now my resolve steadied me. 'I'll just slip it under his door.'

Devon nodded. He didn't ask any questions, for which I was grateful. 'Don't you want to put on real pants?'

I flushed when I glanced down at my pyjamas and hastily changed into jeans in the bathroom. As we walked through the corridor towards Alec's door, my throat started to constrict. This was it. I was breaking up with Alec. I was leaving my home, my life. I was leaving my career as an agent. I was leaving everything I'd held dear for the last two years behind me. Not Holly and not Devon, I reminded myself. Careful not to make a noise, I pushed the piece of paper under the door. I had the urge to open it and look at Alec one last time. Instead I touched my palm against the wood for a second before I turned around and led Devon down the stairs. 'What about weapons? Do we take any with us?' he whispered as we made our way through the darkness.

'I wish we could,' I replied. 'But Major keeps everything locked up in the armoury. I don't have the keys, and breaking in is too big of a risk.'

When we arrived on the ground floor, I didn't steer us towards the front door, afraid that we'd set off an alarm. Instead, I led Devon into the swimming hall and into the changing rooms. I opened the window, and Devon pushed a bench under it. I stepped on top of it and gripped the edge of the narrow windowsill. Devon took me by the waist and hoisted me up. When I was on the other side, he threw my backpack after me, followed by his own bag. I could see the muscles in his arms flex as he pushed himself through the window and landed beside me on the lawn.

We exchanged a quick glance to make sure the other was OK, picked up our bags, and hurried towards the hangar, where we disabled the three helicopters before we moved on to the garage. I had forgotten how many cars and trucks and motorbikes the FEA owned. We'd be busy all night if we tried to cut all the pipes.

'Why don't we take a motorcycle?' Devon pointed at a black BMW. It belonged to Tanner's older brother, Ty. 'This baby goes as fast as a hundred and eighty-eight miles per hour.'

'You sure you can drive that thing?' I asked. The thought of driving that fast on only two tyres made my head spin.

'I've ridden motorcycles before,' he said. He ran his hands over the leather seat of the BMW, an amazed look on his face. 'Of course, never anything this fast.'

'That's not very comforting.' A creak echoed through the hall, and I jumped. My hand darted to my waist, where I should have had a weapon. But of course there wasn't one. I tensed when Devon peered over the cars to get a look at the source of the noise. 'We didn't close the door properly. It's opened a gap. That's what made the noise.'

It was a good reminder that we had no time for arguments. 'We'll take the motorcycle. We don't have time to cut the remaining pipes anyway.'

Devon and I stuffed our luggage into the small trunk attached to the back of the motorcycle before we rolled the bike out of the hangar, the helmets perched on the seat.

'We should push it to the edge of the property. That way we won't be overheard.'

I glanced over my shoulder at the dark windows of headquarters as we crept down the long driveway. Though I hadn't even left yet, a wave of homesickness washed over me. This was goodbye. I wasn't sure if I could ever return. Major would never let me, and I didn't think I'd ever want to.

We reached the spot where the FEA's private street ended and hit a smaller public street that would lead us straight to the highway. Devon handed me a helmet and put the other on before he mounted the bike, and I sat down behind him. The air was stuffy inside the helmet, and I hated how it restricted my field of vision. Devon's warmth seeped into me as I moved closer. Every part of our bodies seemed to touch as I wrapped my arms around his waist. It felt illicit, wrong to be this close to someone who wasn't Alec. But I relaxed into his warmth. 'Where are we heading?' he asked, his voice muffled through the helmet.

Yes, where? We needed to find my mother. She was the only person who knew more about Abel and where he might be, especially if the note in the file was right and she had contacted Abel after I was gone. But first we needed a place to stay and to chart a course and figure out our next moves. 'Let's get some distance between us and headquarters first, then we can look for a motel to spend the night.' I didn't have the slightest clue where my mother was, but I knew where we could start searching. But before we could do that, we had to organize a bit more money and change our ride, because Major would be searching for the missing motorcycle soon.

Devon reached back and patted my thigh before he turned the key and the motorcycle roared to life. My pulse exploded in my veins at the thought of how far the roar had carried. My grip on Devon tightened, and he must have understood because he floored the accelerator. I was sure that Major had heard the engine all the way back at headquarters. I rested my head against Devon's back and let the reassuring feeling of his heartbeat against my palms calm me. The motorcycle vibrated under me as we rushed through the darkness. Our light caught on trees that looked like claws reaching for the stars.

Was revealing the truth worth losing everything I'd held dear?

I would find out soon enough.

CHAPTER 15

We'd been driving for two hours and covered a little over one hundred miles when Devon steered the BMW into a parking lot in front of a rundown motel. It was painted in different shades of grey, except for the green neon letters spelling 'Jimmy's'. A gas station sat beside it – which was fortunate, since we were almost out of fuel.

My butt prickled when I dismounted the BMW. I didn't think my butt had ever fallen asleep quite this much before. I didn't understand how people could enjoy this. We removed our helmets. Devon's face was red and sweaty, his hair matted down against his skull, and I knew I didn't look much better. My usually wild hair was plastered all over my forehead and cheeks. My physical comfort wasn't the only reason I was relieved to be back on my feet: being the passenger on a motorcycle gave you lots of time to think.

'Let's ask how much they charge for a room,' I said, waving at the motel with its bad paint job and dirty windows. My eyes darted back to the road that had taken us here, half expecting a parade of the FEA's black limousines or SUVs to appear at any second.

'Won't they ask for ID or something like that?' Devon asked as we walked towards the door with its ripped fly screen. Gravel crunched under our feet and the wooden steps groaned as we stepped up on to the porch.

I shook my head. 'Motels like this one usually don't care who their customers are, as long as they pay cash.'

Devon looked sceptical, but when we entered the lobby and asked the man at the reception desk for a room, he barely looked at us. He was engrossed in watching a poker game on TV, and, as I suspected, he just counted the bills I'd pushed over to him before handing us the key. 'Have fun,' he said distractedly when we headed out. My skin heated. The guy probably thought Devon and I needed a place to have sex. That's probably why most couples, especially teens, rented a room.

'Well, that was easy,' Devon said as we entered our room. He didn't seem to be one bit flustered by the man's assumption. Two narrow twin beds with flowery blankets, a wardrobe missing a door, and two nightstands crowded the small space. The yellow wallpaper must have been white once; it was peeled off the corners in strips. The brown carpet was littered with unidentifiable stains. I didn't even want to know what they were. A myriad of chewing gum wads dotted the ceiling, some of it grey with age. *Disgusting*. There was only one door, which led into a tiny, musty bathroom.

I sank down on one of the beds, exhaustion catching up with me. Devon took the other bed and stretched out.

'It probably won't always be this easy. The FEA will start searching for us soon. And if Abel's Army figures out that I'm no longer in headquarters, they'll probably send a hunting party after us.'

Way to ruin the mood, I chided myself. But I wouldn't do us any favours if I kept my eyes closed to the inevitable truth. We were the hunted now.

'So where are we going next?' Devon asked between yawns. He tilted his face towards me, his arms stretched above his head. A sliver of tanned skinned showed where his shirt rode up.

I brought my focus back to my shoes and pulled them off. 'We need to find my mother. I don't know where she lives now, but I know someone who might know. Her last boyfriend. Or at least the last boyfriend she had while I still lived with her.'

'Did she have so many?' Devon asked quietly.

'Oh yes, and each one was worse than the last.' I hated remembering that part of my life. It wasn't just that my home life was hard; I hated the way people judged me, as if it was my fault that my mother couldn't get her life in order. Kate used to call me white trash behind my back; once she even did it to my face. But there was no sign of judgment in Devon's blue eyes.

'So where do your mom and this guy live?' he asked.

That was the tricky part. 'In Detroit.'

'Detroit?' Devon repeated, propping his head up on his elbow to watch me in surprise. 'Why don't we just give them a call?'

'We can't,' I said hesitantly. 'My mom cut off contact with me shortly after I joined the FEA. She even changed her phone number to make sure I couldn't reach her.'

Devon couldn't hide his shock.

I had to look away. 'I know that's a long drive, but I wouldn't know who else we could ask.' Except for Major. He probably knew. I should have taken my mother's file with me. Maybe it would have had her new phone number. It was sad that I had to rely on my mother's ex to find out where she lived.

'Do we even have enough money to get there? I've got around fifty bucks in my pocket.'

I hesitated. 'After paying for the room, I have a hundred left. That makes a hundred and fifty dollars between the two of us. That's not enough. We need to get some money and find another ride, preferably a car. It's a thirty-hour drive, so we'll have to stop at a motel once, maybe twice.'

Devon cracked a grin. 'Shouldn't I have paid for the room? Being the guy and all. That's how it usually works.' His dimples flashed, and I felt myself smile back. 'Is that so, Mr Casanova?'

'Definitely,' he said. Slowly the amusement disappeared from his face. 'So how are we going to get a car and more money?'

I wasn't sure. I didn't know anyone who would help us. 'If there's no other way, we'll have to steal.'

Devon sat up. He looked thoughtful. 'We can't drive to my parents. The drive's more than three hours, and it's too risky; that's where Major would probably check first. But we could pay a very quick visit to Uncle Scott and Aunt Celia. You remember them, right?' His voice had gotten strange when he asked the question.

I nodded. I remembered them from my time in Livingston. That barbecue with his entire family had been one of the happiest days of my life – if you ignored the fact that I had been there as an impostor.

'They live about one hour from here. I'm sure they'd help us. They even have a spare car we can probably borrow.'

'Won't they ask questions?'

'I'm sure they will, but we'll just have to give the right answers.'

'OK,' I whispered. I was too tired to keep my eyes open. 'Can you set the alarm for six?'

'That gives us only two hours of sleep,' Devon said, worry in his voice.

'We can't afford more,' I mumbled. 'We have to keep moving.' I didn't bother to undress, just pulled the blankets over my body. The blankets smelled of mould and smoke and cheap detergent.

Devon extinguished the lights. I could hear his

even breathing to my right.

'I'm sorry, you know,' I said in a small voice.

'What for?' he asked. His voice was calm and controlled.

'For everything.'

'Tessa, it's OK.'

My heart broke at the sound of his words. How could I say what I wanted to say? How could I make him see?

'I think you apologized already,' he continued. Tension leaked from his voice. 'You did your job. It was a mission. I get that.'

I nodded, though he couldn't see it in the dark. 'OK,' I whispered.

There was nothing left to add, nothing I could do to take the pain of losing his sister away from him – or his parents. A small part of me wanted to ask about them. But it wasn't my place to do that, and this certainly wasn't the time. I pressed my palm against the *A* over my ribcage. The events in Livingston had left scars on both of us; some were visible, others not.

'For a long time, I was sure you hated me, but . . .' I trailed off.

That got his attention. I could see the outline of his head shoot up.

'I don't hate you.' His tone was gentle – just the way I remembered it.

I wished I could see his expression. 'You don't? But—'

'I don't.'

'OK,' I said quietly. I was tired, but at the same time I was scared of falling asleep.

'Devon, why are you really here?' I whispered into the darkness.

He didn't reply for a minute. Just when I was starting to think he'd fallen asleep, he answered.

'I need the distraction. And I want to help you and Holly.' He paused, and I could hear him breathe. 'I know I should return home, but I can't stand it. It feels so empty and hopeless there. And I don't feel like I belong in headquarters. I don't think I belong anywhere. Not any more.'

He hadn't said it, but I knew that Abel's Army was another reason why he was here. I'd noticed the way his eyes tightened whenever I mentioned them. They were the missing puzzle piece in his sister's murder. He wasn't just here to be helpful – he was after revenge.

I scooted to the edge of my bed and reached out, glad that the beds were so close together. 'I know how that feels. Not belonging,' I said softly. Devon's hand met mine and curled around my fingers.

For a few moments after the alarm rang, I didn't know where I was or what had happened. A wall of cotton seemed to envelop my brain, but with the stench of fuel and dusty fabric, the memory came back, and with it the ache in my chest.

With a groan, I sat up. Devon was already awake. He

was perched on the edge of his bed, his face buried in his hands.

I stumbled to my feet, my head spinning like crazy. Two hours of sleep weren't nearly enough, but I knew Major must have noticed that I was missing by now. We had to keep moving. I touched Devon's shoulder. 'Are you all right?'

He raised his head and gave me a tired smile. 'I'm OK, just exhausted.'

'Why don't you take a quick shower while I organize a classy vending machine breakfast for us?' I asked. Devon smiled. I smoothed down my hair in a feeble attempt to look presentable. There wasn't much I could do about the state of my clothes or the smell of someone who hadn't showered after a sweaty ride on a motorcycle. I headed out of the room and towards the vending machine pressed against the grey wall at the end of the narrow corridor. I passed a dozen shabby doors, my fingertips lightly tracing the cool surface of the metal banister that lined my right side. The air was crisp, and the first hints of grey shone on the horizon; it would be dawn soon.

Despite the early hour, the rest area wasn't as deserted as last night. Two cars occupied the gas pumps. Their owners were probably inside the station. I surveyed the snacks behind the scratched glass of the vending machine and selected two Twix bars and two single-serve packages of Cheerios. Not the most nutritious breakfast, but we could worry about that later. I bent down to pick up the food when I noticed someone watching me. Near one of the gas pumps, a man stood beside the open door of a black truck, looking my way. His eyes were hidden by mirrored, silver glasses – a common trick used by Variants who wanted to hide their strange eyes.

CHAPTER 16

My heart gave a thud, and I jerked upright. The man was still staring at me, glasses reflecting the rays of the rising sun. We should have been more careful. How could I have thought it was safe to come out here alone? And in my own body, no less? *Oh shit.*

I whirled around and hurried back to our room. Devon was emerging from the bathroom with a cloud of steam when I swung the door shut, my pulse pounding in my veins.

'Hey, what's up?' he asked as he made his way over to me and took the chocolate bars and cereal from my hands.

I risked a peek through the blinds, but from my vantage point I couldn't see the gas pumps. 'One of the customers at the fuel station was watching me when I bought the food.'

'And?' Devon asked. He stood behind me, following my gaze outside, his body so close that his heat warmed my back.

I turned and Devon took a step back – he had to or we would have been close enough to kiss. 'He was staring at me and wearing shades. What if it's one of Abel's men or someone from the FEA?'

'Do you really think they'd have found us already? How would they know that we're here?'

'Maybe they saw the motorcycle when they drove by.'

'It can't be seen from the street,' Devon said with a reassuring smile. 'And honestly it doesn't surprise me that the man was staring at you. Your hair is all over the place, and your eye make-up is smeared around your eyes. You look like someone punched you. The guy was probably just trying to see if you're OK.'

I pushed past Devon and rushed into the bathroom to check my reflection in the small mirror over the sink. Devon was right. I looked like an absolute zombie in wrinkly clothes. I let out a relieved laugh and smiled at Devon's face in the doorway. But now that the panic had ebbed away, I noticed that he had moved his towel down around his hips. A droplet of water trailed over his collarbone, down his defined chest and stomach, only to disappear under the towel. He seemed to realize his lack of clothing at the exact same moment, because he shifted uncomfortably and returned to the bedroom. 'I'll get dressed while you take a shower, OK?'

I nodded and closed the door. I allowed myself to relax into the hot water streaming down my body. I rubbed the shower gel over my shoulders, then down my arms, and suddenly froze. The skin below the crook of my elbow felt sore, and then the memory of last night washed over me, how Major had pierced my skin with something. I dug my fingers into the spot until I felt a tiny square object. Something had been implanted into my skin. I shut off the water, my heart thudding heavily in my chest. I wiped the water from my face and peered down at the pale, slightly bruised skin. When I flexed my arm and stretched my skin tight, I could see the tiny black object. A wave of nausea crashed over me.

I knew what it was. A tracking device.

I stumbled out of the shower, ripped the towel off the rack, and wrapped it around my wet body before I stormed into the bedroom where Devon was pulling a shirt over his head. His eyes widened when he spotted me. 'What—'

'I have a tracker in my arm,' I interrupted him, voice panicky.

Devon crossed the room in two long strides and gripped my arm. 'Are you sure?'

'Major implanted it while I was on the pills. I was barely conscious and didn't remember.'

I guided his finger to the spot. His body tensed. 'So the FEA knows we're here.'

I swallowed. I felt dizzy with fear. How could I have been so stupid to forget what Major had done? His pills must have affected my brain more than I thought. 'It's still early. Major thinks the pills put me to sleep. Maybe he hasn't checked on me yet, and even if he has, it'll take them a while to get here.'

Panic swelled in my chest. 'We need to remove it.'

Devon's eyebrows shot up. 'How?'

'Do you have knife?'

He picked up his backpack and took out a small army knife. He unfolded the short blade. He held it up to me, and for a moment I could only stare at it.

'You have to do it,' I said. I didn't have it in me to plunge a knife into my arm. 'You have to do it. It's not a big deal; you can heal me after.'

'You sure?' he asked, taking my arm again. I nodded. 'Just do it quickly.'

Without a word of warning, he pushed the tip of the blade into my arm. I bit down on my lip as burning pain shot up my arm. Luckily the tracker wasn't in too deep. Within seconds, the blood-smeared square sat on Devon's palm. Blood trickled out of the cut in my arm, but Devon put the knife down and wrapped his hand around the wound. Warmth spread over my skin, and we sat there for a minute as I trembled and then relaxed into his touch. When he pulled back again, the cut was gone.

But I still felt shaky. I wasn't sure if it was from the pain or the blood or the knowledge that our escape might be over before it had really begun.

'What do we do with it?' Devon asked, inspecting the tracking device. A few beads of sweat glistened on his forehead. Healing always cost him.

I hurried into the bathroom and left the door ajar, so I wouldn't have to yell. 'We have to get them off our trail. We need to hide it in someone else's car, so the FEA follows them.'

I hastily slipped into my underwear, jeans and T-shirt and pulled my wet hair into a ponytail, then rushed back out again and stuffed my belongings into my bag.

'OK,' Devon said slowly and picked up his backpack.

I opened the door a gap and peeked outside. The man with the glasses was gone. But that didn't mean we weren't being watched. I slipped out, with Devon following close behind.

I glanced across the parking lot, to the tiny store in the gas station. The cashier was reading a book and not looking our way. 'Let's go,' I whispered.

As we hurried towards the parking lot I expected to hear the sound of squealing tyres and catch sight of FEA vehicles at any moment. If Major caught us, he'd never let us out of his sight again. I'd be a prisoner for the rest of my life.

Our motorcycle stood where we'd left it yesterday. 'What if it has a tracker on it too?'

Devon froze centimetres from the bike, then turned to stare at me. 'Would the FEA really have a tracking device installed in all of its vehicles?'

'I wouldn't put it past Major.'

'You're right. Shit.' He ran a hand through his messy blond hair. 'What are we going to do?'

I quickly scanned the other cars in the parking lot. One was a big, clunky pickup truck – not the best escape car. The other was an old black Acura. 'We take that one.' I grabbed a small toolbox from the black luggage case of the motorcycle. I knew I would find an FEA-issued all-purpose utility tool inside. Alec had taught me how to open locks with it, among other things. I strode towards the car and peered inside – candy wrappers on the ground, empty Dr Pepper bottles on the backseat, and no alarm system. Perfect. 'Make sure nobody sees me,' I said as I knelt before the door and began to fumble with the lock.

'Did you learn to steal cars at FEA headquarters?'

'Among other things,' I said. My fingers were sweaty and shaky. I had to calm down. After a few twists, the lock clicked. I opened the door and slipped behind the wheel, turning my attention to hot-wiring the car. Devon watched me with unmasked curiosity.

'Maybe you could slip the tracking device on to the truck,' I said, now working on the ignition with the tool. While Devon went over to the truck, I finally managed to get the Acura running. The engine purred, but in the quiet of the parking lot, even that sound could be our downfall. I shut my door and waited for Devon to take the seat beside me. 'I never thought I'd become a car thief,' he said with a small laugh.

I peeled the car out of its spot and steered it towards the station's exit. 'FEA taught me a lot of strange stuff.' I glanced down the highway. No black Mercedes limousines, no police cars. I pressed my foot down on the gas pedal and turned on to the road.

Devon peered over his shoulder. 'It doesn't seem like they've noticed the car is missing. And nobody is following us.'

'Check the sky,' I said, flooring the accelerator. We needed to leave the motel area as quickly as possible. In a couple of hours, it would be swarming with FEA agents.

'Clear,' Devon said, leaning back against his seat and stretching out his legs. He looked exhausted. We hadn't had more than two hours of sleep and hadn't even had time to eat our makeshift breakfast. 'I miss the bike. It was way cooler than this thing.' He gestured at the mess around us. His stomach let out a growl.

I laughed, but the sound felt wrong. 'In my backpack.'

Devon reached behind my seat, and found the chocolates and cereal I'd bought from the vending machine. We divided them between us, but the snacks were stale, and everything tasted like dust.

'You're a pretty good driver,' he remarked. He sounded surprised.

'I guess I'm a natural. I have hardly any practice. When I joined the FEA I was too young to have my driver's licence, and I've barely driven in class.' I glanced into the rearview mirror. Still no sign of any cars following us.

Now that we had bought some distance between us and the motel, Devon and I stopped to switch places. He knew the way to his aunt and uncle's house better than I did. And we really needed to get rid of our current car as quickly as possible. Soon Major – and the police – would be looking for it.

Devon stayed well within the speed limits, for the most part. Though we were in a hurry, we couldn't risk being pulled over by the police. Devon had his driver's licence, but I was worried that the FEA was linked to the police database and would notice if anyone checked on him. They'd be after us in a blink – if they weren't already. And then there was the little problem of the stolen car. I scanned the sky once more, looking for helicopters. I couldn't shake off the feeling that we were being hunted.

CHAPTER 17

After driving for almost an hour, Devon pulled on to a narrow forest road. The Acura jolted over the uneven pavement, and my stiff legs and back protested painfully. Devon zigzagged to avoid the myriad of potholes filled with muddy water. I could see the tension in his body, the way he held the tightness in his back and stomach. The car groaned every time we encountered a bump. It definitely wasn't made for crossroad trips. The clouds broke open, and heavy raindrops pelted down on us. In that moment a charming house came into view: grey stucco facade, white shutters and a porch with lilac flowers cascading almost to the ground.

When Devon brought us to a stop beside the three cars parked in the driveway, pebbles flew everywhere. The white door flew open, and Aunt Celia, dressed in a bright orange dress and a yellow apron, peeked out, frowning. Of course she wouldn't recognize us as long as we were hidden behind the dirty windshield.

She doesn't know you at all, I reminded myself. After all, I didn't look like Devon's sister, Madison, any more. Devon tried to smooth his hair. He'd nervously run his hands through it so often in the last hour that it was all over the place. I could only imagine what a mess I looked. The ringlets that had fallen out of my ponytail clung to my neck and forehead. The moment Aunt Celia saw Devon, her face lit up. She glanced at me curiously as we walked up the porch before pulling Devon into a hug and kissing his cheek. 'Devon, sweetheart, what are you doing here?'

'Oh, we're just on a bit of a road trip, and we thought we'd stop by,' Devon said lightly.

'And who is this young lady?' She smiled at me. She was paler than I remembered her and slightly older looking. Her blonde hair was up in a messy bun, and she looked like someone who hadn't slept in a while. Just like Devon, she'd recently lost someone she cared deeply about. That wasn't the kind of thing you forgot quickly.

'Hi, I'm Tessa.' I shook her hand with a smile. 'I'm a friend of Devon's.'

'How lovely,' she said, but her voice was hollow, and she cast a nervous glance at Devon. 'Come on in. Your uncle is inside.' The wall to our left was plastered with family photos. A stab of jealousy jolted through me at the sight of them. Devon had a loving family. He didn't have to steal his own family photos from a forbidden file – they were displayed in the open for everyone to see. I reached for the folded photos in my jeans pocket. Just feeling them beneath my fingertips gave me a sense of belonging.

Devon's hand on my lower back urged me to move on. I hurried through the house, but every step felt more like returning to a happy family. As we entered the living room, Uncle Scott looked away from the baseball game on TV. The spicy scent of cigars wafted over to me and burned in my nose. He still sported his trademark moustache that curled around his lips. 'So where are you two heading?' he asked.

'Did you eavesdrop?' Devon asked with a grin. His uncle got up, hugged him, and patted his back.

'No need to. These walls are thin as paper,' Uncle Scott said in his deep, raspy voice. He turned to me and shook my hand. 'So you are Tessa, the *friend*.'

He said 'friend' like he didn't believe for one second that that was what we were.

My cheeks heated. 'That's me. Nice to meet you, sir.'

'So where's your road trip taking you?' Uncle Scott asked again as he sank back down into his chair. He turned the volume of the game down but didn't turn the TV off.

Devon was about to reply, but I cut in before he could say the wrong thing. 'Chicago,' I replied.

Uncle Scott nodded, but I wasn't sure he actually believed me. Aunt Celia walked into the living room at that moment, carrying a tray with cookies and iced tea. 'Is that your car, Tessa?' she asked as she set everything down on the table. I wasn't sure, but I thought I could detect a hint of suspicion in her voice. 'Why don't you kids take a seat?'

Devon and I sank down on the plush sofa. It smelled like the same flowery carpet cleaner his mother had used. 'That's actually one of the reasons why we're here,' Devon began hesitantly. 'I wanted to ask if we could borrow a car.'

'Why can't you take Tessa's car?' Uncle Scott asked.

'It's really old, and the brakes aren't working properly. We don't want to drive such a long distance with it,' I lied quickly. Guilt flashed across Devon's face. We couldn't tell them the truth. They'd find out soon enough that the car was stolen and that we had lied to them.

Uncle Scott put down his cigar. 'You're in trouble, aren't you?'

Devon and I exchanged a look. I turned back to Uncle Scott, smiling coyly. 'We just wanted to enjoy a few days together before we have to be back at the academy.'

'So you're also an artist, Tessa? Devon's mother told me all about your art school,' Aunt Celia said as she handed us both a glass of iced tea.

Artists. I had to stop myself from snorting. 'Thanks,' I said. 'I am an artist – a painter. But it's not that interesting, actually.'

'So, anyway. Do you think you could loan us a car? We'd be back in a couple of days and could drop it off on our way back to campus,' Devon asked. I was glad that he was trying to steer away from the topic of school.

'Of course,' Uncle Scott said, his expression understanding. 'Your aunt and I know this has been a very difficult time for you, Devon, and I'm glad to hear you're taking some time off for yourself. You know we're always here for you. Just don't get in trouble, OK?'

'Don't worry,' Devon said with a smile.

Aunt Celia wiped her eyes and excused herself before disappearing from view. I could hear her rummaging around in the kitchen.

Uncle Scott sighed. 'She talked to your mother this morning—'

'Is she OK?' Devon demanded, tension slipping back into his body. I paused with the glass against my lips.

Uncle Scott frowned, his moustache turning down at the edges. 'She's all right. But they're thinking about selling the house. Your mom can't bear living there any more. And it seems like your dad is always at work.' He sighed again and shook his head. 'I guess that's just his way of coping with things.' He stared distractedly at the TV.

I touched Devon's leg to show him I was there for him. But his face was made of stone. 'I'll call them later.'

'I'm sure they'll be happy to hear from you.' Uncle Scott paused. 'I can give you our old truck. And if you don't have a place to stay, you can always camp out on the truck bed. Just make sure you're safe. Let me get the keys. We won't need it for the next few days, anyway.' He left the living room and returned a few minutes later with keys, a tent and two rolled-up sleeping bags in his hands. He handed them over to Devon. 'Just in case. That way you won't have to freeze if you decide to sleep on the truck bed.'

'Why don't you stay for lunch? You could even spend the afternoon here to relax a bit,' Aunt Celia said, entering the living room, looking more composed than before.

I could tell from the look on Devon's face that he would have loved to take her up on the offer, but of course we couldn't risk spending more than a couple of hours in the same place. Not to mention a relative's house, which was where they'd look first. 'Thank you so much for the offer, Aunt Celia, but we really have to hurry. We're meeting up with friends of Tessa's in Chicago, and we're on a tight schedule,' he lied.

'Why don't we—' Uncle Scott began, but the ringing of a phone cut him off. He excused himself and headed into the kitchen to get the phone. When he returned, he was talking loudly, his brows furrowed. 'No, Linda, calm down.'

At the mention of Devon's mother, my body flooded with anxiety. Devon rose from the sofa, dropped the sleeping bags, and took a step towards his uncle. 'They're here with us. No reason to worry. I can give you Devon right now.' Uncle Scott handed the phone to Devon, who lifted it to his ear after a moment of hesitation.

I shifted to the edge of the couch. This wasn't good. Devon's face fell. 'Mom, I'm fine. Mom, please stop crying. Nothing has happened.' He lowered his voice for his next words. 'Mom, are they still there?' He paled as he nodded. 'OK, Mom. Please trust me. Everything will be fine. I can't talk much longer. But I'll call you soon. Don't listen to them, Mom, they're making a big deal out of nothing. Trust me.' He dropped the phone on the table, his worried eyes settling on me. 'Major and Summers are there.'

CHAPTER 18

'They told my parents that we'd run away and that I wasn't stable. Why would they tell my parents something like that after what they've gone through in the last few weeks?' He smashed his fist down on the table. His glass toppled over, and tea spilled everywhere. Aunt Celia winced, her hands frozen on her cup as she watched us with wide eyes.

'I'm sorry. They want to make you feel guilty and bait you to come back,' I said softly. 'And now Major knows we're here. They'll send the closest agent to come get us. We have to leave immediately.'

'So you *are* in trouble,' Uncle Scott said slowly.

Devon stared at his uncle as if he had only just remembered that we weren't alone. 'It's complicated. But we aren't in any trouble. We just need some time off. Everything is going to be fine.'

Devon and I stood up, picked up the sleeping bags and tent, swiped the keys from the table, and hurried out the door. Confusion showed on Uncle Scott's and Aunt Celia's faces as they followed us outside. 'Where are you going? What's going on?' Celia asked anxiously, but nobody said anything.

'What am I supposed to tell your parents? They're worried about you,' Uncle Scott called after us.

Devon stopped in front of the black pickup truck, casting nervous glances back at his aunt and uncle. 'I'm sorry for causing you trouble,' he whispered. 'But I promise we'll be fine.' I stood with my hands in my pockets, unsure what to do. I could tell that his aunt and uncle kept glancing at me like I was the one who'd led Devon astray. And it was kind of true. Without me, Devon would be living in headquarters, safe and sound, still blissfully unaware of the lies being spewed by Major and the FEA.

'Thanks for your help and for the iced tea,' I said before I slipped into the passenger seat. The inside of the car smelled of old smoke and wet dog, though I hadn't seen a dog inside the house.

Devon slipped into the car and started the engine. He waved at his uncle and aunt as we pulled out of their driveway. They were watching us with stunned expressions. How long would it take for the FEA to come here and question them?

'Damn it!' Devon yelled, slamming his fist down on the steering wheel. As soon as we were out of his relatives' line of sight, he stepped on the gas and we sped down the bumpy road.

163

Devon's knuckles were white from his grip around the steering wheel. 'Do you think the FEA will do something to my parents?' he asked.

I shook my head immediately. 'No,' I said firmly. Devon glanced at me from the corner of his eye like he needed more evidence to believe it. 'The FEA isn't like that. Maybe they manipulate and lie when it's to their advantage, but they'd never hurt innocents. They'll probably try to use your parents as leverage to make you feel guilty or make you do something rash and stupid, but they won't actually do them any harm.' And though I didn't trust the FEA and Major, I knew it was true. Major had certain morals. Sometimes he bent them if it suited him, but that certainly wouldn't make him hurt Devon's family.

'I don't like the thought of Major talking to my parents. He'll just tell them more lies and make them worry. They've been through so much and now this . . .' He trailed off, swallowing hard. His eyes darted to me again. 'Do you think we could check up on them? To make sure they're all right and so they know that I'm OK too?'

I hesitated. I could tell how important this was for Devon. 'We definitely can't go there. They'll probably have the house under surveillance. Same for your dad's vet practice. It's too dangerous. But we could stop at a public phone later to call your parents and try to reassure them.'

Devon's shoulders slumped, though I knew he had expected me to say that. He looked so sad. I touched his arm. His muscles were tense under my fingertips. 'Devon, we need to stay focused. We have to talk to my mother's ex-boyfriend in Detroit and find my mother, that's our top priority. Holly needs us. And I really believe your parents aren't in danger. I promise you they'll be fine. I wouldn't lie to you.'

'I know,' he said and covered my hand with his. 'How long will it take us to get there?'

'Well, I think the drive to Detroit will take thirty-six hours. But we'll have to rest. I could drive, but I don't have a licence, so we better not get caught.'

'It's OK. I don't mind driving. We don't even have to look for a motel. We'll just use the sleeping bags my uncle gave us. That way fewer people will see our faces.' He glanced at me. 'Why don't you just turn into someone else? Nobody would know that it's you.'

'Major would still know if he saw me with you.'

'So what? I could change my appearance. You know, dye my hair black, wear contact lenses, dress differently. And Abel's Army would still be thrown off the scent.'

I stared at Devon's lovely blond hair. 'Maybe a wig would work too. You could buy a few and quickly change your look, if needed.'

'A wig?' He laughed. The giddy sound eased the knot in my stomach. 'Are you serious?'

I smiled, but then I thought of something. 'I don't remember which of the people's appearances that I've stored in my DNA I've used during practice before. If I use a person I've been around Alec or Summers or Major, they could still make the connection.'

'Then you'll have to find new people whose appearance you could use.'

'I guess I could bump a few people on our next rest stop and make sure that I touch their skin,' I said.

'So that's all it takes? Touching someone's skin?' His voice had changed, and I knew what he was thinking of. 'Did you touch her?' he asked quietly.

I stared out of the passenger window. He didn't have to tell me whom he meant. I knew. 'Yeah, I had to. I visited her in the hospital a few days before she died.' I winced. Devon and his parents hadn't found out about Madison's death until after the mission was over. Sometimes I wondered if Devon wished he'd been there for his twin sister's last moments.

'How does it feel?' Devon asked hesitantly, as if he wasn't sure he really wanted to know the answer.

'You mean, to incorporate a person's data?' A moment too late I realized how cold that must have sounded to Devon, but I couldn't take the words back.

'If that's what you call it.' There was an edge to his voice as he kept his gaze trained on the windshield.

'It's hard to describe. I can feel my body absorb the information. It's a bit like a charge, like a flow of energy. My body memorizes the DNA, and most of the time my shape is eager to change immediately.'

'How was it to touch Maddy? Was it different because she was . . .'

166

I didn't know how to answer him. I wasn't really sure if her case had felt much different. That day had been too stressful for me to remember every detail.

Devon rubbed a hand across his eyes, and a heavy silence fell over us. I thought it might suffocate me. But I didn't know what to do.

After a few minutes, Devon cleared his throat. 'I've been wondering since I found out about your Variation: have you ever tried to change into an animal?' I could tell that it was difficult for him to make his voice sound calm and light.

My lips turned up in a shaky smile. 'Oh no. My Variation doesn't work that way. I don't feel anything when I touch animals. My body definitely doesn't absorb their data. It only works on other humans.'

'Why do you think that is?' Devon asked, his shoulders losing some of their tension.

'I assume that absorbing another species' data is unnatural.'

'As opposed to turning into another human being?' I glanced at Devon's face to make sure that he hadn't said it with resentment, but he gave nothing away.

'I know it seems wrong,' I said quietly.

Devon shook his head. 'No, it's not. I didn't want to make you feel bad. We can't help our Variations. It's not perfectly normal to be able to heal people. I know that.'

'Yeah, normal's got nothing to do with us,' I joked. Devon leaned back in his seat, the last of his tension disappearing from his body. 'But honestly, I definitely can't turn into an animal. I've tried.'

'You have?' Devon's eyes flashed to mine, filled with curiosity. 'Let me guess: a cute little puppy.'

I snorted. 'Hell no. You couldn't be further from the truth.' I raised my eyebrows in a silent challenge.

Devon flexed his arms. 'I like a good challenge.' He ran his eyes over me, like that would give him a clue. Did I resemble any kind of animal? If he said hippo or hyena, I'd kick his ass. I felt my neck flush when his gaze hovered on me much longer than it should have. 'A sloth.'

'Now you're trying to insult me,' I said, crossing my arms over my chest. Dimples flashed on his cheeks.

'Hand on my heart. I'd never do something like that.' But I could see from the look on his face that he was looking for an animal that would really make me crazy.

'A spider,' he guessed. Expectation flickered on his face. Did he think I'd start screaming like a little girl?

'Nope. I think my body would implode if I tried to turn myself into something that small.'

He frowned. 'Aren't you afraid of spiders?'

'Why would I be? Except for a few species, they're perfectly harmless. They can't hurt me.'

'What about bugs in general?'

I shook my head.

'Centipedes?'

I shook my head, suppressing a grin.

'Cockroaches?' I shook my head again. He hit the

steering wheel with his palm. 'Oh, come on. There has to be something you're terrified of!'

There were plenty of things I was terrified of. But creepy-crawlies weren't one of them. There were worse things in this world than vermin with eight legs and four eyes. But I wasn't going to tell Devon that, or the light mood would go up in flames.

'Sorry. It looks like I'm a freak in more ways than one.'

'Actually, I think it's kind of cool,' Devon said. 'So will you tell me now?'

'A chameleon.'

'That's it? But with your Variation, you're practically a chameleon already.'

'Not really. A chameleon can adapt to the colour of its surroundings. It can blend in. That was something I never managed.'

'But you seemed to blend in just fine in Livingston,' he said. And I realized he was right.

We'd been on the road for more than eight hours when Devon pulled the car into a small rest area surrounded by forest. Dusk was turning our surroundings grey. He parked the car in a tree-covered spot that was shielded from view, and we got out of the truck's cab. Despite it being spring, the evenings and nights were icy. I pulled on my winter jacket as I scrambled on to the bed of the truck. Devon swung himself up beside me, and together we pitched the tent, so we'd be protected from wind and weather. We crawled into our sleeping bags. The inside of the tent smelled like the great outdoors – reminiscent of bonfires and mould. My nose began tingling.

There wasn't much room in the tent, so Devon and I sat pressed against each other. 'Do you think it'll be freezing tonight?' I whispered.

Devon zipped the sleeping bag up to his chest and turned on the flashlight. Behind the thin material of the tent, I could see that the last sunrays had disappeared. 'It might be, but these sleeping bags withstand temperatures far below the freezing point. We'll be fine.'

I nodded. With Devon's side pressed against mine, his body warmth creeping into me, I knew we would be. 'So you grew up in Detroit?' Devon asked.

'Not really. I grew up in a lot of places,' I said. Devon's eyes searched my face, and after a moment he nodded as if he understood, but I doubted that was the case.

'So what about your mother? If she's a Variant, as you said, is it possible that she could take on other appearances like you do?'

The red stamps reading 'Volatile' flashed in my mind. There was so much I didn't know about my mother. I knew more facts about Devon's family than I did about my own. 'Her Variation is regeneration. I don't think that entails changing into other people. I think she can just make her cells renew themselves, so she looks young again.'

Devon frowned. It was strange how good it felt to be shoulder to shoulder with him. I'd never felt more alone than when I'd found out about Alec's and the FEA's betrayal, but it was comforting to learn I still had Devon. 'Would you even recognize her if she looked, like, twenty?'

I tried to recall my mother's face the last time I'd seen her, but that had been more than two years ago. I leaned forward, heaved my bag on to my legs, and pulled out the photo of my mother that I'd found in the file – but kept the photos with Abel and my brother, Zachary, hidden. 'I think it would actually be easier for me if she looked younger, back when life was made of happy memories. The truth is, I hardly remember how she looked two years ago.' I handed the photo to Devon. He shined the flashlight on it, his eyes scrunching up to get a better look. 'I was one in that photo,' I explained, 'and to the best of my knowledge, my mother was in her twenties.'

Devon's expression softened. 'You and your mom look so happy here.'

I glanced over at it – at the loving smile on my mother's face, at her smooth skin, at the way she held me close to her. My smile was wide, showing off my first few teeth, and I looked like I couldn't be happier anywhere but on my mother's lap. 'I suppose we were happy at that time.'

'So what happened?' He handed the photo back to me, and I stuffed it into my bag, where it couldn't bring up hurtful memories.

I'd asked myself that question so often and always come up short, but now I thought that I might know the answer.

'We moved a lot. Later on I thought it was because my mother was worried someone might find out about my Variation, but now I think she might have been running from Abel's Army.'

'If she was so worried about Abel's Army, why do you think she didn't return to the FEA? You said she'd lived in headquarters for a few years, right?' Devon shifted, and the friction of our shoulders rubbing against each other gave me goosebumps. It was still weird to be this close to Devon; I'd always thought Alec would be the one to stand by me if anything went downhill. I never would have thought that he might be the reason why it went downhill in the first place.

I could feel Devon staring at me. 'I don't know,' I said. 'But I need to find out. That's why we need to find her.' I tried to think back to the happier years with my mother, but the early memories were almost faded. 'I don't think the happy period lasted for long. I think the running got to my mother pretty fast, but what really did her in was when I showed signs of my Variation. It reminded her of everything she'd worked so hard to forget. I think that's when she lost it and started hating me.'

Devon's hand reached for mine, and he laced my fingers through his. He did it with such an ease and casualness, as if we'd been friends – or more – for years. 'She doesn't hate you,' he said softly. But he couldn't know. He had never met my mother, had never seen the disgust in her eyes when she'd caught me using my talent.

I didn't say anything, just closed my eyes.

I wasn't sure how long I'd been asleep, but it couldn't have been more than a couple of hours from the way my body felt. Sluggishly I lifted my head, wondering what had woken me. The beam of a spotlight swivelled across our tent. I peered out of the gap. It was dark outside except for the spotlights, but I could make out the shape of police lights on the roof of a car.

'Devon,' I hissed, shaking his shoulder. He turned around, blinking back sleep.

'What's up?'

'The police,' I said quietly. Devon sat up, eyes wide. 'They're searching for us. You have to get out and hide somewhere. Quick!'

He got to his knees, confusion showing on his face. 'Why?'

'Hurry,' I whispered. 'I'm fine here, but you need to stay hidden.' When the police car pulled into the parking lot, there was a moment when the trees hid the truck bed from their view. 'Now.' I half pushed Devon out of the tent. He landed with a gentle thud on the asphalt, and I watched him dart into the bushes beside the truck, crouching in the brush. We couldn't risk being caught. I wriggled out of my clothes, stashed them in my sleeping bag, then snatched jogging pants and a shirt from Devon's bag and gingerly slipped them on.

The crunching of tyres on asphalt stopped close by. The police car had come to a halt beside ours. I took a deep breath, recalled the memory of Uncle Scott's appearance, and let the rippling wash over me. I heard their steps coming closer and saw the beam of a flashlight growing larger and brighter as they approached the tent. I lay very still except for the shaking of my limbs as I transformed into the form of Uncle Scott. I willed the transformation to go faster. If the police officers caught me mid-change, we'd all be in a shitload of trouble.

When the rippling in my body died down, the police officer stopped in front of the tent opening. He rapped his flashlight against the side of the truck. 'This isn't a campsite,' he shouted. 'Come out.'

I pretended to wake and crawled to the opening of the tent before poking my head out. From the corner of my eye, I could see Devon crouching in the bushes, and in the same instant, I saw a flicker where the police car stood. For the briefest moment its appearance had shimmered and revealed another car underneath. What the hell?

My eyes flew to the man in front of me, and now that I really focused, I could see that something wasn't right with his uniform. It was almost like a hologram, or in the movies, when they tried to use animated characters in the place of real actors. It looked like the real character, but you just knew something was wrong. It was too dark to make out much except for the white glow of his eyes in his black face, but I knew his clothes and the car were an illusion. His arm twitched, and my eyes darted downward. He was holding a syringe in his right hand. The only thing that had probably stopped him from plunging it into my neck was my appearance. He seemed unsure if I was who they were looking for.

I didn't give him a chance to make up his mind. My arm shot out, and I punched him square in the jaw. He stumbled back, and the illusions flickered out, revealing a man in civilian clothes standing before a black car. Was it the FEA or Abel's Army?

He lifted a walkie-talkie. 'She's here.'

CHAPTER 19

Devon jumped out of the bushes, and in the same instant a second man popped into view – out of thin air. I saw a flash of red hair. Holly's abductor! So we were being hunted by Abel's Army after all. I swung myself off the truck bed and aimed a high kick at the man's head. Redhead leaned back, lessening the blow, but I busted his lips. Devon was struggling against the man with the syringe. I aimed another punch at my opponent, but he ducked. He barrelled into me. The air left my lungs in a whoosh, but I didn't fall. I drove my elbow into his eye. His cry of pain was joined by the sound of a body slamming against the car. Devon stood over the other man, who was lying on the ground motionless, his head bleeding. He must have struck hard into the side of the truck.

I turned my focus back to my opponent and tried to kick his legs out from under him, but he stumbled backwards and disappeared with a pop. A second later, he reappeared beside his partner, gripped his arm, and they both vanished into thin air. I was breathing hard, but I didn't let my guard down. They could return at any time. What about their car? Slowly I changed back to my own body. I pulled the strings tight so the jogging pants wouldn't slip off and turned to Devon. My heart gave a heavy thud. He was leaning against the truck. The syringe was stuck in his arm. I rushed over to him and pulled it out. 'Devon?' I said in a panicky voice. 'Are you OK?'

He gave me a weak smile. 'I think there was tranquilizer in the syringe. I feel a little fuzzy, but my body is fighting against it. Meds usually don't take effect because of my Variation. I think that really scared the shit out of my opponent.'

'Come on.' I helped him into the passenger seat before I quickly dismantled the tent enough for us to drive away. I was sure they'd return soon. I slipped behind the steering wheel and drove off. Devon struggled to stay awake beside me.

'Are you sure you're OK?'

He nodded. 'Just let's make sure that doesn't happen again. I really need a good night of sleep.' I forced a smile, but inside I was in full-on panic mode. How had Abel's Army found us? And so quickly? They'd been able to find us before we had any idea how to find Holly.

Twenty-six hours and another night in the tent later, Devon and I reached Detroit. We hadn't been attacked again, but I knew it was only a matter of time before either the FEA or Abel's Army caught up with us.

Carl lived on the outskirts of town, in the same house he'd shared with my mother and me more than two years ago. Telephone lines bridged the street above us, some of the antennas askew. Pigeons walked the pavement, picking the ground for food. It was early in the afternoon, but this part of town, crowded with old warehouses, was deserted. We pulled on to the street that led to my old neighbourhood. I didn't recognize any of the few people on the street, but I hadn't exactly been sociable when I'd lived here.

'That's it,' I said, pointing at a small, brown house with peeling paint, a broken banister, and jam-packed garbage cans. A shopping cart stood forgotten on the sidewalk in front of it. Someone had probably stolen it – or what people around here used to call it: borrowed for good.

Devon pulled up at the sidewalk, but we didn't get out of the truck immediately. I stared at the shabby house that had once been my home. It felt strange to return. Last time I'd sent a letter to my mom at this address, it had been returned. My mother hadn't stayed with a man for longer than two years for as long as I could remember.

I pushed the door open and got out. A dog barked in one of the neighbour's houses. It sounded big and angry. Maybe it was the same mutt that had chased me on my way to school once.

'You OK?' Devon asked as he stopped beside me.

I nodded, though I wasn't sure if it was true. I took a deep breath and walked towards the door. The front garden was missing patches of grass, and a few heaps of dog poop littered the rest of it. I knocked at the door and looked around. It smelled of pee and exhaust. This was nothing like Devon's house. He had a place he could truly call home.

'Do you think someone already knows we're here?' Devon asked, shifting nervously on his feet, hands in his pockets.

I shook my head. 'I don't think so. Major probably thinks I don't have the guts to return to this place, considering how much I hated it and Carl. But we still shouldn't stay here for longer than absolutely necessary. We need to see if he has any information and then keep moving.'

I rang the bell but didn't hear it echo inside the house. It was probably broken, which didn't surprise me, considering the state of the rest of the house. I hammered against the door, then paused to listen for any sign of life inside.

'Maybe he's at work.'

I snorted. If Devon knew Carl like I did, he wouldn't have said that. 'No, he's there,' I said. 'He's probably just in a drunken stupor. It takes a while for him to get out of that.'

Devon gave me an odd look, and I turned away, focusing on the peeling white paint of the door. I rammed my fist against it a few more times, feeling the wood vibrate on its hinges.

'Careful, or you'll break the thing down,' Devon joked.

I stopped and turned to look around at the neighbourhood once more. Nobody had come out of their house to see what caused the noise. No one was concerned by someone screaming and banging in this neighbourhood. Domestic violence and screamed disputes happened here on a daily basis. Suddenly the door ripped open and a wave of sweat and alcohol washed over me. I remembered it well. A smell that was ripe with a life ruined, the scent of hopelessness.

Carl stood in the gap of the doorway. His eyes were bleary and his face unshaven, but at least he was dressed in what looked to be a clean tank top and jeans. I'd seen him worse. He squinted at me as he held on to the doorframe, probably to steady himself. He was drunk. Not a big surprise.

He blinked a few times and then seemed to really recognize me for the first time. 'Tessa, that you?' The words had a slight slur to them, but at least they were intelligible.

'Yes, it's me. I need to talk to you, Carl,' I said.

Carl's eyes flickered over to Devon, who stood so close to me that our arms were brushing.

Hearing my name from Carl's mouth felt strange. When I'd lived with him and my mother, I'd only ever heard him shout it in contempt or anger. Now he sounded almost . . . happy to see me. Nearly nostalgic. Maybe the years of alcohol and loneliness had finally taken their toll.

Carl stepped back to give us room to enter, still gripping

the door. He was unsteady on his legs but managed to keep his balance. 'Come in.'

We walked in and Carl shut the door behind us. The tangy smell of beer was even worse now that the fresh air supply from outside was cut off. 'How about I make some coffee?' I said. I wanted Carl as sober as possible when we had our talk.

'Sure,' Carl said. 'Make yourselves at home. I'm going to wash up upstairs. Why don't you go into the living room?' Gripping the banister, he walked up the stairs. He'd never been this civil to me.

A weight settled in my stomach as I stepped into the kitchen and turned the light on. The sink was filled with dishes, the remains of food crusted on them. The garbage was piled high in the trash bin, ready to be taken outside. Everything was as I remembered it. The memory of my last day in this house flashed in my mind.

Misty white. The glass fogged over, my warm breath eating away at the sheen of frost. Stiff-fingered, I wiped at the clouded glass. The soft glow of the streetlamp flowed into my room. It cast a dim light on the bare walls and stained carpet.

Outside, two shapes disappeared into the shadows. The yellow-white glare grasped for them, but they were wrapped in darkness. Cold clawed at my cheeks and nose. I strained my eyes, but the two forms remained indistinct shapes.

A gentle breeze sent the snowflakes whirling around on the street, past overstuffed trashcans, the three-wheeled car nobody had driven for months, and the shopping cart that Mrs Cross from across the street had stolen from Target a few days ago. My eyes darted back to the place where the two forms had stood – but they were gone.

I pulled my legs up, away from the frigid heater, and pressed them against my chest. If Carl hadn't spent all of our money on booze, it would be warm in here.

The sound of shouting, the words too mangled and slurred to make sense of them, carried through the thin walls into my room.

I felt cold all over again. Mom's high-pitched reply to Carl wasn't even coherent. I pushed myself off my cold perch, and my bare feet landed on the old carpet with its ever-present smell of mould. Something sticky pressed against the sole of my foot, but I didn't bother to check what it was. Probably the beer Carl had spilled when he stumbled into my room instead of the bathroom a few days ago.

The shouting hadn't stopped yet.

I shuffled out of my room and into the hallway, not caring that dust bunnies stuck to my feet. The bathroom was even colder than the rest of the house, and black mould covered the wall near the shower. I pushed the door shut and turned on the light. After a few flickers, the bulb started glowing, and the mirror threw my reflection back at me.

Was it even my face? Maybe I'd lain next to another newborn in the baby ward and decided that her face was better than mine. I moved closer until I could see every fingerprint and toothpaste stain on the mirror. Exhaustion was etched into my skin. I shut my eyes, though it wasn't necessary for the shift. *The familiar rippling washed over me.*

The sensation died down, and I risked a look at my reflection.

The door banged open, and Mom stood in the doorway, her mascara smudged and her lips bust open. For a moment she stared at me as if I was everything evil and bad wrapped into one body. As if I were responsible for whatever had just happened to her. The look of horror changed to anger as she grabbed my arm.

'What are you doing? How often do I have to tell you not to do this? Do you want Carl to find out? Do you want something bad to happen to us? Why can't you be normal?'

Mom flipped the switch and bathed us in darkness, as if she couldn't bear looking at me, before she went on. 'I've been trying to hide your strangeness for so many years, but you never listened. Everything's your fault.' Leaving me in the dark, she stalked off. Guilt burned a path through my stomach. Abnormal. Monster. Thief. That's what I was. A freak who could steal other people's appearances.

I blinked to get rid of the prickling sensation in my eyes. The shape of my face shifted again, and when the tearing stopped, I moved closer to the mirror. Brown eyes instead of turquoise, same auburn hair but thicker and with more waves.

I forced Mom's expression to soften until there was a look on her face I'd never seen directed at me. My lips trembled when I moved them and her voice came out. 'Happy birthday, sweetheart. I love you.' My expression twisted, became more like the one I was used to seeing.

The doorbell jolted me out of the moment, and I dropped Mom's appearance.

'Tessa, get your ass down here. There's someone who wants to see you,' Mom shouted.

I hurried down the steps towards the unfamiliar voices, but Mom grabbed my arm. 'You brought this on to yourself.' Her nails dug into my skin, and I tried not to wince.

Shaking her off, I glared at her. 'What do you mean? I didn't do anything.'

I entered the living room. Two men stood in their prim suits amid the ragged furniture and empty beer bottles. Their faces turned towards me. I took a step back when my eyes locked with a pair of grey ones.

They belonged to the taller and much younger of the two. He had the most amazing eyes I'd ever seen. They kept me frozen to the spot.

I cleared my throat. 'You're here to see me?'

The older man nodded. His slicked-back black hair didn't move a centimetre. 'Yes. I'm Major Antonio Sanchez. I was about to speak to your father about the reason for our visit.'

'He's not my father.' The words shot out before I could stop them.

'Ungrateful brat.'

My skin burned from Carl's words. He'd called me worse, but not in front of strangers. I knew better than to bring anyone home.

'Go get us some cigarettes. I'll handle this alone,' Mom said, surprising me and maybe even herself. I couldn't remember *her voice ever sounding as firm when she spoke with one of her boyfriends.*

Carl glanced between the two men and Mom, probably deciding they would interfere if he hit her, before he stumbled towards the front door. 'Whatever. Suit yourself. The brat's not mine.'

Major Sanchez waited for the bang of the door before he spoke. 'As we discussed on the phone, this is the best for your daughter. She'll be safe and cared for, and she'll live among people like herself, other Variants, and learn to control her Variation.'

The younger guy nudged me. 'Nice to meet you. I'm Alec.' He pushed a hand into his black hair, tousling it even more. 'I heard about your talent. The agency has been talking about nothing else since your mother called us.'

Mom had called them to get rid of me? She'd told strangers about my abnormality? But she'd always tried so hard to hide it.

'So you're taking her with you?' Mom asked, calm and controlled, even hopeful.

Screams built in my lungs.

'Yes. But you can keep in touch and visit Tessa whenever you like.'

She shook her head. 'No. It's for the best if we don't remain in contact.'

My insides collapsed and the silent screams with them. I'd come to terms with the fact that she didn't love me, that she could barely tolerate me most of the time, but that she despised me enough to leave me to the mercy of strangers?

185

'OK, everything's settled then,' Major Sanchez said. 'Tessa, we're taking you with us.' Mom's back was the last thing I saw. She left the room as they led me away, and didn't even turn around once.

CHAPTER 20

'Tessa?'

I snapped out of the past, only now realizing that I was clutching the kettle in a death grip. Devon stood in the doorway, a look of deep worry on his face.

'Sorry,' I croaked. 'I got lost in memories for a moment.'

'I figured.' He approached me slowly, as though he was afraid I might break down or bolt at any moment. I turned the faucet on and filled the kettle with water before putting it on the stovetop. Devon didn't say anything as he watched me wait for the water to boil. I put three heaps of instant coffee in a semiclean cup and poured the hot water on top. I gave it a few quick stirs with a dirty spoon before heading towards the living room. Carl was sitting on the sofa. He looked much more alert than before. I sat the coffee cup down in front of him. 'Extra strong,' I said. 'The way you like it.'

He downed the first gulp of the black liquid. He sputtered and coughed. 'Fuck, that's hot!'

That was the language I was used to from him. No please or thank you, just criticism. I settled on the armrest and waited for the caffeine to kick in. Devon sat down on the armchair across from me. From the state of the living room, no one had cleaned it for months. I wondered if anyone besides Carl had set foot in the house in about as long. Beer bottles, dirty clothes, used tissues and empty cans of meatballs and baked beans littered the ground, and the layer of dust and grime on every surface was as thick as my pinky.

'You've changed a lot,' Carl said eventually.

'People change,' I said coldly. *At least most people do*, I thought. Except for the fact that he had less hair on his head and more on his shoulders – which were sadly uncovered, thanks to his greyish-white tank top – Carl's life hadn't changed.

'Suppose they do,' he said. For a moment, he seemed far away. 'Sometimes all it takes is a little push.' A strange smile flitted on his face, but then he pulled himself out of his zone. 'What do you want? I got no money.'

I had to stop myself from snorting. As if I'd ask him, of all people, for money! 'I'm looking for my mother. I thought you might be able to help me find her, or have some idea where she is.'

'The bitch left me a few weeks after they took you away.'

Devon's eyes grew wide at the insult, but I'd heard far worse from Carl's mouth.

'Did she find someone new?'

Carl shrugged. 'Don't think so. Guess she'd lost interest in me.'

'Have you seen her since then? Or did she tell you where she was heading?' I could see Devon's frightened eyes taking in every inch of the room, and my body heated with embarrassment.

'Nah, nothing. She was glad to get away.'

'You must know something,' I pleaded.

Carl got to his feet and pulled something from behind his back. He was pointing a Glock at us.

I tensed. 'What are you doing?'

Carl ignored my question. He moved a few steps back, then gestured with the gun at Devon. A silencer was attached to its barrel. 'You. Sit beside her. I want you close together.'

'Calm down,' Devon said. 'We don't mean any harm.'

'Shut up!' Carl snarled, spit flying from his mouth. 'Get over there, or I'll put a bullet through your skull.' Devon stood from the armchair and slowly made his way over to me. I never took my eyes off the weapon in Carl's hand. I wondered if he knew that a silencer didn't actually silence a gun completely. The sound of the gunshots would be suppressed, but the neighbours might still hear them. Not that anyone around here would give a damn.

'What did you do upstairs?' I asked.

'A couple of days ago, a guy showed up on my doorstep. Promising money and all, if I called him when I saw you. Thought he was joking, but he gave me five hundred bucks for nothing and promised there'd be a lot more where that came from. Of course, I thought that's all I'd ever get. Didn't think you'd be stupid enough to show your face around here.' He cackled, glee shining in his eyes.

'What have you done?' I whispered. My hands began shaking, so I curled them into fists.

'I always knew something good would come my way. Never figured it would come from you, but I'm happy to be surprised.' He smirked, and I wanted nothing more than to stalk over to him and smash his face. But he still hadn't told me whom he'd alerted to our presence. And there was the problem of the gun.

Devon's fingers brushed my hand. I hooked my pinky with his. 'Who was it? Who was here?' I made my voice come out hard and unafraid, despite the fear turning over my stomach. Was the FEA looking for us? Or was it someone from Abel's Army?

'Dunno,' he said, glancing at the window. I followed his gaze toward the street. 'But the guy should be here pretty soon. I called him when you first got here, and he said he was close by.'

I shifted, every instinct telling me to run. Carl wouldn't shoot us. He wouldn't get a reward if he delivered us dead. Carl chanced another look at the window, and suddenly Devon ripped away from our touch and stormed towards him. Carl was slow, but he raised the gun before Devon had a chance to reach him. A crack sounded through the room, and Devon twitched and swayed backwards. A bullet had hit him.

'No!' I screamed and ran towards them. Devon collided with Carl, and a second shot rang out. The back of Carl's head smashed against the wall, and he crumbled to the ground. Devon lay right beside him. For a moment I wasn't sure who the second shot had hit, then I noticed the bullet hole in the ceiling. Carl's chest was rising and falling – he was just unconscious.

I knelt at Devon's side, trying to squelch the overwhelming panic pulsating through my body. I rolled Devon over so he was facing me. Blood flowed from a wound on his shoulder. There wasn't a second hit. Devon's eyes fluttered, and he gave me a shaky smile. The colour drained from his face, but luckily he stayed conscious. 'Why did you do that?' I whispered as I helped him to his feet. Even if he was wounded, we couldn't risk staying here for much longer. Whoever Carl had called would be here at any minute.

'Remember? I'm bulletproof.' The humour died on his face, and he grimaced from pain as I wrapped his arm around my neck. He leaned heavily on me as I led him out of the living room. 'It doesn't look like that to me,' I muttered. Though I knew I should be grateful. Devon had bought us time and gotten us out of a hopeless situation, but I couldn't forget the stab of panic I'd felt when I'd watched him get shot.

I cracked open the front door and peeked outside. The

street was still empty. I hurried to our car, dragging Devon along with me. I could tell that he was trying to walk on his own, but his legs were too shaky. I pushed him on to the passenger seat, and he gave me a grateful smile. Droplets of sweat beaded on the top of his lip. I walked around the car and slipped behind the steering wheel. Part of me wanted to speed away, but on the other hand this was a good opportunity to get a glimpse at the person who was following us. If it was Abel's Army, it would be good to know the faces I'd have to look for. Again I thought of letting them catch me. If they took me prisoner, at least there was a good chance they'd be leading me to Holly. But what about Devon?

His eyes were closed in pain. No. I needed to stick to the plan. Keep Devon safe and try to find my mother. I put the key into the ignition and started the car. I checked the street. Four houses down, a driveway was vacant and the shades were drawn. It seemed like as good a place as any to hide in plain sight. I reversed the car and slowly drove towards the house. I backed into the driveway. That way I could make a fast escape, if necessary.

'I think you'll have to remove the bullet,' Devon said through gritted teeth. I jumped at the sound of his voice. He didn't even question why I hadn't sped away, but he probably had bigger worries.

'What?' I said. 'But your body heals itself.'

'Yeah, it heals itself, but that's the problem. It'll close the wound and encase the bullet. And then later, once it realizes how bad the foreign material is for me, it'll start rejecting the bullet very slowly by driving it out and then healing again.'

I stared at the wound, which was already starting to close. The bullet was definitely still inside.

'Are you sure?' I asked.

'Yeah, I'm sure. It's better to get it out now and heal all at once.'

I'd never removed a bullet. I'd read about it and seen a video tutorial, but that was as far as my experience went. I hadn't really paid attention when Devon had removed the tracker from my arm, and that had been close to the surface. This bullet was lodged way deeper. I couldn't stop myself from glancing at Carl's house, but he hadn't stormed out to search for us yet. He'd hit his head pretty hard. As messed up as he was, I hoped we hadn't hurt him too badly. My eyes drifted to the end of the street.

'I once managed to get a huge splinter in my knee when I had an accident with my bike and fell on a log,' Devon continued. 'Let's just say that it wasn't a pleasant experience to have my body repel that splinter by breaking open my skin. Hurt like hell.'

'That's not very clever of your body,' I said, turning back to Devon. 'It should avoid causing you pain.'

Devon let out a raspy laugh. 'Agreed.'

'OK,' I said slowly. 'I'll need a knife or anything else that's sharp enough.'

Devon nodded towards his backpack. 'Take my pocket

knife.' I unzipped the bag and rummaged in it until my hands closed around cool steel. I unfolded the blade. I took a lighter from the middle console and flicked it on before I led it across the blade over and over again until I was sure that it was sterilized. Devon stuffed an old shirt into his mouth.

'This'll hurt like hell,' I warned. 'But remember, it's going to be OK.' Devon's eyes pleaded with me to hurry. My gaze flitted over to the house and the end of the street again. Nothing yet. I forced my hands to steady. With a deep breath, I pushed the tip of the knife into the already almost-closed wound. Devon let out a groan, sweat glistening on his skin.

'I guess it makes sense to close the wound first,' I rambled to keep myself and Devon distracted from what was happening. I didn't think I was doing a good job. 'It stops the blood flow, and blood loss is probably a pretty big concern for everybody.' The blade hit something hard. I changed the angle of the knife to wedge the tip under the bullet. Blood welled up and spilled over Devon's shoulder and arm. With a moan, Devon began to shake. His eyes rolled back in his head, and he lost consciousness. I was actually relieved. At least that way he'd be spared the worst pain. The skin around the knife kept closing, making it extra hard for me to get a good look at the bullet, and the blood flow wasn't exactly helpful either. When I was sure that I was below the bullet, I started pushing the blade up until finally the bullet came into view and I was able to pry it out. It landed on Devon's jeans, where it left another bloodstain. As I watched the wound closing, I was incredibly thankful for his Variation. I took a small towel from my backpack and wet it with a bit of water from my bottle. Carefully, I wiped Devon's forehead.

With Devon asleep, I suddenly felt afraid to be on the street alone. I'd been stupid to stay here to watch our pursuers. I put the car into gear and was about to pull out of the driveway when a black town car turned on to the street. It was too posh to belong here. Panic surged through me. 'Shit,' I whispered as I floored the accelerator and swung the steering wheel around. My wrist screamed from the force it took to keep the car in check. The tyres squealed as I shot down the street in the other direction. I checked the rearview mirror. The black car was gaining on us fast.

CHAPTER 21

The car jolted as we shot over a bump in the road. Devon came to with a moan and tried to sit up but was thrown against the door as I turned sharply on to another street. But it was useless. The car was so close to us now, I could see the shape of a man behind the steering wheel. And suddenly I felt cold. I'd hoped I wouldn't have to see his face ever again, but there he was. Alec.

The front of his car was almost touching the truck's rear. My foot on the gas pedal eased as a wave of calm washed over me. He appeared to be alone. All the fear, all the worry, all the urgency disappeared. The car slowed even more.

No, a warning voice inside me said. *Keep going. Run.* But I was so calm. There was no need to worry, no need to be afraid. Everything would be fine. Deep down, I was aware that those weren't my *own* emotions. The car rolled to a stop beside an abandoned warehouse. I knew we should keep going, but I couldn't bring myself to press down on the gas, couldn't fight the overwhelming feeling of calm that had captured me.

Alec parked in front of us and got out, his expression wary. And suddenly the calm let up and my feelings returned like a whirlwind. I couldn't believe he'd used his Variation to control me like that.

I gasped. Before I knew what I was doing, I'd grabbed Carl's gun and jumped out of the car. My arm was steady as I aimed it at Alec's head. 'Take another step and I'll shoot you.' But as soon as I'd said it, I knew I could never do it. And I knew that he could feel it too. His grey eyes were soft, completely unfazed by the weapon aimed at him. I'd just as soon pull the trigger on myself as I would harm him. Despite everything, despite all the lies and his betrayal, I still loved him. And I hated myself for it, more than I could ever hate him. I lowered the gun until it was pointed at his shoulder. He took a small step closer to me, his face begging for understanding. But even if I couldn't shoot him, that didn't mean I trusted him or forgave him. For him, the FEA would always come first. It would have always stood between us.

'You manipulated me again, though you promised not to do it,' I hissed. 'You promised! But you lied!' The last came out as a breathless scream.

From the corner of my eye, I could see Devon open the passenger door of the car. I hoped he'd stay where he was. Alec briefly glanced at Devon, his lips tightening before he turned back to me. 'Tess,' he said. 'It's not that simple. It's not the way you think.'

'Don't! Don't use that tone with me. I'm done being your marionette. I'm done with you and your empty promises. I'm done with the FEA and their lies. I'm done. Done.' I took a deep breath, but my rib cage constricted painfully. I felt as if my chest was in a vice.

Alec stared at me like he couldn't comprehend what I'd just said. 'You don't know what you're getting yourself into. You're in danger. The FEA is your only protection. I want to protect you, that's all there ever was. I care about you, and I want to keep you safe.'

The grip on the gun tightened until my fingers turned numb. 'Liar,' I spit out. 'I was your mission. Your puzzle to survey. Every word and every kiss we shared was a lie. If you think I'll ever forget that, you don't know me at all.' He opened his mouth, but I continued. 'When will Major and the others be here?' I was surprised he'd come alone.

'No one's coming. They don't know I'm here.' I couldn't help but laugh. 'It's the truth, Tess. I came to take you back to headquarters with me. I talked to Major. He'll listen to you, he'll reconsider his decision to send you to the hospital.'

'That's a lie I definitely won't believe, Alec. I know Major. After everything I've done in the last few days, he'll keep me locked away until he's sure I'm brainwashed enough to obey his orders.'

Alec took another step towards me. Dark shadows lingered under his eyes, and he'd lost weight. 'Tessa, I just want to help you. Please come back with me.'

'If you want to help me, tell me where my mother is,' I said. I knew it was a risk, but he was my best chance, and if the FEA knew where my mother was, they'd expect me to go there at some point anyway. Devon hovered near the bumper, uncertainty playing on his face. His left arm was pressed against his chest; moving it probably still hurt.

Alec shook his head. 'Tess, please, listen to me. Abel's Army is hunting you. They're extremely dangerous. They are the enemy. You'll get yourself killed. Please trust me, just one more time. I understand that you're angry with me, and you have every right to be, but I swear I'm just trying to look out for you.' His voice was like a caress. I wanted to go over to him and bury my face in the crook of his neck, breathe in his scent, and rain kisses down on his scar. I pushed against the emotion, not sure if it came from within me or if Alec was manipulating me again. 'When I said I loved you, I didn't lie. I never lied about my emotions for you. I love you. And I know you love me too.'

Something snapped in me. 'Maybe a stupid part of me still does. But let me tell you this: it doesn't matter, because I don't listen to that crazy part any more. You only care about the FEA; it will always be more important to you than I or anyone else could be. That isn't what love is about, Alec. And you know what? Your parents were right.' He tensed, but I didn't stop. 'I bet you loved manipulating them, making them doubt their emotions until they were sure they were losing their mind, just like you did with me.

I bet you enjoyed it even as a young boy. No wonder that they couldn't stand your presence. Nobody likes being manipulated and violated. If I'd been them, I would have wanted to get away from you too.' I couldn't believe I'd just said that. I finally had proved that I was my mother's daughter – just as cruel and careless with my words. I was turning into her; I'd hurt Alec where I knew it would sting the most.

Alec turned his face to the side, leaving me to stare at his profile. He swallowed hard, his jaw tense and throat flexing. I wanted to apologize. I wanted for us to forgive each other for the past. I wanted to let him take me back to headquarters to live a life full of happy lies. But I didn't move. I couldn't. That part of my life was over. Forever. Alec and I could never be together. He was on the FEA's side and would always be. They didn't have my best interests in mind. I was on a mission, and I had a job to do. And in order to do it, I had to forget him and the FEA for good.

There was nothing left to say. I whirled around, ready to go back to the car, but Alec spoke up. 'I know where your mother is,' he said quietly. I stopped and slowly, afraid of seeing his face, turned back to him. He reached into his pocket and pulled out a small slip of paper. He held the snippet out to me, his expression unreadable.

After a moment of hesitation, I walked towards him. Devon shifted on his feet, as though he was preparing to interfere if Alec tried to grab me. It was useless, of course.

Alec was stronger than the two of us together. If he wanted to abduct me, nobody could stop him. But he looked so defeated, I didn't think the thought had even entered his mind. My guilt tasted like acid on my tongue. I stopped two arms' lengths away from Alec and reached out for the paper. Our fingers brushed, and my eyes snapped up to meet his grey ones. There was too much sadness in them. Tears sprang into my eyes, but I didn't allow them to fall. I'd cried so often because of Alec in the past. That time was over. I snatched the paper from his hand and took a few steps back.

'It's because of him, isn't it?' Alec said. I followed his gaze towards Devon, who was watching us with confusion. Alec thought I'd left because of Devon? 'You still don't get it, do you? I left because of *you*. You once told me you'd do anything for me. And it was the same for me. I'd have given my life to save yours. I'd have done anything, absolutely anything for you. But then I found out how you'd betrayed me. I was stupid. I knew I'd never be able to forgive you.'

Devon looked more than a little uncomfortable, but I was glad that he hadn't tried to interject. This was between Alec and me.

With clammy hands, I unfolded the paper and glanced down at the address. It was the name of a bar in Las Vegas. 'A bar?'

'Yeah. Your mother works there.' Alec stared at a point above my head. I wondered if I'd ever manage to turn my face into a mask void of emotion. He'd perfected the art.

But I'd glimpsed behind the mask, through the cracks of his strong appearance. I knew that hadn't all been fake.

'How did you find this? Did she stay in contact with the FEA?'

Alec smiled bitterly. 'No. I know the bar. It's a place I've been before. I thought I might find someone there who could help me find your mother. I didn't think I'd find her there, but I did.'

'What kind of bar is this?' Devon asked. Alec's eyes swivelled to him, and his stoic mask slipped into one of anger and suspicion.

'A bar for our kind,' Alec said, then he met my eyes. 'It's not run by the FEA. The people who go there have no business with the FEA, no alliance to any organization. This is an underground scene that doesn't choose sides.'

So they weren't Abel's Army either. But if Alec knew about the bar, there was a good chance that Major or Abel had figured it out too, and that they had spies there. But I had no choice. This was my only lead and the only way to get to my mother.

'Major will kill you for this,' I said.

'Do you really think I still care?' His voice was hollow. I hesitated as I watched his face. I said my final goodbye in my head. It would have hurt me too much to say it out loud. I turned around and stalked back to the car. 'Get in,' I told Devon. I didn't have the strength to spare a final glance. I climbed into the truck, started the engine, and backed up from the limousine until I had enough room to manoeuvre on to the street. I hit the accelerator, and in passing my eyes were drawn to the rearview mirror, to Alec and the way he was frozen in place, his gaze on me. I knew that look in his eyes would haunt me for a long time, but even so, there was no going back.

CHAPTER 22

'Are you OK? Maybe I should drive?' Devon said carefully.

'I'm fine,' I snapped, hating how the tears trailing over my cheeks betrayed me.

'Do you want to drive all the way to Las Vegas? That'll take an entire day.'

'We don't have another choice. We can't fly there. Major will know if we check in anywhere or board a plane. And it'll take too long to organize a fake ID for you. I could always just steal one and turn into the person I've stolen it from, but you can't.' I didn't mean to sound so reproachful. I was glad for Devon's company, but I was making him sound like a liability. 'I'm sorry,' I whispered.

'No, you're right. Would you rather go on without me?'

'No!' I said hastily. 'Please stay.'

Devon just nodded. 'If we take turns driving, we can take turns resting while the other one drives, and we'll be faster.'

'That's a good idea,' I said, casually wiping my eyes with

the hem of my sweater. 'And I guess I'm a natural. Driving is pretty easy as long as you just go with the flow.'

Devon looked thoughtful for a moment. 'I need to call my parents. They'll be worried sick by now. And Major has probably told them even more lies.'

'We'll have to fuel up anyway. Once we've bought some distance between us and Detroit' – *and Alec*, I added in my head – 'we'll look for a rest stop. I think we both could use something to eat and a few minutes of rest after everything that's happened today.' I glanced at his blood-covered sweatshirt. 'And you need to change. You can't walk around looking like that.'

When we finally pulled into a rest stop, my back and legs ached from driving, but at least I'd calmed down. And as long as I kept Alec's face from popping up in my mind, I would hopefully stay that way. 'I'll get you a new shirt,' I told Devon as I jumped out and walked around to the truck bed, where the bags with our clothes were stored. I snatched up the first sweater my fingers brushed and gave it to Devon before I positioned myself in front of the passenger window, so the people mingling about in the parking lot wouldn't see him change. As he pulled the sweatshirt over his head, my eyes were drawn to his shoulder and the now-unblemished skin.

After Devon put on the new shirt, we filled the tank with gas before parking at the end of the parking lot, far away from curious eyes. Devon went to the public phone to call his parents, and I watched how his shoulders slumped after a while. He shook his head. 'They didn't answer. That's so unlike them.'

I could hear the hint of worry in his voice, and somehow it set my own fears off. 'Maybe they needed to get out for a while. And your dad is probably at work, right?' Devon pushed his hands into his pockets and nodded. 'Yeah, maybe. I'll try them again later.' He took a deep breath and smiled. 'I'm starving.'

'Me too,' I said, though that couldn't have been further from the truth. I had completely lost my appetite; since I'd seen Alec, an abyss had taken the place of my stomach.

Devon and I bought fries and hamburgers in the diner beside the gas station. Instead of eating in the dingy space, with its ripped pleather booths and grimy checkered floor (not to mention the curious glances of the waitress), we decided to take the food back to the car and eat it on the bed of the truck.

The fries were greasy, and the hamburger bun was too dry, but I didn't care. It was the first real meal we'd had in a while, and it all tasted bland to me anyway. I could feel Devon's eyes on me, and a knot of unease built inside me. I hoped he wouldn't bring up Alec. I didn't think I could stomach that right now.

'Do you know the extent of your Variation?' I blurted and winced at how loud and panicky my voice had sounded. I stuffed a few more fries into my mouth. The grease clogged my throat, and I had to take a few sips from my bottle of soda to wash them down.

Devon swallowed the bite and wiped his mouth with a napkin. 'What do you mean?'

'What have you tried? What kind of injuries can you heal? Can you heal diseases? Can you even die?' I grimaced when I realized how insensitive that sounded, but I couldn't help my curiosity. I stuck two fries into the ketchup and swirled them around.

He took another bite. Apparently he didn't mind that the food was bad, or the stench of exhaust and fuel. 'Well, I've never thrown myself in front of a car or set myself on fire to test it. But I'm pretty sure there are limits. I think I'd be dead if my body was torn apart by a bomb or if I was decapitated.'

I wrinkled my nose at the horrible images his words evoked in my head. Devon laughed, dimples flashing. '*You* asked.'

'I know,' I said, smiling. His hair was such a mess. I was glad that I hadn't checked my reflection in the diner's restrooms. I could imagine what a bird's nest my own hair had become. 'So have you ever hurt yourself to see how your body healed?' I set my remaining fries down on the truck bed. I just couldn't bring myself to take another bite.

Devon looked embarrassed. 'Yeah. When I was younger, I used to cut myself, and once I broke my own pinkie, but after that I pretty much stopped. I don't enjoy pain, you know.'

I nudged him with my shoulder. 'Would have never

guessed.' He jerked his chin towards my discarded food. 'You done with that?'

I chortled. 'Don't tell me you're still hungry.'

Devon's blue eyes sparkled. 'Not quite hungry, no, but I could eat a few more bites. Who knows when we'll be able to stop and eat again?'

I pushed the fries over to him. 'Suit yourself. I think the fries-to-grease ratio isn't quite working for me.'

'Whatever,' he said and winked at me. I felt lighter as I watched him eat the rest of my meal. I'd always marvelled at how much Devon could put away. Maybe his Variation made him hungry all the time, and it probably also made him burn the calories the moment they entered his body, because from looking at him you'd never guess how much he wolfed down every day.

'I'm glad you have such a kick-ass Variation,' I said softly. I remembered the night back in Livingston when I'd knelt beside his lifeless body and cried. I didn't yet know about his Variation, and I thought I'd never see him again. It had been a horrible moment.

Devon relaxed beside me, our legs and shoulders pressed against each other. I hadn't even realized how close we were sitting until now. 'Me too.' His eyes scanned my face. I wasn't sure what he was looking for.

I wrapped my arms around myself, wishing I could banish the memories of that day forever from my mind. My arm brushed the scar. Devon didn't know about the mark over my rib cage. Nobody had told him. 'Ryan did something else that night.' My voice was barely audible, even to my own ears.

Devon tensed. I could feel the energy through our touching bodies.

'You remember the *A* he cut into his victims?' I whispered.

'How could I forget?'

'He did it to me too. He renewed the cut while I was pretending to be your sister, and now it's part of my body.'

Devon's eyes widened. 'He marked you?'

I nodded. Slowly, I released my crushing hold around my rib cage and let my arms sink into my lap.

'Can I see it?' Devon whispered.

I moved on to my knees, never taking my eyes off Devon's. His were so soft and worried, they gave me the support I needed to stay calm. I looked around the parking lot, but except for a man who was pumping gas into his car with his back to us, there was no one outside.

I curled my fingers around the edge of my shirt and pulled it up until the red *A* was visible. I shivered as the cold air hit my skin.

Devon just stared at the mark, something dark clouding in his eyes. 'Why didn't you tell me about this before? I could have healed it.'

I avoided his penetrating gaze. 'I felt guilty for the mission, for pretending to be your sister. I guess I was scared of your reaction. Part of me felt like I deserved this.'

Devon reached out but didn't actually touch me. His

fingertips hovered about a centimetre from my skin. 'Do you want me to heal it?' His blue eyes were soft as they gazed at me. I swallowed and gave a small nod, not trusting myself to speak. He pressed his palm against the *A*, his skin warm against mine. Goose bumps flashed across my skin, and I couldn't take my eyes off Devon's face. His brows dipped in concentration, and a tickling spread through my rib cage. I felt closer to him in that moment than I ever had before.

'Done. See?' He shifted his hand so I could see the now unblemished skin where the A had been. But he was still touching me. His hand rested gently on my waist.

His gaze searched my eyes, then darted to my lips. My mouth became dry. I knew that look. I knew what he wanted to do. But I wasn't sure if I wanted him to. The wound of Alec's betrayal was deep. I wanted to move on. I wanted to forget. But was I ready for something new?

Devon leaned closer, his eyes never leaving my face, looking for a sign that I didn't share his feelings. He gave me enough time to pull away, to say I wasn't ready, but I didn't move. The kiss was short and sweet; neither of us tried to deepen it. He pressed his forehead against mine. 'I hope that was OK?' he whispered.

I wasn't sure. This was too soon. I didn't know anything right now. But I cared about Devon. Devon must have seen the conflict on my face, because his expression dropped. 'I shouldn't have done that. I'm sorry.'

I shook my head hastily. 'No. I'm just confused. I need more time.'

Devon nodded.

'Thank you,' I said. We were still so close that I could feel his breath on my face.

'No one's ever thanked me for a kiss before,' he joked, a hint of hesitation in his tone.

I laughed and punched him lightly. 'Not for that.'

'I know,' he murmured. Silence settled around us. I listened to our even breathing and closed my eyes.

My mind drifted to Holly. I hoped that wherever she was, Abel's Army wasn't hurting her. She was useful to them, I assured myself. She was an asset, and they would keep her around.

Suddenly Devon tensed and held his breath. I peered at him. 'What is it?' I whispered.

He put his finger against his lips. I shut my mouth and listened intently. There was a distinct sound in the distance. A whirring like helicopter blades. The hairs on my neck stood on end, and slowly the little hairs on my arms rose as well. I searched the sky with my eyes. A black helicopter was flying low, a red light flashing and spotlights illuminating the ground beneath it. 'Is it the FEA?' Devon whispered.

'I don't know. It could be a lot of things.' The helicopter was drawing closer. It didn't look like it was landing, but that could change in a blink.

'They're definitely looking for something,' Devon said.

I hopped off the truck bed. 'We should leave.'

'Won't we draw attention to ourselves if we drive off the moment the helicopter appears above our heads?'

I froze. He had a point. We couldn't win a chase with a helicopter. 'Let's sit in the car. That way they can't spot us as easily, and we can drive off, if necessary.'

Devon nodded, but he never took his eyes off the helicopter. We huddled inside the car, our eyes trained on the sky. The circles of the helicopter were becoming wider, and slowly it moved away from the rest area. We waited a few more moments before we pulled out of the parking spot. I wasn't sure if the helicopter had been the FEA, but this encounter had made something very clear: we were being chased, and we weren't safe. We had to get to Vegas as soon as possible, and we couldn't let down our guard.

CHAPTER 23

We had almost a thousand miles ahead of us. Less than twenty-four hours before I'd see my mother again, after more than two years of her silence.

I wrapped my arms around myself and started to fall into a slumber.

Devon woke me three hours later. We were parking at another rest stop. 'I need to stretch my legs.' After a moment, he added, 'And I'm starving.'

I sat up, rubbing the sleep from my eyes. My legs and back were stiff. 'Good idea. I'll get us some snacks.'

I got out of the car, and the blood rushed back into my calves. Sucking in a deep breath of fresh air, I jogged towards the small rest stop on the other side of the parking lot. A man was fuelling up his minivan, but I wasn't worried about him; I could see three kids in the car. I doubted he was a spy. The bell above the glass door jingled shrilly as I stepped into the shop at the rest stop. The air inside was stale. With a small nod towards the cashier who'd looked up when I entered, I headed straight to the snack display and picked up a few granola bars and two bags of chips.

I walked up to the counter and froze when a familiar face stared back at me from the front page of several newspapers. I put the snacks on the counter, reached for a newspaper, and quickly scanned the headline and the report. Senator Pollard had been found dead. It was still unclear whether he'd killed himself.

I felt the cashier's eyes on me and gingerly put the newspaper back down, realizing he was waiting for me to pay. I handed over the money and hurried out of the rest stop, snacks clutched against my chest. Devon was walking around our car, his arms lifted above his head. He glanced my way and froze. 'What's up? You look as if you saw a ghost.'

I slipped into the car without a word, and Devon followed. 'Someone killed Senator Pollard. It was in the newspapers,' I said the moment he closed his door.

'The guy you pretended to be?'

I nodded and handed Devon the snacks before I started the car and sped away from the rest stop. 'The press thinks it might have been suicide, but I'm sure it was Abel's Army.'

'Why do you think they killed that guy?' Devon asked. He unwrapped one of the granola bars and took a bite, his blue eyes never leaving me.

'He was an expert on organized crime, and Abel's Army's has strong ties to the mob, if Major was telling the truth.' He definitely hadn't told me everything, considering the secrets I'd unearthed so far. 'He was also responsible for leaking information regarding the FEA prison. He had to make sure that they followed federal rules or something like that. But Major said that he wasn't actually the one who got people locked up, so revenge is out of the question.'

'There's an FEA prison?'

'The FEA takes care of Variants, even the ones who are too crazy or too criminal to walk free,' I said bitterly. 'Major said it's for Variants who lost control of their Variation or who used it against others to harm them. But after everything I found out about the FEA, I'm not sure if only criminals end up there.'

'Are many members of Abel's Army currently locked up there?' Devon asked.

I thought back to my conversation with Major about the FEA's high-security prison. He hadn't said much. 'Stevens, definitely. And I'd guess he isn't the first member of Abel's Army that got caught. But I have no idea how many others there might be.'

'Maybe they let him get caught on purpose,' Devon said thoughtfully.

'Doesn't make much sense. Why would they risk it? He could have given away important information.'

'Not if it's true that Abel's Army has a Variant who can alter memories. They could erase any memories that would be dangerous for them, or maybe even alter people's memories in a way that would lead the FEA on a false trail.' My head was spinning. The thought of someone doing that

215

with my memories seemed less and less enticing. What happened to a person who had their memories altered? If they thought their life had unfolded in a different way, did that change who they were?

'But Major has to know that he can't trust Stevens. What would Abel gain by getting him captured? I just think Stevens was their last priority, and that's why he wasn't rescued.'

'I guess we'll never know,' Devon said. He sounded exhausted, and I wondered if he'd started this discussion to distract himself from his parents.

'Unless my mother knows more.'

'She hasn't seen your father in, what, fourteen years?' Devon raised his eyebrows.

'I don't really know,' I said in a small voice. 'There was a note in the file. Major thought they'd been in contact after I joined the FEA.' But the fact remained that in nearly all the years I'd been alive, Abel hadn't given a shit about me. He'd left my mother and me because he had no use for us. And now that he'd seen how useful my talent was, he wanted it for himself.

The FEA didn't even know where Abel's Army had their headquarters. Hopelessness washed over me. How was I ever going to find Holly?

Devon grabbed my hand, tearing me out of my thoughts. 'Do you miss her?'

'My mother?' I wanted to snort, but then I paused. 'I don't miss the mother I remember. I miss the mother from the photo, the young, happy mother who held me on her lap with a smile, the mother who loved me. The mother who still had hope. Sometimes I'm not sure if that mother ever existed.' My voice caught in my throat. 'Maybe I'll just have to accept that I'm unlovable.'

'Don't say that,' Devon whispered. 'Nothing could be further from the truth.' His grip on my hand tightened. I squeezed it right back. The thought of our kiss flashed through my mind, and warmth crept up my neck. Devon's closeness felt good. Was it so bad to move on? To find someone else to love? What difference did it make how much time had passed? I already cared deeply about Devon, and Alec was definitely a thing of the past. Still, part of me knew this was too fast.

'Sorry. Thinking about my parents makes me depressed. I'll just have to deal with it.' I turned the radio on and let the music carry away my thoughts.

We spent the next few hours without talking, but shortly after we crossed the border to Nevada, Devon's voice split the silence. 'Maybe we should stop for a while. I think we both could use the rest. And I'm starving.'

I bit my lip. We were getting so close, and we'd wasted so much time already.

'And if we keep driving, we'll arrive at the bar around lunchtime. I doubt they'll be open that early.'

He had a point. As we approached the next exit, I pulled off the highway and into a rest stop. Once I was out of the car and able to stretch my legs and gulp down some fresh – albeit gas-tainted – air, I felt much better. We bought sandwiches, a few bags of chips and several chocolate bars before we returned to our truck. 'I'd thought it would be warmer in the desert,' I said as I sat on the end of the truck bed, legs dangling down.

'Not at night,' Devon said as he ripped open a foil bag and practically inhaled a handful of chips.

Reno was only a few miles away. 'Holly's parents live near Reno,' I said.

Devon froze mid-chew. 'Do you want to visit them?'

'Maybe. I don't know,' I said hesitantly. 'They'd think it was weird if I was visiting without her. I don't think they know about her yet. And maybe they'll never have to find out. If we can manage to save Holly, then everything will be fine.'

Doubt crossed Devon's face. Of course it was ludicrous to think we could free Holly that easily. I unwrapped my chocolate bar and took a huge bite. The sweetness soothed my stomach.

'Maybe we should take a quick nap,' he said. 'So we have enough energy when we arrive in Vegas.'

We crawled into our sleeping bags and stretched out on the bed. Devon moved closer to me until our faces were only centimetres apart. His eyes searched mine. 'You need more time, right?' he whispered. 'Because of what happened with Alec.'

I nodded. Not just because of Alec. That was part of it,

of course. Everything was still too raw, and I hadn't let go yet. I could feel it deep down. But I also needed time to figure out what I was feeling and why I was feeling that way. Was I just latching on to the next person who was kind to me? Was I looking for someone – anyone – who might love me? That wasn't healthy, and it wouldn't be fair to Devon.

'Tell me about the first time you healed someone,' I murmured, resting my head on his chest.

'I was maybe seven, and I was playing in the garden,' he said. I could hear the smile in his voice, and it filled me with comforting warmth. 'Our cat had caught a bird. When I finally wrangled it away from her, it was dead. I was so sad when I saw this ball of feathers in my palms. And then my fingers began to prickle and become hot, and the bird stirred. I was so stunned, I actually dropped it, but by then it was OK. It took another minute to collect itself, then it flew up into the forest.'

'Did you try to tell your parents?'

'Oh yes. I thought I had done magic and was convinced I'd get a letter from Hogwarts in no time.' His chest shook under my head as he chuckled. 'My parents thought I was exaggerating. They stopped reading me *Harry Potter* that same evening.'

I smiled. 'So did you get a letter?'

'No, but I didn't give up for a long time. I got pretty obsessed with owls. Eventually Dad told me that I had to be patient. He reminded me that Hogwarts letters would be delivered on my eleventh birthday. Well, by then I'd figured out that I wasn't really a wizard. I also realized that I couldn't tell them the truth.'

I squeezed his arm and inhaled his scent. Somehow things didn't look so bleak anymore.

I was exhausted, but we couldn't risk more than two hours of sleep at a time. I entered the address of Holly's parents into our GPS. I knew it would be risky to visit them, but since their house was practically on our way, it didn't seem like it would hurt to make sure they were OK. It would take us only about fifteen minutes to reach their house. Devon took a sip from a bottle of water before he asked, 'Have you ever met them?'

'Holly's parents?' I asked. He nodded. 'Yes, once, about six months after Holly and I joined the FEA.'

'You joined the FEA at the same time?'

'Pretty much. Holly moved in a couple of weeks before I did. And when Major finally allowed her to see her family again, I went with her. Summers too. Someone had to keep an eye on us, after all.'

'And that was the only time you saw them?'

'That was the only time Holly or I saw them. Major didn't want her to visit them. She called them and sent emails, but Major didn't approve.'

'That's tough. How could Major expect her to forget her family?'

'That's how the FEA works,' I said bitterly.

Neither of us said anything for a while after that.

'What about you and Alec?' Devon said carefully.

My hands around the steering wheel tightened. Where had that question come from? 'What do you mean?'

'I'm sorry if it's a touchy subject. I just don't know the whole story. What went down between the two of you?'

I thought of the sadness on Alec's face after I'd told him I understood why his parents hated him. But the resignation and acceptance had been worse. It was as though his worst fears had been confirmed, as though he'd suspected it all along. How could I have said that to him? My stomach clenched so tightly, I was sure I'd throw up. 'There's no such thing as Alec and me any more,' I said. But the lie was so blatant. It showed in the way my voice shook, in the way I couldn't even look at Devon when I said it. I didn't think there would ever be no such thing as Alec and me. My heart didn't care about the betrayal. Maybe in a few years my feelings would fade, dulled by years gone by, nothing but a distant memory. But that wouldn't change the fact that Alec was a part of me – good or bad. 'He took care of me when I first joined the FEA. He listened to my stories, and he was there when I cried. He understood what it was like when your parents turned their backs on you. He was my everything.' I realized how stupid that sounded. How stupid that made me sound. 'I guess I just latched on to the first person who showed me some kindness.' It was more than that, but I didn't want to explain.

'That makes sense, I suppose,' Devon said. But of course

he could never understand. He had his parents, Linda and Ronald. He had a family who loved him no matter what. He'd never felt the hollow pain of deep betrayal, of believing you were worthless, that feeling you only get if the people who'd brought you into this world, the people who should love you more than their own life, can't even look at you without disgust.

I nodded. It wasn't Devon's fault that he couldn't commiserate. He understood pain and loss. It was just a different kind of pain. I took his hand. It felt strong and warm.

We pulled into the street where Holly's family lived. Rows upon rows of identical-looking small grey houses stood perched on even tinier square lawns. I pulled the car up beside the curb, and we got out. The grass was yellow, the flowers in the beds burnt by the sun. The front door was ajar. I slowly walked up to it and pushed it open. There were no sounds emanating from anywhere in the house. There was utter silence. Devon followed me inside. 'Hello?' I called, but the word echoed in the quiet. I poked my head into the living room. The drawers were open, and their contents littered the ground. My heart pounded in my chest. I hurried up the stairs and found the bedrooms in a similar state of disarray. The closets in the master bedroom and the rooms of Holly's siblings were all empty. The furniture was still there, undisturbed.

'What happened here?' I whispered.

Devon poked a potted plant with the tip of his sneaker;

it had fallen to the ground and scattered soil and dried leaves all over the beige rug. 'Whoever was here, they were in a hurry.'

We went back downstairs. In the kitchen, a milk carton sat forgotten on the counter and gave off the rancid smell of spoiled milk. Through the window, I could make out a neighbour watering his tomato plants. I hurried out of the house and towards the man. He looked up when Devon and I approached and pushed back the brim of the black hat that was protecting him from the sun.

'Where are . . .' I racked my brain for Holly's last name. 'Have you seen the Mitchells lately?'

The man's eyes narrowed slightly. He put the watering can down and wiped his big hands on his blue overalls. 'I've never seen you around.'

'I'm a friend of their eldest daughter, Holly.'

'The boarding-school girl,' the man said. Then he let out a sigh. 'The Mitchells left a few days ago. We heard their car drive off in the middle of the night. Nobody knows anything about where they went. I know they were having financial troubles, but to run off like that . . .' He shook his head.

'That's all you know?'

He nodded.

'OK, thanks.' I took Devon's hand and dragged him back to the car.

'What do you think happened here?' he asked as we got back into the car.

'Either Major brought them to a safe place – which I doubt, given the state of the house – or Abel's Army kidnapped them to guarantee Holly's cooperation. Or . . .' I racked my brain to come up with another idea. No matter how you sliced it, it didn't quite make sense.

'We should leave,' Devon said, looking around the neighbourhood nervously. 'Now.'

I hit the gas, and we sped down the street. Panic clutched at my chest. What had happened to Holly's family?

'We shouldn't jump to conclusions. It makes sense that the FEA would bring them to a safe place, not just for their sake, but for the safety of the FEA too. They would have to protect them. Plus, Holly will be less inclined to give away secrets if her family isn't at risk,' Devon said in a calm voice.

I wanted to believe that. Devon reached over and plugged the address of the bar into the GPS. Suddenly an image materialized before my inner eye, almost like a vision. My fingers tightened their grip around the steering wheel as the road disappeared from my view. The image in my head was all I could see: *a small boy with turquoise eyes stands on a wooden stool and bends over a crib, staring down at a tiny baby. He moves closer and kisses the baby's cheek. The baby opens her eyes. They're turquoise, just like his.*

'Zach,' a man says, 'don't wake your sister. She just fell asleep.'

'She's awake,' Zach quips. The man comes into focus beside the boy and ruffles his hair. He too has turquoise eyes. He wraps an arm around the young boy and bends over the crib like the

boy did. The man reaches out and pushes his finger into the baby's tiny hand. She curls her hand around his finger.

'Tessa!' Devon's voice burst through my vision. I gasped and tried to blink away the images. The road came back into focus, and the car swerved violently as Devon gripped the steering wheel to rip the car back to the right lane and stop us from colliding with oncoming traffic. A car rushed past us, honking repeatedly, and the driver gave us the finger.

'Tessa, what's the matter?' Devon's voice was panicked, and he was still holding on to the steering wheel.

'I've got this,' I assured him, and he released his grip. The images of the baby girl were still in the back of my head, vivid as the road in front of me. They were memories; I knew that now. But how had they suddenly appeared in my head? I glanced into the rearview mirror and went cold. A black limousine was two car lengths behind us.

Another image burst into colour behind my eyes. This time Zach was on the ground, cradling the baby against his small body, smiling up at someone.

I pressed my foot down on the gas pedal and passed the car in front of us with centimetres to spare.

'Tessa, what the hell is going on?'

'My memories, someone is manipulating them,' I yelled.

Devon threw a glance over his shoulder, his body coiled with tension. I didn't slow. I passed one car after another, ignoring the honking and the angry hand signals of passing drivers.

The images in my head faded, flickered and disappeared. 'The black limousine, where is it?'

'It's a ways back, six cars behind us. It's trying to keep up with us.'

I wouldn't let it. The car was jerking back and forth every time I passed another car, but I kept my foot pressed down on the gas pedal until I couldn't feel the images nibbling at my mind.

'They're gone,' Devon said, relaxing against the seat.

'For now,' I whispered. My throat felt tight, and my eyes burned. The images, the memories, were they real? It didn't matter. Someone was trying to mess with my mind, to take control of my thoughts and manipulate my consciousness. But this time, I wouldn't let them.

CHAPTER 24

It turned dark when we reached Las Vegas. For the rest of the way, we didn't have another encounter with the black limousine, and not a single strange vision had tried to burst into my mind, but I caught myself trying to conjure up my memories, looking for the image of Abel and Zach leaning over me in the crib. It was something I'd always wanted, to remember a loving father and brother, but could I even be sure the images were based on something that had really happened?

I pushed my thoughts aside. I had to focus on Holly now.

In the distance the stratosphere tower rose up into the sky, and around it skyscrapers in all shapes clustered together. There was a faux Eiffel Tower and Statue of Liberty and a roller coaster curling around the buildings like a snake.

Though I wasn't sure what lay before us, I was glad to be back in a city and for the departure from the harsh landscape we'd passed. After a while, the thorny cacti and spooky tumbleweeds got old. The navigation system told us we'd have to cross the city to reach the outskirts where the bar was situated. Devon made a little detour over the strip because I'd never been there before. On any other day, the luminous advertising, water shows and fake gondoliers steering their gondolas through the Venetian landscape would have made me giddy with excitement, but I couldn't get past the lump in my throat.

Las Vegas Boulevard was crowded with people in flashy outfits. The skirts were a bit shorter and the shirts a bit more unbuttoned than I'd seen in the rest of the country. People here were desperate for fun, for the thrill of losing or winning money. Maybe if my life had been a bit more normal, the thought of risking a few hundred bucks at a roulette table would have given me a thrill too. But after what I'd been through in the past year, the thought of mere gambling didn't really make my heart race.

Even so, it was pretty clear why a bar for Variants belonged so close to this place. A few people who acted or looked strange wouldn't draw much attention to themselves in a surrounding as big and exaggerated as this.

'You've been here before?' I asked, my eyes already struggling against the burst of colours.

'A couple of years ago. Mom and Dad took Madison and me here for the weekend. We went to see a show, the Cirque du Soleil, and spent most of the day at the pool, and in the evenings we stuffed ourselves at the huge buffet at the Bellagio. I've never seen plates piled higher with crab legs in my life. It was kind of disgusting.' He laughed but then fell silent, and a wistful look crossed his face. I knew he was thinking of his sister.

We spent the rest of the drive in silence.

Eventually the hotels became a little less opulent, though not less flashy. The buffets got cheaper, and so did the rooms, and the flow of people thinned. A few seedy-looking strip clubs and bars shared this part of town with motels that had seen better times.

'It's supposed to be around here somewhere,' Devon said.

My eyes were drawn to an alley that turned off the street we were on. 'I think that's the right street.'

Devon steered the car to the right, and we followed the narrow road to the very end. 'This is it.' We pulled into a small parking space in front of an unremarkable grey building with a flat roof. There wasn't a flashy sign atop the door or ads for cheap rooms and food. Actually, there wasn't anything that indicated a bar was hidden inside.

My stomach tightened as we got out of the car. The air was warm and dry. I pulled my sweater off and straightened my T-shirt with shaky fingers before I scanned our surroundings. Our truck wasn't the only car in the lot. Three spots, all closer to the door, were occupied by ordinary looking cars. I wasn't sure what I'd expected to see, but this was definitely underwhelming. I'd thought something would be different about a place frequented by

Variants. An air of otherness. Unless this wasn't a bar for Variants, and Alec had lied to throw us off course. I glanced at Devon. 'What do you think?' My words seemed to carry and echo over the parking lot as if I'd used a microphone.

Devon unfolded the paper Alec had given me. 'Stanley's. That's what the bar is called. Do you see a sign anywhere?'

I shook my head. The front of the building didn't have any windows, and the only sign that you could actually enter it was a steel door that looked like it wouldn't open unless you pulled very hard. I fingered the gun in my back pocket, regretting once again that I didn't have a holster. It was much easier for the weapon to be detected this way, and just as easy for it to slip out of my pocket. 'Maybe we should just check.'

Slowly we made our way towards the building. My ballet flats scratched over the pavement. It sounded as if I was grinding hundreds of tiny grains of sand into dust. Devon's body was coiled with tension, and the closer we got to the building, the more aware I became of the reassuring pressure of the gun wedged against my butt. Of course, I didn't have many bullets left, and I didn't know where I could get more without a fake ID.

The facade of the building was grey concrete, matching the unadorned steel of the door. I pressed my ear against it, but if someone was inside, not a sound travelled through.

I took a step back. My eyes once again scanned the windowless front. The steel door seemed to be the only way in or out. I didn't like the odds of that. 'Let's go around the building. Maybe there's more to see,' I said.

Suddenly the door swung open, and I had to stumble back or it would have nailed me in the forehead. Devon gripped my arm protectively, and his other hand flew to the knife under his jacket. My own hand was already on the gun. But the average-looking guy who stumbled out of the building didn't even glance at us. He staggered towards his car. The stench of alcohol and sweat wafted after him. It took him several tries to get the key into the lock. I didn't think he was in a state to drive, but right now that wasn't my problem.

Devon nudged my arm, and I finally noticed that we weren't alone. Another guy was holding the door open and eyeing us. His eyes were entirely white except for the black dots of his pupils. *Variant.* So maybe this was Stanley's bar after all. I dropped my gaze from his eyes when they narrowed. He was scanning my face but lingering on my eyes for much longer than was appropriate. The turquoise of my irises was probably the reason why he opened the door a bit wider. 'You wanna come in?' His voice was thin and high.

Devon shrugged and walked in, glancing over his shoulder to check that I was following. With a pang of unease, I did. But this wasn't a bar. It was a narrow, claustrophobia-inducing hallway with a low ceiling. The hallway led to a second door behind which I could hear laughter and music. If I'd extended my arms, my fingertips would have brushed the black-painted walls. My unease grew. I could feel the man who'd invited us in keeping close behind me. His breath pressed against my neck, wet and hot. He was only an inch taller than me and even thinner, and yet he seemed to be the bouncer in charge of guarding the place. I guessed that when it came to Variants, appearances didn't necessarily reflect how dangerous someone could be. His eyes alone made me unwilling to cross him. My ignorance about his Variation only added to my fears.

The only light source was a torch-like lamp on the wall, which gave off a bluish glow. It was right at eye level and messed with my vision. I moved closer to Devon to get some distance between the creepy bouncer and me. That's when I noticed that the bouncer wasn't the only person in the hallway with us. Tucked into an alcove, a woman sat on a high barstool, her pale legs curled under her body on the round red leather seat. She was bowed forward in a deep hip bend, her eyes closed. It was a miracle that she hadn't toppled over yet.

'I haven't seen you before. How did you find us?' bouncer guy asked sharply.

I jumped at how close beside my ear his voice was. He must have closed the distance to my back again as I'd been busy watching the woman. 'Umm, a friend gave me your address,' I said quietly. Somehow it felt wrong to raise my voice in this place. Devon's hands were curled into fists at his side; he looked ready to wrestle the guy to the ground.

'We're looking for someone,' Devon said.

The bouncer's stance became wide-legged and suspicious. In the bluish light of the torch, his eyes shone in his face like two halogen lamps. 'Who sent you?'

'No one. We're on our own agenda here,' I told him, growing tired of his interrogation. 'We're no threat to you. Why do you ask so many questions?'

Bouncer guy's white eyes locked on mine, but I didn't feel anything. I was sure he couldn't access my mind. He just wanted to intimidate me with the creepiness of his stare. 'First your blood.'

The muscles in Devon's arms tensed, and he took a step forward.

'Excuse me?' I asked.

'Your blood. To make sure you are what you claim to be.' Bouncer guy nodded towards Devon, one side of his mouth curled up in a nasty smile. 'Especially him. No Normals allowed.'

Normals? I didn't even want to know what would happen if Devon or I were found to be Normals.

'What are you going to do with it? Send it to a laboratory for tests?' Devon said in a challenging tone, crossing his arms. The air was practically crackling with tension.

I gripped his biceps to shut him up, but without turning away from bouncer guy. Bouncer guy glared at Devon over my shoulder.

'It'll take only a minute,' he said, finally turning his attention back to me. He positioned himself beside the girl on the bar tool. His shoes scratched over the rough concrete. He wore black-and-white wingtips, like an old-time movie gangster. Maybe he thought it gave him a more dangerous look.

'Finja,' he said in a soft voice. He hadn't once used a civil tone with us, but around her, his face shifted into something kind, devoid of menace. The girl didn't react at first. She seemed to be in a deep meditative state, her chest rising and falling; if not for that, I'd have thought she was dead. He shook her slightly, and slowly she unfurled, her head rising, eyes peeling open almost in slow motion. She had an elegant long neck, and her collarbones jutted out of her creamy white skin. The black of her flimsy dress stood in stark contrast to her paleness. I couldn't make out the colour of her eyes, but they were very dark. I had a feeling that everything about that girl was dark, inside and out. She tilted her head like a baby bird, her long lashes fluttering as she peered at bouncer guy, who carried an almost tender expression. 'I need you,' he said. It took her longer than it should have to process the words, then she turned her head towards Devon and me. 'Bring them to me,' she said in a voice like smoke. The hairs at the nape of my neck stood on end.

Bouncer guy waved us closer. Though my body bristled, I moved into the alcove. It wasn't big. There was only a second stool in it, probably the perch for bouncer guy, and a small table with a radio that played soft classical music. It mingled with the beats coming through the heavy door leading into the bar.

Close up, I could see how young the girl was, maybe fifteen or sixteen, like me. Her eyes hovered above my head, though she had to crane her neck for that. Before I had time to react, bouncer guy took something from the table. I saw the blade gleam blue before he took my hand in a crushing grip and pierced the skin of my thumb. I released a harsh breath as the pain unfurled in my finger.

'What the hell are you doing?' Devon snarled, lurching forward, but I put a hand against his chest to stop him from doing anything rash.

'It's OK,' I told him. Then I held out my thumb. 'What now?' Bouncer guy used a small plastic square to catch the droplet of blood from my wound and held it out to Finja. For a long moment, she stared at it. It reminded me of a time when I'd seen a zookeeper feed a snake. He'd put the mouse into the terrarium right in front of the snake, but for a long time it had silently watched its prey before suddenly darting forward to deliver the deadly blow. Finja's expression wasn't unlike that of the snake. She lifted a spindly arm and took the plastic square with bony fingers. I noticed that her pinky stuck out at an unnatural angle, as if it had been broken and had grown back together without tending to it. My attention was torn from her fingers when she brought the square to her lips and her tongue darted out, instantaneously licking my blood off of it. I let out a sound of disgust and stumbled back, into Devon's hard chest.

'Fuck,' he breathed out. I didn't think it was because I'd

hurt him. My breath was lodged in my lungs.

The girl closed her eyes and hummed. Then she made a strange sound deep in her throat. I wasn't sure if it was a growl or a moan. Her eyes snapped open, still unfocused, and she released her breath very slowly. Then she nodded without looking at any of us.

'You're clean,' bouncer guy announced. Devon held his hand out, and the whole procedure started again. Only when the girl had nodded after tasting Devon's blood did bouncer guy relax. Finished with her duties, Finja curled into herself on the stool again and quickly lost track of what was going on around her.

Bouncer guy gestured towards the black door. 'You're good to go.'

'Really?' I cringed at how surprised I sounded. 'I mean, because we're underage,' I said quickly.

The man gave me a look as if he thought I was stupid. 'We don't follow human laws here. We have our own, so you better listen: No using your Variation to kill. No using it to injure someone. No human police. No mention of Variant politics. You break 'em, I'll break you. Understood?' I blinked at him. I wondered how long he'd worked on that little quote. He seemed unnecessarily proud of it. Devon and I exchanged a look and nodded. He'd only mentioned not killing or injuring someone with a Variation. What about using guns or knives?

'And the cold steel stays here,' he added, as though he had read my mind. Reluctantly I handed my gun to him.

Devon hesitated so long that bouncer guy did something to the air that made my skin tingle and blood-licking girl jerk up with panicky eyes. I snatched the knife from Devon's hand and handed it over before I pushed Devon towards the second door, desperate to get far away from the hallway and the strange vibes that now filled it.

I'd thought the hallway encounter was weird enough. But the moment we stumbled through the second door, I was sure I'd entered a new dimension.

CHAPTER 25

This had to be some kind of strange parallel universe. Bluish light seemed to float on the plumes of smoke in the air. I was glad that my eyes had had the chance to get used to the strange lighting back in the hallway or this would have given me vertigo. The inside of the bar was far more crowded than the parking lot had suggested. Maybe some of the customers had other, less conventional means of reaching the bar. The beats of the music I'd heard faintly through the door now throbbed like a pulse in my veins.

I began to scan the room full of patrons, but my eyes were drawn to the huge water tank in the middle of the bar. It was a gargantuan glass cylinder reaching from floor to the ceiling.

'Wow,' Devon whispered beside me.

'Yeah,' I said, slowly walking around the water tank. Spots on the ground of the tank threw bluish light into the water, making it glow, and jets set in two narrow lines on both sides of the cylinder sent pink glitter whirling around. But that alone wouldn't have warranted that slack-jawed look on Devon's face. Two identical women, each dressed in a skimpy pink bikini, moved inside the aquarium. They had strawberry blonde hair that floated in the water as if carried on a gentle breeze. Their make-up was heavy – pink lipstick, blue-rimmed eyes and blue eye shadow, topped off with thick black lashes. They turned and twisted in the water in a rhythmic, silent dance. Their bodies squirmed and coiled, but while many customers had their eyes trained on them, the women only had eyes for each other, caught in their own sisterly trance. Apparently this was what qualified as Vegas-style entertainment in a Variant bar.

'I guess their Variation is that they can breathe underwater,' Devon said, his eyes still glued to the water-dance show. Once I stopped gawking at the aquarium and took in our surroundings, I noticed how many eyes had turned our way. Even in the presence of the water show, it seemed we were the main attraction. We couldn't have acted more suspiciously if we'd tried. Everyone could see that we were new here. And from the look on many of the faces, new guests meant trouble. Groups of customers put their heads together conspiratorially. Few of them were paying attention to Devon, I realized with dread. Their curious gazes latched on to my eyes, then darted away quickly, only to be back again seconds later. They'd seen turquoise eyes before. They knew what it meant.

I grabbed Devon's arm and pulled him along. 'Come on. Let's go to the bar.'

Sunken into the floor were spotlights in the same blue tone as the aquarium, and more blue torches lined the high-ceilinged walls. That explained why the smoke from the cigarettes and cigars was glowing like an apparition from Atlantis. Tall private booths lined the walls, separated from one another by black velvet screens. The customers sitting on the blue leather benches within the booths had a good view of the aquarium and the bar, but most of them were either deep in conversation, lost in their own worlds, or else staring at us. Scattered around the interior ring of the vast bar were small round tables with chairs around them. Most of them were empty. Apparently the booths were the way to go.

We arrived at the bar, which was made of deep mahogany wood and was the only area in the room that departed from the blue colour scheme. The seats of the red leather bar stools were exactly the same colour that the lamps on the bar's shelves gave off.

'This is so crazy,' Devon whispered in my ear. I would have agreed with him if a very tall, very thin man hadn't popped up beside me in that moment.

His fingers flitted over my arm like ghost touches. My body recoiled violently, and I balled my hands for a fight.

'Want some spittle?' he breathed. His hair was cut so short that his scalp shone through, and the red of the bar lights reflected in his damp eyes.

I was too stunned to speak. Either this was the worst pickup line of the century or this guy had lost his mind.

Devon moved closer to me until his warmth was all over my back. I snatched my arm away from the man. 'No.'

He pulled out a vial containing a strange, milky liquid. 'It makes you fly,' he crooned. From the way his eyelids twitched, I was convinced he'd already taken one too many flights.

'No, thanks.'

'Leave them alone, Spleen,' yelled the woman behind the bar. That was the perfect name for the guy. His eyes darted to the barkeeper before he slinked off towards a staircase shrouded in darkness to the left of the bar. It too was cast in a deep reddish glow.

'Thanks,' Devon said, relaxing his stance. The barkeeper was a tall woman clad in black shorts and a black tank top that showed off her tattooed arms, neck and legs. I couldn't spot an inch of her skin that wasn't inked; only her face was free of tattoos. There was a long string of words written all over her body in tiny script. There must have been hundreds of words snaking over her limbs, but I couldn't make out what they said.

She stood wiping a glass, still glaring at the spot where Spleen had stood a moment before. Eventually she turned to us. 'First time, huh?' she asked, a piercing flashing in her mouth. 'I'm Penny.'

'I'm Tessa, and this is Devon,' I said. I couldn't help but wonder if her tattoos were just for show or if they were there to hide something. A clever disguise for scales, or a cover-up for a scar, like Alec's dragon. I felt a twinge in my stomach at the thought of him. *Stay focused*, I reminded myself.

She noticed me staring and set the glass down. 'Took years to get it done,' she said proudly. 'And hurt like hell.'

'What does it say?' I asked with genuine curiosity.

'All kinds of things.' She shrugged. 'Quotes that mean something to me.'

'Do they have something to do with your Variation?' Devon asked. Our minds seemed to work alike.

Something on her face shifted, like a shadow passing. 'I'm not a Variant.'

'You aren't?' I blurted and felt instantly bad. How could I be so insensitive?

But she just smiled, even though I wasn't quite sure if she meant it. 'My father owns the place. He's a Variant. But I'm just a Normal. Yet another instance where genetics screwed me over.'

'So what exactly is this place?' I asked instead.

'A safe place for Variants to have a good time. A place where you aren't in danger of getting caught in the crossfire of politics.'

'You mean between the FEA and Abel's Army.'

At the mere mention of those names, her face lit up with alarm.

'Don't,' she hissed, eyes darting around. 'My father has banned those words. You better not speak them if you don't want to find your butt on the street.'

'So people who come here aren't part of either group?' Devon asked. He said it in a way that suggested there was no alternative.

She gave him a look like she thought he was crazy. 'People around here are doing their damn best to stay under the radar. Because if they know about you, you either join them or else you disappear.'

'You're talking about Abel's Army,' I whispered. She frowned at me but didn't correct me for saying the name again.

'I'm talking about them both. They're just two sides of the same coin.'

'But the FEA doesn't force people to join them, do they? They don't coerce or kill people?'

'If they find you, you join. End of story. They don't kill you, but they force you to follow their rules or else they throw you into their prison because you're a security risk, and you rot there until you die. What's the difference?' She put her palms against the counter, leaning closer to us, dark eyes sparkling. 'But enough of that. Politics has no place here.'

I was about to protest, but she spit out her next thought, leaving me no chance to get a word in.

'The stuff Spleen tried to sell you isn't the only way to have a good time.'

'What is it, anyway?' Devon asked.

'What it says. It's the spit of a Variant, which contains

endorphins and ephedrine and other things. People mix it into their drinks.'

This was too disgusting for words. My toes curled at the thought of purposely putting someone's spit into my soda.

'And your father doesn't mind that Spleen sells the stuff?'

'Of course not. He's the Variant who produces the stuff,' she said with a twisted smile.

'Oh,' I said stupidly, glancing at Devon. A slow smile spread on his face.

'This is so weird,' he whispered.

'Anyway, if you're not into the spittle, we also have the option to give you sweet dreams. We have a dream-catcher who'll give you the dreams you want. For a few bucks, we'll provide you with his services along with a few sleeping pills to extend the experience. Everything is possible.' The experience sounded almost too good to be true, but Penny wasn't much of a salesman. If she really wanted to sell anything to us, she probably shouldn't have sounded so disgusted and bored by it all.

I rested my elbows on the bar. 'Why do people buy spittle and manipulated dreams?'

Penny shrugged. 'The same reason Normals use typical drugs and alcohol. To forget, to remember, to be someone else, to be themselves. There are so many reasons,' she said. I followed her gaze. Many of the people in the booths looked as if life wasn't exactly kind to them: they were dotted with scars, worry lines, crumpled clothing, jittery demeanors. I suppose that's what you got for hiding from forces as strong as Abel's Army and the FEA. Would Devon and I end up like them?

In the presence of so much weather and worry, I somehow suddenly knew why my mother was working here. 'I'm looking for someone. She was once called Heather, but she might go by another name now. She has brown hair that's sort of wavy, like mine, and brown eyes.'

Penny narrowed her eyes at me. 'What do you want from her?' There was a hint of protectiveness in her tone. So my mother really worked here. My stomach knotted painfully, suddenly unsure if I could face her.

Devon took my hand. The warmth and strength of his grip helped me relax. 'She's my mother,' I said.

Penny froze in place. 'Oh shit,' she whispered. Her eyes scanned my face, then she turned around and walked towards the red-lit staircase. 'Heather!' she called. She cocked her head as if she was listening for a sound. But there was no reply. No one came down. She glanced at me. 'Maybe she's asleep.'

But I knew my mother. 'She and your father are a couple,' I said, without a hint of uncertainty. My mother hadn't been single for more than a few days for as long as I could remember. She needed a man at her side, especially one who bossed her around. For the first time, I wondered if it was because they reminded her of my father. I pushed past Penny and climbed the stairs two at a time. Her fingers grazed my arm, but I shook her off. 'Don't,' she whispered.

Her expression brimmed with pity.

I charged up the stairs. Penny and Devon remained close behind. I reached a corridor lit by more red torches. 'Where?' I demanded. 'Where is she?'

Penny hesitated.

'Where?' I screamed, and she actually took a step back. Devon touched my shoulder, but I jerked away.

Penny waved a hand at the end of the corridor. I strode towards the closed black door, my heart slamming against my rib cage, and put my hand on the handle. Every muscle in my body tensed. I swallowed. I was strong, I reminded myself. I could deal with whatever came my way.

Bracing myself, I pushed the door open and stepped inside.

CHAPTER 26

A wave of patchouli hit me, and the smoke of recently burned incense swirled in the room. My nose tickled with the urge to sneeze. But then everything seemed to go still, even my heart and pulse.

My eyes glided over the unmoving form tangled amid red satin sheets on the bed. My mother.

Her brown hair hung limply around her slack face, which was tilted towards the door. An arm was lazily thrown over her head. Drool had dried in the corner of her mouth and on her chin. I could see her eyes move under her eyelids, flitting back and forth like she was watching a tennis match in her mind. I forced myself to cross the room towards the king-size bed. The red carpet was so plush, my feet seemed to sink deep into it. Parts of it were matted and stained. As I made my way closer to her, my shin collided with the bedframe.

I stared straight ahead, at a scratch on the dark wooden headboard, and focused on my breathing. But focusing on anything but keeping it together was so hard. All the feelings seemed to bubble over. My mother's lashes fluttered, and she shifted and stirred. Her arm slipped off the bed and brushed my leg. I bit down on my lip to stop myself from making a sound.

Just breathe, I reminded myself. *Breathe. This doesn't mean anything to you. She's just a means to an end, a way to get to Holly. Nothing else.*

But in her daze, she looked so much like the mother in the photo. The mother who'd once held me with a smile. I perched on the edge of the bed. I could feel Devon's and Penny's eyes on me, could practically feel their pity radiating off of them in waves.

I uncurled my fist, felt the blood return to my fingers. Slowly I reached out, hand shaking – body shaking – and brushed a strand of hair from her passive face. I trailed it over her eyes, which twitched once more, and cupped her cheek. 'Mom?' I asked. I didn't recognize the sounds that formed that word, didn't recognize my own voice. I sounded like a small, scared child. For a moment, my mother leaned into my touch. *She's drugged*, I reminded myself. *She isn't in her right mind; this means nothing.* Then why did a feeling of happiness flood through me?

She moaned, her lips parting. She rolled over, revealing bruises on her arms and shoulders.

I jerked back, gasping. My throat, my rib cage, even my body felt too tight. I let out a cry – a cry so foreign that it made goose bumps flash across my skin. And suddenly my body seemed to explode. Rippling, shifting. I flew through the transformations. The bodies became a blur. My bones ached, my head throbbed, but I kept changing bodies. Faster and faster. Someone wrapped their arms around me, warm and reassuring, and the transformations slowed until they finally stopped and I was myself again. I breathed in Devon's scent and closed my eyes.

But the moment was interrupted as the door was flung open. 'What's going on?' a deep voice demanded.

I pulled back. A tall, heavyset man with a bald head and seedy yellow eyes stood in the doorway. The resemblance to Penny was undeniable. I tore myself from Devon's embrace and moved without actually realizing what I was doing. But suddenly I was in front of the man, and my fist collided with his cheekbone with a satisfying pop. He had given my mother his drug – and the bruises. I didn't dare to consider what she'd done in return for the spittle.

His eyes rolled back, and he hit the door – which was thrust shut upon impact – before sinking to a heap on the ground. He held his cheek, a stunned expression on his face. Penny shook off her stupor and knelt beside him. 'You all right?' She touched his arm, but he pushed her away. Hurt flickered across her face, but it was already gone by the time she straightened.

'I'm fine. Get Benny,' he snarled. 'He can kick the bitch out.'

'If you throw me out, I'll immediately tell the FEA about your existence,' I said in a thick voice. I hoped I'd managed to sound stronger than I felt.

He bared his blood-covered teeth in a terrible jack-o'-lantern smile. His eyes squinted at me. 'If you weren't on the run from them, you wouldn't be here, girl.'

I took a step closer to him. I didn't know what I wanted to do, but his gaze stayed frozen on my eyes. A horrible look of recognition crossed his face, as if he'd seen them before, and his entire face went white. 'Your eyes,' he muttered, then he shook his head. 'No. That's impossible.' He stumbled to his feet and stared at my mother. 'Heather, what the fuck is going on?'

My mother raised herself up on her elbows, blinking dazedly. 'Stanley?' The word was drawn out like a long sigh. Her eyes brushed over me without recognition. She didn't know who I was. But in that moment, I wasn't even sure she knew who *she* was. Heat gathered behind my eyeballs. Why did she still have the ability to make me angry? Why did I still care about her after all she'd done? Why couldn't I stop loving her when she had never as much as cared about me?

Stanley tried to walk past me to get to the bed, but I stepped in his way. I was a full head shorter than him, and he tried to push me away. His hands collided painfully with my collarbones, and I lurched to the side, barely keeping upright. Devon gripped his arm and twisted it, but Stanley swung a fist at him. In a swift move, Devon ducked, so the knuckles only grazed the top of his head, and he landed a punch in Stanley's stomach. The man gasped and stumbled and had to catch himself on the shabby wardrobe. He panted, his face red. Penny came forward and gripped his forearm. 'Dad, that's enough. We don't need any more trouble.'

'More trouble?' he cried and pointed a shaking finger at me. 'I'm not the one causing trouble. That girl is trouble worth a lifetime!'

Penny stared at me, but she didn't seem to make the connection.

'I'd recognize those eyes anywhere. She's one of *his* spawns.' Fear and disgust played out on his face, fighting a battle for which was the stronger emotion.

Penny seemed to know exactly who the word 'his' referred to. Her eyes grew wide, and she started tracing the words of her tattoos like a spell that would give her consolation.

I glanced down to where my mother was struggling to get into a sitting position. The strap of her flimsy nightgown slipped off her bony shoulder, and the neckline plunged. I leaned over and helped her to lean up against the headboard before I put her strap back in place. Her brown eyes darted over my face, and panicked recognition settled in them.

Mom glanced down at herself like she only now realized the sorry state she was in, and her face crumpled. I wrapped my arm around her back and pulled her up to her feet, taking care that the nightgown covered her. 'Come on, Mom. We'll get you cleaned up.'

'Don't tell me you've pissed the bed again,' Stanley growled.

'One more word,' I said harshly, 'and I swear I'll call my father and have him take this place down.' I couldn't do that. At least not without revealing myself to him. And even then I wasn't sure he cared about me enough – or at all – to do me any favours.

But from the terror on Stanley's face, he believed I could. I relished the feeling of triumph, but my mother grew heavier in my arms, her legs giving way. 'Is there an antidote to whatever she's on?' I asked.

Stanley glared at me, but Penny replied, 'Yes. I can pick up a vial.' She quickly slipped out of the room, and he followed her without another word.

Devon came up beside my mother and me. 'Do you want me to help?' His eyes were soft and sad but also pitiful.

'No,' I whispered. 'I can do this alone.' I could tell that he didn't believe me. 'Really,' I said firmly. Penny returned with a tiny plastic vial. 'Just make her drink this, and she should be back to normal within a few minutes.' I took the vial and pushed it into my pocket. 'Where's the bathroom?'

Penny opened a small door beside the wardrobe. I led my mother inside. There wasn't much room. The seams between the white tiles were yellowed and partly black with mould. There was a shower cubicle, a toilet and a sink, which left hardly enough room for my mother and me to stand. Penny hovered in the door, uncertainty colouring her face. 'I don't need help,' I said again, loud enough so Devon could hear it too. He seemed reluctant to let me deal with this by myself. 'If you want to help, could you please get some clean clothes for my mother?'

Penny snapped out of her stupor and nodded resolutely. 'Don't worry. I'll take care of it.' With that, she closed the door and left me alone with my mother.

My mom hadn't said a word to me yet. Maybe there wasn't anything to say. I closed the toilet lid and made her sit down on top of it. Only when I was sure that she wouldn't topple over did I let her go. I tilted her head back and brought the vial to her lips. She gulped down the liquid without protest. She was probably used to being given the antidote. Who knew how often she'd overdosed on spittle or whatever else they sold around here.

I pulled the shower curtain back – it was clammy and stained – and rinsed the floor of the shower with hot water. From the corner of my eye, I could see my mother watching me. Her head was still bowed, but I could feel her eyes on me through the fringe of her eyelashes. Maybe it was my imagination, but she already looked less dazed than moments before.

'I'll help you undress now, OK?' I said. She didn't react, and I took it as silent permission. I was glad that she was wearing only her nightgown and panties. She let me pull the gown over her head and even raised her arms on her own. Our eyes locked as I threw the garment to the ground. 'You've grown,' she whispered. Her voice was like broken glass, but at least she was talking, and her words were intelligible.

I didn't know what to say, so I reached for her last piece of clothing, but she shook her head. 'No. I . . . I . . .' She trailed off, embarrassment twisting her hollow cheeks. I stepped back, bumping against the door to give her room. Her movements were clumsy and slow, and as she bent over to push her underwear past her knees, she almost fell forward. But I didn't embarrass her by helping her any further. She gripped the edge of the tiled shower cubicle and slowly stepped inside. She leaned against the dirty tiles, face drawn from exhaustion. 'Why don't you kneel down?' I suggested. A blanket of numbness seemed to settle over the emotions raging war inside me, and I was glad for it.

She sank down, her bony knees hitting the shower floor with a thud. It must have hurt, but her face didn't show a sign of pain. I turned the water on, making sure it was hot enough, just on the verge of unbearable. I knew she was always cold after waking from a drug daze; the effect probably wasn't so different with Stanley's spittle. She let out a small sigh when the hot stream hit her back. I massaged shampoo into her hair, and she relaxed into my touch. She looked small and vulnerable with her shoulder blades peeking through her skin. The only towels I could find were in a heap on the floor. I picked up the cleanest of the bunch and wrapped it around my mother.

'What's taking so long? I want answers!' Stanley bellowed

from the bedroom. Penny's soothing voice followed his outburst, much calmer and quieter.

'Why do you let him treat you like that? You deserve better,' I said through gritted teeth.

Mom's fingers curled over my shoulder to steady herself, water dripping down her neck. 'We both know that isn't true. I deserve this.'

I searched her eyes. Was she sorry about the way she'd treated me? 'Nobody deserves that,' I said. She'd treated me almost as horribly as her changing boyfriends had treated her. She hadn't hit me or physically abused me, but her silent treatment, hurtful words and disgusted looks had left their scars, too. 'I don't get it. Why do you always choose such assholes?' She didn't reply. Maybe she didn't know the answer.

I pushed those thoughts aside and guided my mother back into the bedroom. Stanley, Devon and Penny were there, each one standing apart from the others. Devon pushed himself off the wall he'd been leaning against.

'Out,' I ordered, avoiding everyone's eyes. Penny grabbed her father's arm and dragged him out; Devon followed with a sympathetic look at me. I couldn't help but wonder how Alec would have handled the situation, but I knew it was no use dwelling on that.

As promised, Penny had found my mother's clothes. They were spread out on the bed, and though they could have used ironing, they were clean. 'Do you live here? Or do you have an apartment somewhere else?' I asked.

I peeked through the curtains down at the parking lot to make sure we weren't about to get any unwanted visitors. A few more cars had parked there by now. I heard my mother's breathing grow laboured from the effort it took her to dress herself. 'I had a place, but I lost it a while back,' she said, frowning like she was struggling to remember when that had happened. She probably hadn't paid rent. It had happened before and had led to a few middle-of-the-night moving schemes when I was a kid. From what I'd seen so far, I didn't think she earned any money here at Stanley's. I wasn't even sure if she was in a state to work on a regular basis.

When she was finally dressed, she sat on the bed, hands clutching the crumpled sheets. Her eyes were glued to me. I rubbed my hands, feeling out of place. 'I know about my father. I know who he is.'

If the news shocked her, she hid it well. Maybe the constant use of drugs had messed with her ability to show emotions. 'You shouldn't be here,' she whispered.

CHAPTER 27

Her words stung in my chest like acid, but I tried not to let it show. 'I know. You made it perfectly clear the last time I called that you don't want anything to do with me. And don't worry, this isn't a mother-daughter reunion. I'm not asking anything of you, I just need some information.'

She blinked. 'I said that for your own protection,' she said. I scoffed. 'It's true. I was worried that – this place isn't safe. People will recognize you here.' I didn't believe that was the only reason. She'd barely been able to stand my company when we'd still lived under the same roof.

'Why worry about me now? Were you worried about me when you ignored me for days when I was too young to get it, when you told me I was a freak and that I disgusted you, when you were relieved that the FEA finally picked me up and took me away?'

Her gaze settled on my eyes. 'You're right. I was glad when you were gone.'

There it was: the admission. Of course, I'd always known

it, but hearing the words from her mouth hurt more than I'd thought they would. I should have left it at that, should have steered the conversation toward something that could lead me to Holly, but I couldn't. 'Why?' I croaked.

'Your eyes,' she said quietly. Something dark flickered on her face. 'They reminded me of your father. They reminded me of a past I wanted to forget. I thought I could leave it all behind, especially your father. I once loved Abel, a long time ago. He was smart and charming and kind. He was so charismatic, almost nobody could resist him. He just had something special about him, something powerful.'

I frowned. Then why had she left him? She watched my face for a reaction before she continued. 'I'm sure you don't remember, because you were just a baby then, but it wasn't always easy with Abel. He had his good side, but the one thing I wanted most was the one thing he couldn't deal with: normalcy.'

That was something I could understand. I'd often longed for a normal life, but my childhood had been far from it. Maybe my mother and I were more alike than I'd known. But maybe she and Abel were more alike than she wanted to admit. Because despite her desires, normalcy definitely wasn't something my mother had ever accomplished.

She continued in a soft voice, 'He and I wanted to live a life without the FEA's supervision. They took away our choices, our freedom, and gave us rules that your father didn't agree with. We made the decision to run away. He wanted to try it for me, to build a normal family, live a normal life. Well, that was my dream when we left.' She paused, her expression wistful. 'And at first it looked like it might work. But I could tell that your father struggled with normal life. He didn't know how to function in normal society. And he didn't feel safe on his own. He thought the FEA would come after us at any moment and lock us into their prison for treason. Then his brother – your uncle – came to town. He'd been on the run from the FEA for years, and he convinced your father to work alongside him, for rich businessmen. Your father knew he needed money if he wanted a chance to build a safe place for Variants away from the FEA, away from the crushing grip and the watchful eyes of the FBI. He didn't want to be used any more.

'I didn't know much about their work. I was scared to ask. I think Abel got in over his head with his brother. It got harder for him to reconcile his ideals with his work, but he never stopped trying. I think that was what I admired most about him. And when your father's brother started to spend all his time with us and began talking about building their own group, a group that would destroy the FEA, I tried to talk Abel out of it. I pleaded with him to stop the madness. But his brother had too much influence. Abel thought he was doing the right thing. There was no reasoning with him. Your brother had already showed signs of a Variation, and I knew that Abel would never let him go. But for the first few years of your life, you seemed to be normal. I can't tell you how much I wanted that. And so I took you, and I ran. I don't think Abel ever followed us, but I was always careful not to stay in the same place for too long, just in case.'

'But then my Variation began to show,' I said.

My mother nodded. 'I knew I'd been stupid to think there'd ever be a normal life for us. I can't tell you how often I regretted running away from Abel, but at the same time I knew I couldn't return to his life. It would be too dangerous for the both of us. I wanted normalcy, safety, even just the pretense of it. If Abel had found us, I knew I'd have been too weak to resist him.'

'So that's why we always moved?'

'Yes. That and the FEA.'

'The FEA? Why? You didn't seem to mind when they took me away.'

'You would never be free with the FEA. I knew that. They promise a virtuous life, but they keep their agents in a golden cage. I didn't want that for you. But once they found us, I had no choice but to let them take you. Major wouldn't have listened even if I'd said no. Maybe I should have called Abel then, as I'm sure he would have taken you in before the FEA could, but I didn't want to admit to him, or to myself, that my life was in shambles. I should have known that my plan was doomed. You're either with the FEA or with Abel's Army. At least that's what I thought back then. I didn't know of the many Variants living in the underground, far from the FEA's radar. But with your eyes, we couldn't have kept your identity a secret for long.'

'I could have taken on another appearance,' I said.

'For weeks?' she said sceptically. 'Forever?'

I nodded. 'I've been on a mission that took weeks to complete.'

For a long time, my mother looked at me. 'That wouldn't have changed much. I still can't change my appearance. They would have recognized me.'

'But you could have made yourself look younger.' The lines around her eyes and mouth were even deeper than I remembered them. She hadn't used her Variation in a while.

She touched the crow's-feet with her fingertips. 'When I left your father, I swore never to use my Variation again. I'd seen what people like us can do, but I'd also seen what it does to them. I didn't want to be like that any more. I wanted to be normal.'

'But you were an FEA agent once. You had a home at headquarters, a future, a job. Why didn't you go back there? Wouldn't that life have been better than sharing your life with drunks and spending the nights passed out from drugs?' She winced. My words had been harsh, but they were the truth. We both knew it.

'You and I would have belonged to the FEA. I'd have to use my Variation whenever they wanted, however they told me to. I wanted to be free. That was all that mattered to me.'

'Even more than your own daughter? Don't you think my life would have been easier if I didn't have to grow up around endless beer bottles and a string of violent guys?'

Her eyes were fierce. 'Maybe. But I was selfish back then. I still am. But you're on the run from the FEA now too, aren't you?'

'Yes,' I admitted. 'I found out that I can't trust them. They had someone I trusted more than anyone keep an eye on me with his own Variation – he was reading my emotions to see if I was stable enough to be an agent.'

'You really liked that boy, didn't you?' she said in a resigned voice. I wasn't sure how she knew. Maybe my expression or voice had given me away. Or maybe she had enough experience with heartbreak to recognize it instantly.

I shrugged. I didn't trust my voice to answer.

'I'm not surprised Major doesn't trust you. Not with your background. Too much has happened between Major and your father.'

'So it's personal?'

'Major's too professional to get emotional. But Abel and his brother are a different story.'

'Why didn't Major force you to join the FEA when he took me with him? He knew you were a Variant, and he could have thrown you into prison if you'd refused.'

'He could have,' my mother said quietly. 'But he and I go way back. Maybe that was one of the rare instances when he didn't follow the rules. And he knew I was a mess. I'd have brought trouble with me, and that was the last thing Major needed in headquarters.'

I gasped. 'Don't tell me that . . . you and Major?' I

couldn't even say the words.

'It was a long time ago,' she explained. 'When I joined the FEA back in the seventies, Major was a good-looking young man.'

My face must have shown my shock, because she lowered her eyes. 'It sounds strange, I know. But I was drawn to his seriousness. He was very intense. He was so much older inside than his age suggested, but things didn't go well for long. Maybe I was too erratic. And when your father joined the FEA years later, I fell in love with him. I don't think Antonio ever forgave me for that.' I wasn't sure if she realized that that was the first time she'd used Major's real name. 'Maybe that was why he didn't want me anywhere near the FEA when he found you and me. It reminded him of what happened back then.'

It was too much to take in, and it didn't really matter. I had to find Holly. That was all that mattered now. 'I need to find Abel's Army,' I said.

My mother gave a small shake of her head. 'You don't have to look far. If you stay in one place for very long, they're liable to come find you. But you don't know what you're getting yourself into, Tessa. Change your appearance, go to Europe or somewhere else, and live a normal life. Enjoy yourself. Live by your own rules. I think you could do it. You are stronger than I ever was. You are your father's daughter.'

'But Abel's Army kidnapped my best friend. I have to find her.'

My mother didn't seem surprised. 'They won't hurt your friend. He wants *you*, Tessa. I don't think he ever forgave me for taking you away from him.'

'Are you still in contact with Abel? I heard a rumour that you are.'

Her eyes grew wide. 'Maybe someone in the bar has been spreading rumours.'

'Mom,' I said firmly, drawing her eyes back to me. 'Are you? Do you know where Abel's Army is located?'

'I saw your father once, a few weeks ago. When he contacted me, I just had to meet him. I knew you were safe, so why not?' She sighed. 'He was still everything I remembered. Charismatic, strong, charming. Smart. We talked about you. He'd found out that you were a Variant, that you were with the FEA. He was angry with me. He couldn't believe I'd handed you over to them. He'll never forgive me for that.'

'But where are his headquarters?'

'I don't know. That's restricted information, and he didn't tell me. We met in a small restaurant outside of Vegas.'

'Did he tell you anything that will help me find him?'

She laughed mirthlessly. 'No. But some of the customers talk. There are always rumours about Abel's Army and the FEA making the rounds. I'm not sure how much of it is true. I never really bothered to find out.'

I wondered how she could be like that, how she could so easily turn her back on her past and everyone in it. 'Then

264

why did you wind up here? If you were so desperate to be normal, why did you get into a relationship with another Variant? You gave me up to have a chance at a normal life.' I didn't bother to hide the bitterness that I felt.

Hopelessness blanketed her expression. 'It seems normal is out of my reach. You can't help who you are. No matter where you go, no matter how fast you run, Tessa, you can't escape yourself.' She sniffed.

She pressed her fingertips against her temple. Exhaustion marked her face. She probably needed some rest after her drug haze. I perched on the bed beside her and took her hands in mine. Her eyes widened, but she didn't pull back. Maybe she didn't have the energy to do so, but I tried to tell myself that she stayed because she enjoyed my closeness. 'Please. If you know about any way I can find Abel, you have to help me. I need to find my friend.'

Her eyes became distant. 'Abel's Army can't be found; they find you. That's what people say, and it's true. Abel found me, and he will find you too. If you let him. I think he's met his match in you.' She paused. 'But it's possible that Stanley knows something. He hates talking about it, but he belonged to them once. To Abel's Army.' She started to get up, but her legs shook and she sank back down. I walked to the door and found Stanley in the corridor, arguing with Penny. Devon spotted me and immediately came over and touched my arm. I wanted to press myself against his chest, but I knew this wasn't the time or place. 'You OK?' he asked.

I gave him a small smile. 'I'm fine. My mother doesn't know where Abel's Army is, but she thinks that maybe Stanley does.'

Devon looked doubtful. 'I don't think he'd tell us even if he knew.' Especially after I'd threatened to call Abel on him earlier.

'Stanley,' I yelled out. 'I need to talk to you.'

His narrowed yellow eyes cut to me. He said something to Penny, and she disappeared down the stairs. Stanley strode towards me, a reddish-blue bruise marking the spot on his chin where my fist had struck him. If I'd known I needed him, I wouldn't have hit him, but it was too late for that. My eyes darted to my mother, collapsed into herself on the bed.

'You still here? I don't want you under my roof,' Stanley growled. Like he hadn't known that I'd been helping my mother all this time.

'I don't want to cause any more trouble,' I said. 'As soon as you tell me what I need to know, I'm gone. And you'll never see me again.' I retreated into the room. That was a promise I wasn't sure I could keep, and he probably knew it. I couldn't leave my mother in this place, but I couldn't exactly take her with me either. I had to save Holly first, but then who knew if I'd be back.

He followed me into the room, scanning my mother without a single emotion on his face. 'What do you want?' Devon trailed after us, his eyes never leaving Stanley.

'You have to tell me how to find Abel's headquarters.'

His mouth twitched, and then booming laughter burst out of him. My hands curled into fists at my side, but I let him have his moment. Devon glanced at me, his eyebrows raised.

'*You* want me to help you find Abel?'

'Yes. I won't leave otherwise.'

His eyes hardened. 'Oh yes you will.'

Devon took a . threatening step towards Stanley. 'Listen, you'll have far less trouble if you just tell us what you know.'

The man jabbed a finger at Devon. 'You know nothing about trouble, boy. That girl of yours is getting you into a shitload of it. Better run while you still can.'

'Just tell us!' I shouted.

His small eyes twinkled angrily. 'If you want to meet up with your daddy, you'll have to let him catch you. There is no other way.'

Maybe I should just let him catch me, I thought. The odds of us finding Holly without being captured were incredibly slim. My mother had made him sound OK, and the photo of him holding me showed a softer side too. But he was still an unknown entity: he had kidnapped Holly, and I didn't know what his plans were for me. I had to try to get Holly to safety, and then I could decide if I wanted to risk a meeting with my father. 'That's not going to work. He won't let me leave once he has me. I need to get inside their headquarters without their knowledge.'

'Didn't you listen? You can't find them. Very few people

know where they're located. They have their ways of making sure that no one can reveal it.'

'You mean their Variant who can alter memories? Do they make sure that no one can remember where they are?'

He stared at me for a moment. 'Not as clueless as you pretend to be, eh?'

We were getting nowhere with this. Devon ran an impatient hand through his hair. 'This is all bullshit. Can you help us or not?'

I gave him a warning look. 'Tell us what you know. My mother said you knew *something*.'

Stanley glowered at her, but she had curled up sideways on the bed, and her eyes were now closed. 'Your mother doesn't know what she's saying. But I'll give you some advice: get the hell away from here, and stop looking for Abel. If you're not willing to be part of his army, you shouldn't get near them. They won't leave you with any other choice.'

The door was ripped open, and Penny stumbled inside, eyes widened in panic. 'They're here!'

Stanley went very still.

'Who?' I whispered, fear slicing through me. Devon stepped up beside me, and I slipped my hand into his.

'Abel's Army. One of their cars just pulled up in front of the bar. Benny is sure it's them. They're just waiting. They haven't gotten out yet.'

'They won't wait for long,' Stanley said.

My eyes flew to Devon. He let go of my hand and

hurried towards the window to peek through the gap in the curtains. I pressed myself against his back and peered down into the lot. A black limousine sat right below the window, its engine running.

I whirled around. 'Did you call them?' I demanded, narrowing my eyes at Stanley.

He glowered back. 'Do you think I'm desperate for trouble? Someone must have recognized you in the bar. With those eyes of yours, it's no surprise.' He released a harsh breath. 'I told you to leave. You should have listened!'

'What do we do now?' Devon asked softly. I glanced at my mother, still passed out on the bed, then at Devon. There was no other way. If I let them capture me, they would leave Devon and my mother alone. They would take me to Holly.

I looked at my mother and then back at Devon. 'Hide her or get her away from here,' I told him.

'No, I won't let you go alone.'

'It's the only way.'

'What? Letting yourself get captured? Tessa, you've got to be kidding!' he said desperately. 'You don't know what you're getting yourself into. You'll both be prisoners. How is that going to help Holly?'

I knew he was right. 'Is there only one car out there?' I asked.

Penny shrugged. 'It's the only car we can see. That doesn't mean there aren't more hiding out of sight.'

I touched my mother's shoulder, but she didn't react.

She must have spent all her energy talking to me. Now her body needed time to recover from the spittle and the antidote. I couldn't just leave her here. But I knew she couldn't come with me. 'I'll keep her hidden,' Penny said suddenly. Stanley, who had been staring into nothing, snapped his head around. But Penny glared at him. 'We owe it to her, Dad.' Then she turned to Devon and me. 'You should really leave now.'

I pressed a brief kiss against the top of my mother's head, then followed Stanley into the corridor and down the stairs. Patches of sweat had spread under his arms. 'There's a tunnel in the basement that leads to another bar. I have something of an agreement with the owner, so he doesn't care who enters or leaves.'

I knew he wasn't doing this for our sake. He just wanted to get rid of us as fast as possible and without causing a big stir. But Stanley froze the moment we reached the bar area. He stopped so short that Devon and I almost ran into his back.

'What's—' I never finished my question, because a boy with eyes like mine had just entered the bar. He was unmistakable, even after all these years. My brother, Zach.

CHAPTER 28

He was tall and slender, with the same auburn hair and turquoise eyes as me. His skin was milky, but not quite as pale as mine. He wore black from head to toe, right down to his sneakers. Two men entered the bar after him, also dressed in black. But they hovered somewhere behind Zach, so I couldn't make out their faces or see if they were armed. I'd have to be careful. Slowly Zach scanned the room, his face like steel, until he found me. Devon grabbed my hand in a painful grip and tugged. But as my eyes locked with my brother's, I couldn't move. His face softened, and something stirred in me. I had a brother. He really existed. He gazed at me with warm eyes. It reminded me of the expression I'd seen in the photos and in the recent memory.

'Damn,' Stanley muttered.

Zach's lips pulled into a tentative smile, as if he was happy to see me. But my face was frozen, unsure of how to feel. He was part of Abel's Army. Maybe he was responsible

271

for Holly's kidnapping. The softness of his expression made me want to believe otherwise, but I knew better than to trust someone's face. One of his men – I recognized him as the guy with the red hair who had disappeared with Holly – said something, and every hint of happiness slipped off Zach's face. His eyes cut through the room, and my heart stopped as I followed his gaze toward a booth at the end of the bar. Tanner and Kate were slowly rising from the blue leather seats.

Where was Alec?

Bitter realization set in. After what I'd said to him in Detroit, he was done with me. The FEA still wanted to rescue me, but not Alec. He no longer cared what happened to me.

The other customers started to whisper nervously, and most of them got up and moved closer to the only exit, which Zach and his men were still blocking. Where were Benny and Finja? Was there no other form of security?

'This is all your fault,' Stanley said miserably. His hands hit my back, and I stumbled into the middle of the room. 'Here, take her. She's why you're here. Take her and leave.'

I caught my fall with my hands and slowly straightened. Stanley and Devon were fighting. Punches were flying, and Devon was trying to get the older man in a headlock. Stanley was spitting, probably to put Devon in a drug haze. But that wasn't my main problem. Devon was a good fighter. And it was better for him to be part of a brawl with Stanley than to get into whatever was about to go down

272

between Kate and Tanner and Zach and his men. I could only hope that Penny would stay with my mother upstairs. My eyes darted between my brother and my former agent colleagues. Whatever I did, escape was unlikely. One of them would inevitably triumph.

Maybe the FEA was the lesser evil or maybe not. After everything I'd learned, I couldn't be sure anymore. Abel's Army was the great unknown. Could what awaited me with them possibly be worse than being thrown into the FEA's loony bin and having my life controlled by Major? The unknown held the potential for danger, but it also held hope. And my brother was my ticket to Holly, and she was all that mattered.

Tanner held out his hand. Today his mohawk was blue. Good old Tanner – but his face was missing his trademark grin. 'Come on, Tessa. We can get you home safely. This can all be over now.'

'What home?' I retorted bitterly.

'Home is the FEA, where you belong. Major wants you back. Alec is waiting for you,' Tanner said, his eyes flitting between me and Zach, on the other end of the room.

'Major just wants to control me. And if there were a chance for Alec and me, he'd be here with you. Don't start lying to me too, Tanner.' I really wished Benny hadn't taken my gun when we'd entered the bar. Even when it came to fighting Variants, I'd have felt much safer with it in my hand.

'We're your family,' Tanner said. Kate rolled her eyes,

and I almost wanted to do the same. Strangely enough, she was the one person in the FEA I resented the least right now. Without her, I'd still be clueless. She had set this whole thing in motion, but at least she had told me the truth.

'A family doesn't do what the FEA did to me,' I said quietly. And yet part of me still wanted my old life back at headquarters, that feeling of belonging, of having a place where I was safe. I longed for my life the way it used to be: movie nights with Alec, banter with Tanner, laughter with Holly, and breakfast with Martha cooking in the kitchen. Maybe I could have forgiven everything if Major had apologized, if he hadn't planned on locking me away, but even then, broken trust was hard to mend. Especially if there was a lack of trust on both sides. As Abel's daughter, Major would never trust me completely.

Everyone in the room had fallen silent. The tension was so thick I could almost reach out and touch it.

Zach's eyes focused on me with strange intensity. 'You have a real family, Tessa. You don't need them.' He nodded towards Tanner and Kate, resentment hardening his eyes.

I turned to him. 'You only want me because of my Variation. When you thought I was normal, you didn't even come looking for me.'

Zach took a step towards me, and Tanner and Kate tensed. 'That's not true,' Zach said. 'We didn't have the same resources we have now. Dad never stopped searching for you.'

I wanted to believe him, and maybe it was true. My mother had said that Abel would never forgive her for taking me away. What if that meant he really cared for me? Devon appeared at my side, hair rumpled but otherwise uninjured. When our eyes met, it took him a second to focus. 'Did Stanley hit you?' I asked.

Devon shook his head and blinked once, hard. 'No, the bastard just spit on me. His spittle is strong stuff.'

'But you're OK?' I whispered, never taking my eyes off Zach and Tanner, who had both taken a few steps towards me. Stanley had disappeared.

'I'm fine. My Variation can take care of the stuff.' Devon's gaze settled on Tanner. They had joked around a lot in the time they'd spent at headquarters together, and now they were facing off like enemies.

'Why should I believe you?' I asked, turning my attention back to Zach.

He opened his arms in a disarming gesture. 'Blood's the strongest bond in this world. You should be with the people who love you for being a sister and a daughter and not for the value of your Variation.' He sent a brief glare towards Kate and Tanner.

'Don't let him manipulate you,' Tanner warned, taking another step in my direction.

I snorted. 'Because you and the FEA would never do that, right?'

Devon's body brimmed with tension beside me. He was eyeing the redheaded guy with the transport Variation, and

275

I felt stupid for having almost forgotten about him. He looked relaxed, the way he was standing with his arms crossed in front of his chest, but I didn't buy his act. 'What about him? Will you let him kidnap me the way you did with Holly?'

Zach's face looked puzzled, and for a horrible moment I was sure he didn't know who Holly was because they'd killed her the moment they'd found out she wasn't me. 'Jago won't touch you. I won't force you to join us. I want you to come because you want to,' he said. Jago gave a small mocking bow, his red hair falling into his eyes.

'Enough already!' Kate hissed. 'This is ridiculous. Tanner, now!'

My gaze flew to Tanner. He looked reluctant to do whatever Kate wanted him to do.

'Now!' Kate snarled. The guns that Benny had taken away from us soared over Zach's head and landed in Kate's and Tanner's outstretched hands.

One of Zach's men guffawed. 'How very human of you to use guns!' Now that he wasn't half-covered by Zach any more, I realized he was the suspicious-looking guy who'd watched me while I had been giving my speech as Senator Pollard.

'Shut up, Will,' Zach hissed. But Kate raised her weapon and fired at Zach as all hell broke loose. My chest constricted with fear. What if Kate had hit Zach?

A few Variants started scuttling through the room in panic, but others joined the fighting. Bolts of electricity shot through the room, taking out several light bulbs and whoever was in their way. The smell of sulphur flooded my nose. More shots were fired, and knives soared through the room. Kate tried to make her way over to me, but other Variants and bolts of electricity kept getting in her way. The light flickered, turned from blue to red then back again. Someone bumped into me and sent me flying to the ground. My tailbone collided with the stone floor, sending a twinge of searing pain up my spine.

Devon gripped my arm and pulled me to my feet. 'Come on. We have to find the tunnel and get away.' But some part of me didn't want to run – the same part that wanted to believe that Zach's words had been the truth, that he and my father had been searching for me for all those years. The part of me that wished we could be a real family.

'Tessa, come on!' Devon urged. Fighting was happening all around us, but Kate had almost reached us. Zach and Will were crouching on the ground. But I couldn't see Jago anywhere. Suddenly Zach nodded in Will's direction. Will sprang to his feet and thrust his arms outwards. Every mirror and glass in the room shattered with an ear-splitting shriek. A crack tore through the thick glass of the aquarium, the sound like nails on a chalkboard, and then the ground began shaking, just like it had done when I'd pretended to be Senator Pollard.

Devon pushed me to the ground and threw himself on top of me. My breath whooshed out of my lungs. Screams and the hissing of water burst through the room. I lifted my head, only to see a wave crash over our heads. The water swept over our bodies, rushing into my nose and mouth, leaving us soaked. Devon rolled off me, and I pushed myself to my knees, disoriented. My hands, which hadn't been protected by Devon's body, stung. Small splinters of glass stuck in my skin. I brushed them off as best as I could. Luckily the wounds they left were tiny. One of the water twins lay curled into herself a few steps away from me, cuts littering her back. They didn't look life-threatening, but she'd probably have scars.

I stumbled to my feet and turned to Devon. My heart skipped a beat. His shirt was ripped, and his back was far worse than that of the woman. It looked like someone had dragged a rake across him. I helped him to his feet and we surveyed the scene. The room was a mess. The lamps and the glass bar shelves had exploded. Only a few of the spotlights on the floor seemed to have survived the shockwave and gave off an eerily bluish light. It was hard to make out much. Broken glass crunched under my feet as I turned around to get my bearings. Some people huddled against the wall, while others were motionless on the ground. The smell of chlorine and copper hung heavy in the air. Had people been killed by the flying shards? I stumbled forward, looking for Tanner and Kate. Even if I didn't trust them, I didn't want them dead or injured.

I detected Kate on the ground. She was sitting with her face in her palm. I stumbled towards her to see if she needed help. Suddenly someone gripped me from behind. I twisted around, ready to punch whoever it was, but I found myself looking into turquoise eyes. Devon came up to us, shoulders squared. Zach's gaze levelled on the wounds on Devon's shoulders, which were rapidly healing themselves, and realization settled on his face. Then he turned to me. 'Come with me, please,' he whispered.

'You could have killed people. Why did you do that?'

'I didn't start firing. I didn't have a choice. We were just talking, and, as usual, the FEA attacked.' I opened my mouth to argue, but what he'd said was true. 'Please, Tessa. There'll be enough time to explain it all, but not right now. And I knew nobody would die. The shards Will's shockwave creates are too small to do any major damage, and Devon can help the injured, right?'

I didn't say anything, but I never looked away from his eyes – they could have been my eyes. His hand on my shoulder was warm and soft. We were family. 'I've been waiting for this day for so long.'

'Me too,' I said, because it was true. I'd always wanted a loving family, had looked everywhere for it, except for the one place where I was most likely to find it: with my real family. Yet a cautious voice deep inside warned me not to trust him too easily. I didn't know enough to let down my guard.

Zach smiled, and I could tell it was an honest smile, without pretence. Don't let emotions blind you, I reminded myself. A figure was staggering towards us. Zach's head turned. 'We have to leave now,' he whispered. 'The agents will have called for reinforcements. Major could arrive at any second.'

Devon stepped up behind me and put his hands on my shoulders. His grip was warning. 'Tessa—'

'I have so many memories I want to share with you,' Zach said quickly. 'Memories of our dad and how we spent our first Christmas together. You have a family, Tessa. Whatever the FEA told you about us, it was a lie to secure your loyalty.'

I searched his eyes in the dim, bluish light. He took my hand gently. I should have pulled back. 'We could be a family and have a real home.'

A home. A family. Devon's expression reflected uncertainty but also determination. 'Have you ever met a Variant by the name of Ryan?' he asked suddenly. 'He could make fog.'

I gave Devon a grateful look. At least one of us was using their brain. *I* should have asked that question.

Zach hesitated. 'Never heard that name.'

'He claimed that your Army turned him into a raging killer. He murdered my sister.'

Zach opened his mouth but I cut him off. 'I want the truth. If I wanted lies I could go back to the FEA.'

He cast a nervous glance at the chaos around us. 'We didn't turn anyone into a killer,' he said eventually. 'It's true, we tried to recruit Ryan for our cause. But he didn't want to follow the rules. He was out of control.'

'Then why did he cut AA into his victims? That stands for Abel's Army, right?' Devon asked.

'I don't know why Ryan did what he did, and I'm not sure I even want to know. Maybe he wanted to impress us, or blame us for the murders – who knows. But we were shocked when we found out what he's done.'

Devon frowned. 'But—'

A male voice screamed out an order, but I couldn't make out the words over the crackling of electricity. It was a miracle that we hadn't all been fried. People began to emerge from their hiding places.

'Please, Tessa. We have to leave,' Zach urged. 'Holly is waiting for you. Once you talk to her, you'll see that Abel's Army isn't what Major made it out to be.'

Tanner came into view, the display of a phone glowing in his hand. He searched the area around his until his eyes settled on me. In the distance, I could hear the sound of helicopter blades.

'Tessa, quick!' Zach hissed. Holly's name echoed in my head. I had to see her. I gave Devon a pleading look. I needed to do this. And not just for Holly. I had to find out if it was true. If a family had been waiting for me all those years, if everything I thought I knew about Abel was just a web of carefully constructed lies.

Devon gripped my hand and gave a nod. 'OK. I'll come with you.' He glowered at my brother. 'But I want answers. I want to know everything you know about what happened in Livingston. You had spies there. You must know more than you've let on.'

Zach glanced at Tanner, who was now joined by Kate. She had a wound on her forehead that was dripping blood over her left eye.

'I'll answer all your questions,' Zach assured Devon. 'But we need to go. Now.'

Before I left, my eyes were drawn to the stairs. I hoped Penny was taking care of my mother. I wasn't sure if Zach knew about our mother being here.

Tanner was stumbling towards us over the remains of the aquarium. 'Devon, Tessa, don't!' he shouted, despair ringing out in his voice.

Guilt stabbed through me. I knew I was betraying the FEA, but they'd made their choice, and I'd made mine. I'd been longing for this all my life – for a family to call my own. Even Devon couldn't possibly understand how strong my desire for parents like his was. And now I had the chance to live my dream. No matter the risk, I would never forgive myself if I let it slip through my fingers. And it was my only way to get to Holly. Devon and I followed Zach past the remains of the aquarium.

'Tessa, don't!' Tanner tried again, but I didn't stop. Zach led us into the narrow hallway between the bar and the parking lot. Neither Finja nor Benny was in their spots. But Jago was there, peering outside. 'Two helicopters on the way. They'll land in a couple of minutes. We don't have much time.'

'Get my sister away from here,' Zach ordered. My body

filled with warmth when he called me his sister. I tried to squash the emotions. I needed to stay alert. But when he pulled me into a quick hug my resolve crumbled. 'Jago will bring you to safety.'

'But what about you and Devon?' I asked in panic as I heard the first helicopter touch down. Before Zach could answer, Jago had gripped my arm, and I felt like my body was split in two.

My surroundings started slipping away, and my hand was ripped from Devon's. His face became distorted, worry still etched into it. Then my vision started to blur.

CHAPTER 29

The ripping sensation was worse than anything I'd ever felt before, but then it suddenly stopped, and I landed on black leather seats. My vision was still blurry, and my stomach felt upside down. I pressed my eyes together and waited a few seconds before I dared to open them again. Jago sat beside me. He didn't seem disoriented in the least, but his face had paled, and red blotches dotted his cheeks and neck. A myriad of pale freckles dusted his nose. Close up, I realized with a start that he wasn't much older than me. His light red hair was plastered to his sweaty forehead. He leaned forward, perching between the front seats to talk to the driver. 'Drive! I'll go pick up Zach.'

'What about Devon?' I asked, but Jago disappeared from my side without another word. Hadn't he heard what I'd said? I tried to catch a glimpse at the man behind the steering wheel, but I was thrown back into my seat as he floored the gas pedal and the car shot forward. I glanced out of the window, clutching the seats to stay in place.

Outside the car was an unfamiliar street and a big motel sign, which bathed me in a pink glow. This wasn't the bar parking lot. 'Where are we?'

'A few blocks from the bar,' the man replied. 'Jago transported you here.' He had a gruff voice, like a few too many cigarettes had taken their toll. It reminded me of a voice I had heard before.

'Why didn't Jago take me to Abel?'

'Because that might kill him. He can transport himself over long distances, but not a second person. For a double transport to work, he has to be within a mile, better yet in view of the object.' He shook his head. His hair was black and curly, his skin very dark.

'Who are you?' I asked, more to distract myself than anything else.

'I'm Luthor,' he said, watching me through the rearview mirror with a kind smile. There was a cut on his lip. 'No need to introduce yourself.'

'My eyes,' I guessed.

'Yep, among other things.' He frowned as he glanced at the clock on the dashboard. 'You should make some room back there. When Zach and Jago return, they might land right on top of you if Jago messes up like usual.'

I didn't ask what messing up meant. Had people ever been ripped apart during a transport? Or was he referring to the time he had transported Holly and accidentally taken the wrong person? I pressed myself against the door. In the distance I could see a helicopter drawing circles in the sky.

I could imagine Major sitting in it, barking orders into the radio, face contorted with fury. He couldn't possibly spot us from that distance. We were blending into the parking lot and too far away from the bar for that.

Luthor's frown deepened as the seconds trickled by. I watched him through the rearview mirror, getting more nervous by the second. He kept glancing back and forth between the clock and his cell phone resting in the middle console. Suddenly the air crackled around me, and someone collided with my arm. I was pushed against the door, and Zach suddenly leaned against me, groaning as if in pain. He was bent forwards so I couldn't see his face, but his right sleeve was ripped, and blood dripped from a long cut. I hastily ripped the rest of his sleeve off and used it to bandage the wound. When I was done, I noticed Zach watching me with a stunned expression.

'You really looked worried,' he said quietly.

'Of course, I *was* worried. We're family.' That word sent a rush of happiness through me and left no room for doubt and anxiety. I realized that Jago was still there next to him. His eyes were closed, his face chalk-white. 'Hey, you need to get Devon,' I said, but he didn't react. I turned to Zach. 'What about Devon?' Panic rang in my voice.

Zach looked away, his eyebrows pulling together. He took a moment too long to reply. 'Devon changed his mind.'

I froze. 'What? He wouldn't do that. He would have told me.'

'Maybe he felt bad and didn't want to disappoint you.'

'Zach, why isn't Devon here? Tell me the truth!'

He lowered his head and nodded toward his wound. 'The FEA agents got us. When Jago appeared, he could only grab me. They had already wrestled Devon to the ground. The last thing I saw was Major entering the room. I couldn't stay. I'm sorry.'

For a moment, my vision turned black. I gripped the seats and inhaled deeply. 'This is all my fault. I shouldn't have involved him.'

What would happen to Devon now? I shouldn't have let Jago separate us. It was possible Major would forgive Devon if he decided to return to the FEA. Devon was still new; Major would probably blame everything on my bad influence. I tried to console myself with the fact that Devon couldn't have gone into hiding for the rest of his life anyway. He had his parents to consider. Yet the way I'd left him gnawed at my conscience. I could still feel the warmth of his hand in mine. I *had* to do something.

'I'm sure he'll be fine,' Zach consoled me. 'I bet Major will give him a simple warning. If they catch Will, though, he won't be so lucky.'

'Will escaped?' I asked.

'Yeah. He knew that Jago couldn't have transported him too, so he fled with another car. He's good at running away. That's what he did all the time before joining Abel's Army.'

I buried my face in my palms, overwhelmed by my conflicting emotions: worry for Devon, relief about Holly, profound happiness over having found my brother. 'Is there a way we can find out what happens to Devon?' I asked, lifting my gaze.

Zach's lips quirked up in a small smile. 'That won't be a problem.'

'You have a spy in the FEA?'

'Maybe,' Zach said.

'Who is it?'

He considered me for a couple of seconds. 'A guy named Ty. I don't know if you know him, but—'

'As in Tanner's brother Ty? Tall, dark?'

'That's him.'

'Does Tanner know?'

'I don't think so. Ty is a recent recruit.'

An idea popped into my head. 'If you have a spy then we can rescue Devon. There has to be a way.'

Zach looked like he regretted bringing up Ty. 'It's almost impossible to sneak someone out of FEA headquarters, assuming that's where they are even keeping him. If it were easy, we would have got you out sooner.'

'But Major won't guard Devon as heavily as he did me. I was the big safety risk. Promise me, you'll talk to Ty. I need Devon. Please?'

Zach nodded. 'I'll do everything I can.'

I wrapped my arms around him then quickly pulled back, still unsure how to act around my brother. Zach seemed to share my uncertainty; the moment I let go of him he turned to Luther. 'When will we arrive?'

'A couple of minutes,' Luther replied.

'Where?' I asked.

'Our helicopter. We flew here. There's a secure base not far from here.'

I leaned back, but my muscles were coiled tight. Zach was watching me with a strange look. 'What?' I whispered.

'I can't believe you're really sitting beside me. I've been dreaming about this for years. Whenever I lost hope, the memories of you kept me going. I knew that one day we'd be reunited.'

'You remember our time together?' I asked in amazement. I hadn't even remembered his face, much less any shared happiness between us. Before I'd found the photos in the files, I barely remembered anything at all. He was only two years older than me. Did that make such a big difference?

'Yeah, I do,' he said softly, then shifted in his seat to face me. He lifted his fingers up to my temples. I flinched from the touch and immediately felt like a fool. Zach wasn't going to hurt me. He gave me an encouraging smile before his fingertips tightened on either side of my head. The skin contact allowed images to scroll through my mind. They materialized behind my eyes like a vision, the same way they had a few days ago in the car. There was the memory of the day I was born in a windowless, white room. Abel was holding my mother's hand and beaming with pride. Then a later memory in which my mother had me nestled in her arm. She was lying on a narrow bed in the same small but sterile bedroom, looking exhausted and sweaty. A little boy knelt on the mattress beside her. His eyes were turquoise, and he was stretching out his tiny arm to touch the baby's hand. Abel sank down on the mattress beside them, looking almost as tired as my mother. The boy snuggled against him as Abel slowly, gently stroked a finger over my head until I opened my eyes. Turquoise, just like his.

I gasped, and Zach dropped his hands from my temples. Those memories felt so real, like a vivid dream, as if I was experiencing them right in that moment. It was almost too much, to finally see and feel what I'd longed for. Tears sprang into my eyes. 'The boy, that was you. But how can you remember it so clearly? You were only two.' I knew, of course, but I wanted to hear him say it.

Zach relaxed as if he'd been dreading my reaction. 'That's part of my Variation. I never forget. I can store memories and replay them for others.'

'A few days ago, a memory entered my mind while I was driving. Did you do that?'

He lowered his head. 'Yeah. I know it wasn't OK of me to do it without your permission, but I wanted to show you what you were missing. I'd hoped the memories would convince you to join us. I wanted you to come to us acting on your own free will. Obviously that didn't really work out how I'd planned. You are a tough opponent.' He chuckled, but I was lost in thought.

'You didn't need to touch me then, why did you do it now?'

'I usually need to touch people to use my Variation. The

only person with whom it's never necessary is our dad, so I thought that might work with you too, and it did. Maybe it's because we share the same DNA, I don't know.' He paused, scanning my face, which probably still showed my confusion.

'So they were real memories? Not fake?' Fear bubbled up in my stomach.

'Of course,' Zach said immediately. 'I wanted to show you what I remember every day.'

Alec's words about a Variant who could manipulate memories came into my mind. Maybe the rumours had exaggerated the truth, like they often do. 'Can you alter memories too?' I asked reluctantly.

We pulled into a private airport, and Luthor parked the car near the landing strip. Zach still hadn't replied. He gave Jago and Luthor a nod, and both of them exited the car, giving us a moment of privacy. Zach rubbed a hand over his face. 'If I focus very hard, then I can alter memories. It's very difficult to do, though, and I feel drained for hours afterwards.'

I tensed. 'But that's horrible. You can't just change people's memories!' Alec had manipulated and monitored me with his Variation. I didn't want the same thing to happen again.

'Some people ask me to change their memories. Many Variants have experienced horrible things in their life and think they need to forget in order to have a fresh start, and sometimes that's really the case. If the past keeps weighing you down, it might be best to drop it.'

'So you're telling me you never altered someone's memories without their permission?'

Zach glanced out of the window. Luthor and Jago were waiting for us, their backs turned to the car. 'On a few occasions, I had no choice. It was to protect myself and those I care about. I didn't like it, and it's always my last resort. What would you do if it was your only chance at keeping the people you care about safe?'

I shrugged. 'I guess I would do it. I don't know. I've never been in that situation.'

'Sometimes I hate this life of secrecy, but as long as the FEA is hunting us . . .' He trailed off and nodded towards the door. 'We should go now. Dad is waiting for us.'

My pulse sped up at the mention of Abel, at that word: *Dad*. I wasn't yet sure what to call him. It was so much to process at once.

As soon as we stepped out of the car, it disappeared. 'Did you do it?' I asked Luthor. He nodded. I narrowed my eyes. 'It was you! You were the guy with the syringe who attacked me.' I thought back to our night out camping and the flickering vehicle.

Luthor rubbed the back of his head and glanced at Zach, who rolled his eyes. 'Sorry about that. When we found out that you were on the run from the FEA, we tried to track you, but it wasn't easy. Dad sent out almost our entire organization to search for you. We knew you'd visited Devon's aunt and uncle, and we sent out scouts to track you in the area. Eventually someone in a diner said they'd seen you. Luthor followed up on the hint, because I wasn't close by. Since I wasn't there to talk to you, Dad permitted Luthor to use a sedative. That obviously didn't work out too well.'

Luthor smiled sheepishly. 'You're a good fighter, girl.'

'You gave me a concussion,' Jago said reproachfully. Did he want an apology?

'You scared the shit out of me. That's not really the most effective way to convince me to join you.' But I wasn't even angry any more. I couldn't believe that Abel had cared enough to send all of his men out to search for me. With the FEA out searching in tandem, that had been a big risk. 'Your Variation is cool,' I said to Luthor. Jago rolled his eyes and turned towards the helicopter.

Luthor grinned. 'Yours isn't too shabby either.'

Zach smiled, but it was tense as his eyes searched the sky. 'We use Luthor's Variation to disguise our helicopter, too.'

'But didn't it appear on the airport radar?'

'Nope. Luthor's Variation prevents that. And we have connections to the people who track that sort of thing,' he said evasively, then gave me a quick smile. 'Come on. We should hurry. Soon the area will be crowded with FEA helicopters.' He took my hand, and I followed him towards a helicopter that looked like it might be used by the military. Instead of skids, it had three tyres and was painted in a brownish-green colour.

Zach and I sat together in the back, while Luthor and Jago took their places in the cockpit. They exchanged grins as we lifted off the ground. As we rose into the sky, I could see the FEA helicopters in the distance. They were looking for me, but with Luthor's Variation, they'd never find us.

I couldn't help but wonder who was in the helicopters. Had Major come to make sure I didn't slip through their fingers again? I'd always been grateful to him for saving me from a neglectful home. But having seen my mother today, I wasn't sure whether the FEA hadn't been part of the problem from the start. Her years as an agent might have turned her into the wreck she was now, and the FEA had silently hunted me, probably from the day I was born. Even if my mother hadn't wanted to give me away, the FEA would have forced her to eventually. What would it have been like if my mother hadn't wanted to live a normal life? If she'd stayed with Abel? Zach seemed so normal and kind, not like the crazy Volatile Major made him out to be. What if Zach was telling the truth, what if Abel had been searching for me all those years, if he'd honestly missed me? If he loved me? Had the FEA kept me from a loving family?

My mother said she left Abel because she wanted a normal life and he couldn't bear it. She hadn't run from him because he had been cruel to her.

Zach touched my arm, and I jumped. His turquoise eyes were curious. He looked so much like me, I couldn't believe it. My brother.

'So Holly is really OK?' I whispered.

Zach nodded. 'She's more than OK. She's happy with us.'

'She doesn't want to return to the FEA?'

He stared out of the window for a moment. 'No one does once they meet our dad. People realize that Abel's Army is the better choice.'

'What about her family? I went to their home. Well, you probably know that since you followed me in the car.'

'Holly was worried that the FEA would target them to get to her. She was worried that one of her siblings would turn out to be a Variant and that the FEA would find out. She wanted them safe, so we relocated them. They're perfectly safe.'

'What did you tell them? Why would they leave their home and everything behind? Why did it look like there had been a struggle?'

'We discussed it with Holly, and she knew they'd never be safe as long as they were in contact with her. We moved them out very quickly. We gave them new identities and a new house and new jobs, far away from the FEA's reach. Trust me, they're happier than before.'

'You changed their memories, didn't you?'

He hesitated a heartbeat. 'It was for the best, really. They'll never find out. They can lead a normal, happy life without worrying about their daughter. Plus, their new circumstances are much more comfortable than before.'

I sucked in a breath. 'You removed Holly from their memories.'

'She wanted us to,' he said quietly. 'If there's ever a time of peace, she can return to her parents. We'll give them their memories back, and everything will be fine.'

I doubted that everything would be fine that easily, almost as much as I doubted that there would ever be peace between the FEA and Abel's Army – not as long as Major was there, and even then . . . 'I can't believe Holly gave up her family like that.'

'Sometimes we have to let go of the people we love to keep them safe,' Zach said.

I wanted to believe him, but I wasn't so sure.

The FEA helicopters became small black dots in the distance as we left Las Vegas behind. This was it. I was pretty sure there was no going back. I had really and truly crossed the line, and Major would never forgive me for this. Even if I decided to escape with Holly and not stay with Abel, Major would treat my actions as treason. And maybe they were. Because saving Holly was only one reason for my willingness to go with Zach. More than anything, I wanted to meet my dad.

'You're angry with me.' He touched my hands, which were balled into fists in my lap. I uncurled them and rested my fingers loosely on my thighs.

'I'm not angry. It's just a lot to take in.' I shook my head. 'Why did you kidnap Holly? Was it an accident?'

Zach snorted. 'That's what happens when Dad or I don't

take matters into our own hands.' I cocked an eyebrow in silent question. 'I wanted to be part of that mission. I knew I could make you see that the FEA was the wrong choice, but Dad didn't want to risk it. He knew Major would be close by, and he feared that I would get captured. Everything would be lost if Major ever got his hands on me.

'The mission didn't go as planned. Will sent a too-powerful shockwave and knocked out two of our own men. Then everything got out of control. They were just trying to save their own skin, and then Jago spotted a girl in black. He said he had seen her appearance flicker; she looked like FEA, and since he had only one chance, he grabbed her,' Zach continued. 'Of course, we figured out pretty quickly that it wasn't you, but we were glad that we had Holly. She's a great addition to our group. And we knew we could kill two birds with one stone. Holly is your best friend. We were sure you would be part of a rescue mission. We actually never considered you running away from the FEA on your own.'

I wasn't on my own, I thought. *I was with Devon*. My heart ached when I thought of him. I really hoped Zach would find a way for Ty to get Devon out of headquarters soon. I couldn't leave Devon in the hands of Major.

'What about Stevens?'

Zach frowned. 'You mean Harold?'

I bit my lip. I didn't even know his first name. 'The agent that you kidnapped in Livingston.'

'We didn't kidnap him.' Zach chuckled, giving me a

297

wide grin. 'He came all on his own. He wasn't happy at the FEA. He didn't like how he was treated and that he was forbidden from keeping his relationship with a normal woman.' He sighed.

I nodded. It was strange to think about saving someone from the FEA. The FEA had always been the epitome of good for me. But I hadn't known any better.

I closed my eyes and let my head fall back against the seat. The vibrations of the helicopter went right through me, and the whir of the blades gave me a headache. This was all too much for my brain to compute. Thinking about the FEA hurt. Every time a memory of the happy times I'd spent there entered my mind, I felt like my heart was ripped out. And Alec. He'd been my friend, my protector, my love, and now? What would he become? My hunter? My enemy?

'I didn't think I'd ever see you again,' Zach murmured. 'I thought my memories were all I'd ever get.' I turned to face him and tried to memorize every part of his face, just like he seemed to do with mine. His nose was a tad wider, and the shadow of stubble showed on his chin and cheeks, but our similarities were striking.

'Do you miss our mom?'

Hurt flickered in his eyes. 'Sometimes. But I can't forget that she left. She took you, but she completely gave me up.'

And I realized then that we'd experienced the same heartbreak. Our mother had failed us both. 'She wasn't much of a mother to me either,' I whispered.

Questions clouded his eyes.

'She tried to be normal, but she couldn't get her act together. She was drunk or stoned more days than she was not. And she had more boyfriends than I care to count. Every new guy was worse than the one before him.' I felt bad for talking about my mother like that after seeing her this last time. But it was the truth. She'd never been a caring mother. Her neglect would have broken me if I hadn't gone to the FEA.

Zach's face tightened. 'Did they ever hurt you?'

'Apart from the occasional insult, they pretty much ignored me. The loneliness and disgust from our mother was much worse.'

'Disgust?' Zach asked. I realized he'd taken my hand in his. He cared about me. Heat pressed against my eyes.

'Because I was a Variant. When she found out I wasn't normal, she called me a freak and told me I'd ruined her life.'

'That's bullshit!' Zach's face flashed with anger. 'She's a Variant too. Dad said she always hated herself for it. And that's why she didn't want me or him.'

'I'm sorry,' I whispered.

Zach shook his head. 'It's OK. Now we have each other.'

'I can't wait to see our father,' I said. Zach looked out of the window, his lips tight.

'Is something wrong?'

He shook his head with what was probably meant to be a reassuring smile. 'No. The last few weeks have been

299

exhausting. You didn't exactly make it easy for us. And Dad was getting more desperate every day. I was worried he'd do something stupid.'

Zach must have seen the confusion on my face. 'The hatred between Major and our dad is like a festering ulcer. It can blind you to what's right and wrong.'

'What do you mean?'

Zach looked like he regretted ever bringing it up in the first place. 'Our uncle, our dad's twin, has been locked up in the FEA's high-security prison for twelve years. There hasn't been a day that our dad hasn't thought of him. They were really close, and now he hasn't seen him for more than a decade. In all these years, Dad's hatred towards the man who imprisoned his brother has only grown.'

I suspected my mother's involvement with my father and Major only fuelled the hatred.

I had an uncle in the FEA's prison. I remembered what my mother had said about him.

'He must have done something to be thrown in jail, though, right?'

Zach's expression twisted. 'Many people who are locked up in the FEA prison haven't done anything more than refuse to work for the FEA. They think having a Variation makes you the property of the FEA and thus the FBI.'

Major had ordered Alec to make sure I was under control at all times, so Zach's words made sense. Every Variant was a possible weapon, and if a weapon didn't fire for your side, you'd better lock it up. But I also realized that Zach hadn't exactly answered my question. 'But what about our uncle?'

'Look, I don't exactly agree with everything he's done,' Zach said slowly. 'But our father loves him, and I can see how much it pains him to know his twin is locked up without ever getting a fair trial. Sometimes love for someone can make you blind.'

No one knew that better than me. Even now the memory of Alec's grey eyes, of his laughter, still made my heart clench. But my love hadn't blinded me so much I'd hurt others. What did our father's love for his brother make him do? I opened my mouth to ask, but Zach sat up suddenly. 'We're here.'

I leaned over him and stared down, but there was only barren land and mountains of glowing red rock surrounding us. We headed right for one of the rocks. 'I don't see anything. Is it disguised?'

'Yeah. The entire complex is underground. The base of the mountain is actually the entrance.'

My eyes widened. It would be difficult to escape from an underground headquarters. The helicopter was steering straight towards the sharp rocks. I clawed at the seat as the red of the mountains filled the entire width of the windshield. Any moment we'd collide with the rock.

CHAPTER 30

Our blades hit the rock wall, but they didn't make impact. They passed right through the surface, and so did the rest of the helicopter, as if the mountain was made of smoke. After a moment of darkness, we entered a huge hangar, and I realized we were inside the mountain.

'What happened?' I asked, dumbfounded. I twisted around to look back to where we'd just come from. There was the same red, solid rock, but now we saw it from the inside.

Luthor landed the helicopter in the middle of a platform emblazoned with a red cross. Trucks, tanks, helicopters and cars filled almost every free space of the cave. The rough red of the bare rock walls glowed like fire under halogen lamps, which were affixed to the ceiling.

Zach pointed at a guy sitting in a glass booth perched at the base of one wall, his feet resting on a desk. He waved at us, made a bubble with his chewing gum, sucked it back in, and kept on chewing. 'He watches what's going on outside from screens inside the booth. And if it's one of us, he dissolves the solidity of the rock, and we can pass through it like smoke. Not bad, huh?'

I blinked. That was the understatement of the year. This was amazing. He opened the helicopter and jumped out, then held the door open for me. I followed after him and let my eyes wander over the equipment. There were three helicopters, bazookas, missiles, machine guns, and countless crates with tags like 'ammunition' or 'explosives'. It looked like they were planning for war. 'You've got a lot of . . . stuff.'

Zach shrugged. 'We need to be prepared. Keeping headquarters safe is a big responsibility that we take very seriously. Too many lives depend on it.'

Then he took my hand and led me towards an elevator embedded in the rock wall. Luthor and Jago didn't follow us. They stayed back to take care of the helicopter, but I didn't miss the curious glances they threw our way. If this place was anything like the FEA, people would probably talk about nothing but out family reunion for days. We stepped into the large metal-and-glass elevator. Twenty people could have fit inside, but when the doors closed, the room still seemed much too small. I leaned against the cold metal, trying to stop the palpitation in my chest. Ten buttons lined the side of the elevator.

'I'll take you to our common area first. You can meet Holly there,' Zach said. Excitement flooded me at the thought. He pressed the button for -3, and my stomach plummeted along with the elevator. Zach didn't seem to mind the enclosed space or the fact that we were dozens of feet below the surface. Had he grown up in this place? I couldn't imagine a small boy running around between ammunition and tanks. There was so much we had to talk about. I couldn't wait to find out more about him and his life.

The elevator came to a halt, and the door slid open, revealing an enormous room with an open kitchen across from us. Pans and pots hung from stainless steel hooks attached to the ceiling. A sole cook was stirring something in an enormous copper pot. It wasn't mealtime, which probably explained why he was alone. His gaze briefly darted towards Zach and me before it returned to the six massive flat-screen TVs that lined the wall to my right. They were muted, but were showing horse racing.

Tables and chairs were scattered around. They weren't white plastic or stainless steel, like you might expect to find in a cafeteria. It looked as if every member of Abel's Army had taken their dining room furniture with them and put it here. There were round and square tables, some big, others small, made from wood ranging from maple to oak, and some of the chairs had old-fashioned flowery covers, while others were upholstered with trendy leather. There was even a small pink table with four matching pink chairs, which looked as if they were meant for kids. Were there children in headquarters?

I didn't get the chance to ask Zach. A door opened at

the other end of the common area, and Holly stepped through it – just as I remembered her. Short, red hair and a wide smile. She looked healthy – and happy. We started running at the same time, and I almost slipped on the smooth granite floor before we finally fell into each other's arms. I hugged her as tightly as I could, until she made a small sound of protest. I pulled back and quickly scanned her face. She wasn't pale, and her eyes were bright with joy. 'Are you OK?' I whispered. I didn't want Zach to overhear us, but when I glanced back to where he'd been, he was gone. Apparently, he didn't want to supervise our reunion.

'I'm fine,' Holly said. Relief surged through me.

'Are you sure?'

She let out her bell-like laugh. 'Of course I'm sure.'

'I was terrified when you were kidnapped. Did they hurt you?'

Holly led me to a dark wooden table, and we sat down. 'They didn't do anything to me – except make me realize that I was on the wrong side.'

My eyebrows shot up. 'Wrong side? You mean the FEA?' It wasn't as if I was thrilled about the FEA's actions, but hearing Holly say it came as a shock. She didn't know about the extent of their betrayal yet.

For a moment, anger flashed across her face. 'The FEA has been holding me back. I always felt like a failure with them. *They* made me feel like less, especially Major. I've been with Abel's Army for only a couple of weeks, and they've already helped me perfect my Variation more than the FEA ever did. I feel like everything's possible, like I can do great things.'

I touched her hand. 'That's good,' I said tentatively. 'So you want to stay *here*? You don't want to return to the FEA?' I still wasn't sure what I wanted, or at least my brain was undecided; my heart was a very different story.

She tensed, her eyes hard. 'I won't ever go back to the FEA. Why?' Suddenly she sounded worried. 'Do you want to?'

'I—' Before I could reply, the elevator opened with a bing, and Zach stepped out. His eyes found me, and he smiled hesitantly.

'I think he wants you to go with him. Abel's probably waiting for you,' Holly said, rising from the chair. My expression must have dropped, because she added, 'Don't worry. We'll see each other later.' She gave me a quick hug. I turned slowly, unwilling to leave her behind, but she was already heading towards the cook. She looked as if this place had been her home all along. Could it become mine too?

'So how was your reunion?' Zach asked the moment I reached him.

'It was good.' Holly looked at ease as she talked to the cook, who'd finally torn his gaze away from the TVs. This wasn't how I'd imagined my rescue mission would end.

Zach didn't press for more, but I could tell that he

was curious. He led me into the elevator and pressed the button marked −6.

I took his hand and squeezed. It felt surreal to be able to do that after all these years, and I needed his support. His turquoise eyes scanned my face. 'Are you all right?'

I squared my shoulders. 'Yeah. This is just a lot to process.' I swallowed. 'And I'm nervous. This is the first time I'm meeting my . . . my dad.'

'I know,' he said with a smile.

The elevator halted, and the metal doors slipped open with a soft whoosh. I took a deep breath as I followed Zach out. Except for the lack of windows, this room didn't look like we were underground. The walls were painted a bright, clean white and the floor was covered with birch planks. I could smell vanilla and maple syrup. The room we entered was huge – at least eight hundred square feet – and square. From the looks of it, it was a living room, kitchen and workspace at once. Several doors led to other rooms. One of them opened, and a man stepped out. He was smiling.

'Finally,' he said. 'I thought the pancakes I made were going to get cold. I didn't know what you like, but I figured everyone loves pancakes.' He was tall, with short greying brown hair and, of course, those turquoise eyes. I froze. I couldn't move, couldn't say anything.

'They're made from a mix, though, and probably burned, so don't get too excited,' Zach said, looking over his shoulder at me. There was something in his eyes I couldn't place. Maybe excitement mixed with anxiety. We'd all been waiting for this moment. I really didn't want it to get awkward, but I was tongue-tied and could feel my eyes tear up.

Abel raised his eyebrows. 'You like pancakes, don't you?' He talked to me like it was perfectly normal for us to be in the same room, perfectly normal for him to be offering me pancakes, like we'd been spending all our lives together, like we weren't practically strangers. And maybe for him I wasn't a stranger. He could remember the memories Zach had shown me, and probably many more. I only wished I could remember them too.

I gave a jerky nod. 'I love pancakes.' My voice was so quiet I wasn't sure he'd heard me. He was striding towards me, his smile warm and welcoming. There were crinkles lining the corners of his eyes. From smiling too much? I wished I'd shared more of the moments that had carved those lines into his face. I felt a lump rising into my throat.

'I've waited so many years for this day,' he said as he stepped in front of me. He left a few feet between us, like he was worried that coming closer might spook me. I looked up at him. Tiny worry lines appeared around his mouth. I probably looked like I was going to burst into tears at any second.

'Have you?' I croaked.

He bridged the distance between us and wrapped his arms around me. I relished the feel of his heartbeat against my ear. He felt warm and strong. My dad. This was how it was supposed to be, how it should have been all my life.

My mother and the FEA had kept this from me. After all the years of searching for something, of feeling like there was a piece missing in me, I had all the pieces of my story. I finally felt whole. Warmth filled me up as I tightened my hold on him, and he in turn did the same. Tears squeezed out of my eyes. 'Soon our whole family will be together again. The FEA has kept us apart for long enough. Once we convince your mother to join us, and free my brother, everything will be well.'

I pulled back with a sad smile. 'I don't think Mom will ever agree to join us. She told me that she hated being a Variant, that all she wanted was a normal life.'

His expression darkened. 'Normal life. Who's to say what's normal and what's not?'

I shrugged.

'The FEA has destroyed many lives,' he said bitterly. He shook his head and gave me a bright smile. 'I shouldn't bring this day down with my feelings.'

'But you're right,' I said quietly. Sadness overwhelmed me. 'In the last two years, Major used me, made me feel like I was safe, only to break my trust. Everything I believed in was taken away.' It still hurt thinking about it. It hurt a lot. I wrapped my arms around my chest as if that could help hold me together. Zach had been picking at the pancakes that were piled up on the kitchen counter, but now he came over to us.

Abel touched my cheek tenderly. 'You went through a lot. Your life until the FEA had been full of heartbreak and neglect, and then when you finally felt safe for the first time in your life, they took that away too. I hate to see you suffering. That's too much of a burden for someone as young as you. We could help you. We could make it all better.'

I stared into his turquoise eyes, I knew what he meant. Alec and I had discussed it, back when there still had been an Alec and I; Zach could make all the horrible memories go away, could erase the hurt, the betrayal. This could mean a new beginning.

Alec had said he'd never remove his past because it was part of him.

But I *wasn't* Alec.

Zach moved closer and brought his fingertips up to my right temple. I tensed briefly, but the look in my father's eyes banished my worries.

'But only the bad memories,' I said quickly. 'I don't want to forget the good times with Holly, or Martha, or Devon. Can you just tweak the bad memories so they don't hurt so badly?'

Zach exchanged a brief look with Dad before he gave a terse nod.

I could feel a tug at my memories. They flashed through my mind as Zach browsed through them like a catalog. Alec and I watching a movie, laughing, kissing. Kate telling me about Alec's Dual Variation. Alec admitting he'd lied. Major giving me the pills. My mother having a shouting match with one of her boyfriends. The files with the notes about me. One by one, they all turned murky. The images were coming quicker, blurring in my mind. My mother's face when I helped her shower, the brief flash of tenderness on her face.

Zach's touch loosened for a second, but then his fingers pressed against my temple again. Alec kissing Kate. Alec telling me it was complicated. Major telling me I'd have to go to the loony bin. My memories started trickling away. I felt better already. But what would be left of me if all the horrible experiences from my past were gone? Who would I be? Alec always said that his past made him who he was. Who would I be once my past was taken away from me? I searched Zach's eyes. I could see my own memories reflected in them as he swallowed them up. My head began throbbing, and emptiness spread in me, and with it came a bone-chilling cold.

'Hold on,' Zach said softly. 'Sometimes cold is a side effect. It'll be over soon.' My teeth started chattering, but I trusted his voice. He hadn't betrayed me. More scenes flashed in Zach's eyes. There was a funeral. There was the house in Livingston, and a boy with blond hair who lay in a puddle of blood. There was fog and a boy with a knife. There was a guy with grey eyes and a dragon tattoo on his shoulder. But I didn't know who he was.

'You'll feel better soon,' Zach whispered. Images followed his words. Memories – happy memories – snuck into the empty corners of my mind, filling them with warmth and light. There was a boy running through a sprinkler in underpants, yowling as the water hit him, and a toddler in diapers, a few feet away, sitting on the grass laughing. There was a Christmas tree with multicoloured lights that bathed the room in rainbow colours. There was Dad carrying me on his arm, setting me down on the ground, handing me a present. My tiny fingers ripped at the wrapping paper. Zach knelt beside the baby, beside me, and unwrapped his own present. There was laughter and warmth and smiles and hope. I blinked. The memories crowded my brain, filled me with a sensation of wholeness, of belonging.

The fingertips dropped from my temples. Someone stroked my cheek. I turned my head and stared at a man with turquoise eyes. His hand cupped my head, and warmth flooded me. I leaned into the arm that held me. Slowly my vision cleared, and I focused on the face in front of me. 'Tessa?' said a familiar voice. A good voice.

I smiled. 'Dad?'

'I'm so glad you're back.'

'Welcome home,' said another voice. Zach. He was smiling too.

I relaxed.

Home.

I was home.

Acknowledgements

Writing a book is a solitary activity, but preparing a book for publication isn't. A heap of people are involved and I wish I could thank every single person by name, but then this would turn into a novel.

Yet I'd like to take the time to thank my wonderful agent Jill Grinberg and her team (with a special mention to Katelyn and Cheryl). And my sincerest thanks go to the Hodder team, especially my wonderful editor Naomi Greenwood. I'm so glad that Tessa found a good home in the UK!

As usual, the biggest thank you goes to my husband. I couldn't do this without you. To put it in the words of Snape: 'Always.'

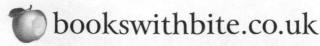